DEA

The laboratory was in partial darkness. There was no longer any movement inside the cage: the last rat was dead, lying on its back like the others, its legs stiff and its eyes dulled to a dusty black. The rats were the first living things to succumb to the new man-made organism - against which man would be powerless to fight by any means known to medical science.

DEATHWATCH

A Novel

Elleston Trevor

A Star Book
published by
the Paperback Division of
W. H. Allen & Co. PLC

A Star Book
Published in 1985
by the Paperback Division of
W. H. Allen & Co. PLC
44 Hill Street, London W1X 8LB

First published in the USA by Beaufort Books, Inc., 1984
First published in Great Britain by W. H. Allen & Co.PLC, 1985

Copyright © 1984 by Trevor Enterprises, Inc.

No character in this book is intended to represent any
actual person; all the incidents of this story are entirely
fictional in nature.

Printed and bound in Great Britain by
Anchor Brendon Limited, Tiptree, Essex

ISBN 0 352 31574 1

To my Sempai

ART WEINER

CHAPTER ONE

The snow came drifting in massive silence across the Lenin Hills, blown from the north and spreading rumpled ermine over the city, torn here and there by the spikes of the church steeples and jeweled by the street lamps, with the gold domes of the Kremlin burning against the black horizon to the south. With the snow came the silence as the rush-hour traffic was slowed to a crawl, its echoes smothered by the deepening drifts, leaving only the muffled boom of the locomotives hitting the buffers in Savelovsky Railway Station like the tolling of unknown doom.

Lopatkin was jammed in with the rest of them, skidding his little two-door Zhiguli over the ruts along Lavochkina-ulitsa and jostling for position with the front wheels losing grip on the treacherous surface and a loose snow chain beating like a lone drummer on the underside of the mudguard, while the heater fan blew oil fumes against his face and ruffled the loose papers that had slipped out of the file on the seat beside him.

More police appeared, waving their illuminated paddles, and he veered to the right past the ropes and lanterns and flags and the piled frozen clay that had been there for six weeks now because the new sewage pipes still hadn't arrived from Smolensk —the idea, you see, is to dig your trench and then order the pipes, so that if by any chance (and there is every chance) they don't arrive in time, you can at least have the satisfaction of

1

fouling up the traffic and confirming your absolute indispensability as minister of public works.

Lopatkin swerved again to miss a Special Medical Aid van that had stopped to pick up another drunk and haul him along to the drying-out station, two of the uniformed men heaving him through the barred doors at the back with one shoe flying off and a bottle of liquor smashing against a leaning pickax and spreading a red stain on the snow. Lopatkin cleared the obstruction and pushed his way into the left traffic lane, his thin shoulders hunched at the wheel and his hollow face with its laboratory pallor catching the light reflected upward from the frozen ruts. He wanted to get home and into a hot bathtub, out of this disorderly night where nothing could be controlled the way he controlled the base sequences and enzymes and the DNA strands under the stark tubular lamps all day. Disorder of any kind frightened him; it was out of place in an orderly universe.

But not a bad day, not bad at all. After eight months they'd finally synthesized a workable gene segment and spliced it into the phage, and the Kushevat Forest bacillus was already replicating the clones and all they had to do now was sit back and bite their nails to the quick and tell desperate jokes until the pattern of dark spots across the X-ray film told them whether they were right or wrong this time, whether they'd pushed their way through one of the major frontiers of medical biology or had simply cost themselves eight months of tedious benchwork that those bloody Americans could have done in less than one day with their new automated synthesizer, according to whispered rumors in the canteen at the Klinik.

It would also depend, of course, on rats 9 to 27, which were last seen frisking nimbly on the treadmills and darting past the water troughs without stopping to drink: a promising sign at this stage. Dobrynin, who was running the *in vivo* tests himself, had made the injections early this morning, and three of his staff were watching the batch in assay 5; but no one would know anything until tomorrow, unless of course any of the rats began dying.

It was nearly seven o'clock before Lopatkin was kicking the snow off his boots against the wrought-iron grid outside the apartment, his breath clouding under the big grimy lamp as the door came open and Elena was there, reaching with her warm flour-covered hands to pull him inside: she'd heard the noise he was making with his boots.

"What took you so long?"

"We worked late. And there's the snow again."

"Did something go wrong?"

"With the car?" There was always something going wrong with the car.

"No, at the Klinik."

"Mother of God forbid!" he said as she pulled his heavy fur coat off and hung it up.

"Then that's all right." She kissed his cold cheek and in an instant brought him into the warmth and excitement that was most of what she was, and now he was home. "Petr called from Kiev—you just missed him! And you're freezing! Go and soak in the tub while I finish the *pirozhki*!"

"Who's coming tonight?"

"Ludmila! Why else should I be doing *pirozhki*?"

"We should have them every night!" he called from the stairs.

"You'd get sick of them!"

"You always assume things—it's unscientific!" But in his tone was the pleasure that their daughter was coming to see them, worn out by her day at the hospital, no doubt, but full of her plans: she would one day qualify as a laboratory assistant and try to get into her father's Klinik; he would ask Smirnov to make himself useful for a change and pull a few strings. The man was normally a pest; he'd buttonholed Lopatkin again today while he'd been trying to eat an onion sandwich in peace during the lunch hour.

"As a member of the Soviet Academy, Lopatkin, you should also hold a Party card. It goes without saying, and I'd be honored to propose you, of course."

"The honor would be mine," Lopatkin had said carefully, "but look at all those meetings I'd be expected to go to while there's work to be done. Besides, politics confuse me, you know that. I don't know the difference between a committee and a commissariat." It was the endless meetings and committees that kept a stranglehold on any hope of new equipment and supplies for the labs, where all the real work was done. The top brass of all the major research institutes were high-ranking Party members, a damned sight more interested in their large apartments and dachas and vacations on the Black Sea than in what was happening in the laboratories.

Smirnov had leaned closer to him, the war medals hanging askew from the lapel of his blue serge suit and his breath rich with onion. "You're an important figure, you know, a highly respected scientist; you ought to be supporting the ranks of the Party." In the face of Lopatkin's silence, he'd resorted to downright bribery. "Don't you want a bigger car? Vacations on the coast? Couldn't your wife do with a better maidservant?"

"She has a maidservant already."

"Who doesn't wash."

Never averse to calling a spade a spade, your Comrade Smirnov.

"I'll tell you what I want more than all those things," he'd told the man, "and that's an automated synthesizer." He'd been about to say, "like the Americans have got over there," but that would have been risky. No one was supposed to know too much about what went on in the decadent West, and a remark like that would have been noted. Only a couple of months ago they'd lost Galkin from assay 2; he'd quietly disappeared, and a replacement was there at the bench. Of course Galkin had asked for it, writing that kind of thing about Pavlov, calling him "understandably limited in the light of present-day thinking." Sacrilege! He'd be in Magadan by now, in Siberia. One had to be careful. Smirnov was all right, not a hardliner, but he was in the Party all the same, and it was wise to keep on the good side of him in any case; he'd steer Ludmila's labor application through when she was ready, just to demonstrate his power.

Soaping himself in the bathtub, Lopatkin decided he wasn't

sorry he'd missed the telephone call from Petr just now; the boy would have talked endlessly about mechanics while he had to stand there in his coat and boots with Elena calling questions from the kitchen. He was a good boy, of course, but instead of following his father into biomedical research he'd gone off to work in the second Kiev Clock and Watch Factory. Not a bad start at his age, but what possible interest could there be in cogs and ratchets, compared with the infinitely delicate and unpredictable life that floated in the culture dishes and danced through the complex arterial systems of the white Ukrainian rats? A cog was a cog. It worked or it jammed. True, Petr had rigged up a wind generator on the roof of their old apartment when he was only thirteen, using a bicycle dynamo and a model airplane propeller and producing current to light three bulbs in the kitchen, and in those days this had saved them a few kopecks; but even then he'd never found a way to stop the bearing freezing up from October to May when the light was needed most. Mechanics were so appallingly *limited*.

But a fine boy, Petr, yes; and Ludmila was a fine girl; and Elena . . . well, Elena was everything to him, and to them all. Heaving himself out of the scummy bathwater he began counting his blessings, as he did quite often, perhaps to banish for a moment the pervasive shadow of anxiety that had been with him since he could remember. He had no real worries. His work fascinated and obsessed him, bringing him the status that allowed him this four-roomed apartment, a telephone line, the Soviet-made Fiat outside the door, and shopping privileges at the special *beriozka* stores reserved for diplomats and foreign tourists. He had a lot to be thankful for, compared with most men of his age.

This was before the telephone call.

By eight o'clock he was ensconced in the warmth of the living room, its enormous brass stove smelling of forest pine as they sat down to their meal, Ludmila's dark hair flying out just like her mother's as she swung her head to look at them each in turn, full of her news from the hospital. "Most of the women doctors are so far behind the times! They're still prescribing herbal remedies instead of the new drugs; but some of the men are quite brilliant, especially Boronov, who's absolutely *awed* by the fact that this humble trainee's father is the famous academician at the Gestov-Klinik!" She reached impulsively to squeeze his hand. "I'm so proud of you, Daddy, when people find out!"

"And I'm proud of you, my precious." He waited until his wife had put down the second dish of little salmon loaves, hot from the oven. "But you should read your *Meditsinskaya Gazeta* more carefully, you know. It's just reported that the chief of the Lithuanian pharmaceutical industry accuses doctors—including your brilliant Dr. Boronov—of not even knowing the exact properties of the new drugs they use with so much enthusiasm. Quite frankly, I'd rather have a good cup of comfrey tea in my stomach than a shot of your hydrocortisone."

The resulting discussion was fierce, noisy and inconclusive, while Elena sat between them wondering why she'd spent the last three hours in the kitchen kneading and stuffing *pirozhki*, a whole dish of which were getting cold on the table. She wished Petr were here to finish them while he turned a deaf ear to the argument. "Papa can talk of nothing but *bugs*," he'd so often say. "But there's no *precision* in bugs. They can even die on you while you're trying to make them work. I think they're just a mess."

"Penicillin, after all," Aleksandr was telling their daughter, "was only the mold on bread at one time. Did you know that, my precious?"

Then the telephone began ringing.

"It'll be the Klinik," he told them, getting up. "I asked Dobrynin to keep me informed of things." He crossed the room and unhooked the black receiver on the wall. "Yes?"

"Is that you, Aleksandr?"

"Speaking. Is that—"

"This is Vladimir. Listen to me, Aleksandr. Listen carefully." The man's voice sounded slow and heavy through the scratching of the telephone line. "Something has happened."

"Well, then? I'm listening."

"Something has gone wrong, here at the Klinik."

The shadow of anxiety that Aleksandr had lived with all his life took on sudden substance, enshrouding his heart, but he shook off the feeling and waited for the heavy voice to sound again.

"There was a mutation. Can you hear me, Aleksandr?"

"Yes, yes. A *mutation?*"

He heard the sudden change in his own voice now; it had become low and hushed; and at this moment Elena, taking the dishes from the table into the kitchen, dropped a knife, and didn't stoop to pick it up, but stood watching him, her dark head turned to look across her shoulder. The room had gone very still.

"All the rats are dead," the voice came again on the line. "For the moment we have to assume a wandering plasmid in the first batch. We have begun rigorous testing, but we already know enough about what this means."

Aleksandr went on staring in front of him, not focusing on anything in particular but seeing the whole room, as if through a fish-eye camera lens, with his wife and daughter both watching him, not moving, as he felt the blood draining gradually from his face. It came to him with absolute clarity that he would always remember this scene, with the big hand of the clock over the dinner wagon reaching the hour.

"What about the films?" he asked, suddenly angry. "You must—"

"It was the first thing we did," the heavy voice came. "And they're perfectly conclusive. It's a mutation. A new life form."

Aleksandr closed his eyes for a moment, standing quite still and listening to the thudding of his heart while he tried to think rationally. Vladimir Dobrynin was an experienced biologist and he knew what he was doing. He wouldn't have panicked when the rats began dying; he would have started on the tests right away, and he would have made absolutely certain before going to the telephone and alerting the chief scientist at his home.

So it was real. They'd made a mistake. A bad one.

There was so much to be done.

He opened his eyes.

"Aleksandr?" his wife was saying. She hadn't moved; she was still standing there with the dishes, and the knife was still on the floor near her foot.

"It's all right," he said, and spoke into the telephone again. "Vladimir?"

"I'm here."

"Have you told anyone else?"

"No."

"Then tell Director Smirnov, immediately. Tell him we need a *cordon sanitaire* thrown around the Klinik as soon as possible. The police must be told it's an extreme emergency. The Klinik must be sealed off, and no one inside it must make contact with another living person. Nothing must be emptied into any of the sinks; the toilets must not be used; you must set up temporary sanitation bins, using disinfectant." *So much to be done. What else?* "Vladimir, who else left the Klinik after the cloned material came out of the containers?"

There was a pause, either because Vladimir was trying to remember, or because he was trying to take in the enormity of what had happened. Then his voice came: "Gregor left here an hour ago."

"Only Gregor? No one else?"

"I'll look at the register."

"Very well. Anyone who left there after that critical time will have to be put into immediate quarantine at their domicile, and the place cordoned off. Have you got that, Vladimir? And think of everything else that will need to be done. But inform Smirnov first. *Don't leave anything to chance.*"

He juggled the receiver hook until the voice of the woman operator came on the line, then he asked for the chief of the metropolitan police. It was almost two minutes before someone said:

"Deputy Shibayev. Who is this?"

"My name is Dr. Aleksandr Lopatkin, chief scientist at the Gestov-Klinik. Listen carefully. This is a medical emergency.

We must seal off the Gestov-Klinik at once with a *cordon sanitaire* and no one must be allowed to enter or leave. The same goes for the Klimov Park apartment block on Shmitovskij Prospekt number 1617 East." He was aware of Ludmila getting up slowly from the table, and Elena putting the dishes back there; they stood together staring at him. "You must also seal off the domicile of Dr. Gregor Pokryshkin, who lives at number 2890 Panfilova-ulitsa, and inform him he is to go into immediate quarantine. I will telephone him there as soon as I can. Now do you have all that?"

"I shall need more authority for this. I can't just take a telephone call from someone who says he—"

"Then you must telephone Director Geydar Smirnov, who is head of the Gestov-Klinik." He told him the number, dabbing at a trickle of cold sweat that had started from his temple, itching against his skin. "And Deputy Shibayev, I must tell you that at this moment the city of Moscow is exposed to the risk of a major epidemic and that the sooner you act, the more lives will be safeguarded."

He hung up the receiver before the man could ask any more stupid questions and stood wiping the sweat from his face with a rumpled handkerchief, thinking of Vladimir with the Klinik turned suddenly into a madhouse—or a morgue; thinking of Smirnov and what he had to do, thinking most of all of the two people who stood here in the room with him. The easiest part had been dealt with, now came the hardest. He got it over quickly, going straight to the little hallway and taking his heavy fur coat off its hook and shrugging himself into it.

"You mustn't come near me, please. Elena, would you just put a few things in a bag for me—my toilet things, razor and so on? I don't want to stay here any longer than I can help; I might be infectious, you see." As his wife hesitated an instant and then hurried up the stairs, he looked at his daughter. "It may not come to anything, my precious—and you must tell your mother this when I've left here—it may not turn out as bad as it sounds; that will depend on a lot of things at the Klinik." Seeing her young face like that, bewildered and frightened, he yearned to go to her and hold her close and comfort her, and he even took a step in her direction before he stopped himself. "You must disinfect the telephone, Ludmila. Don't use the toilet or empty anything into the sink—*no water or refuse must go out of the apartment, you understand?* I know you've done a little training in epidemiology. When you draw water for washing, empty it into the bathtub every time, with the plug in. You'll be able to think of other things like that: this place is in quarantine, that's what it amounts to." He looked at the stairs. "Hurry, my darling!"

Ludmila was moving toward him, either because she wasn't thinking or didn't care. "Daddy, will you be all right?"

"*Don't come near me.*"

She stopped, as if tripping, and he turned away, clenching his fists and savoring the pain as the nails dug into the palms. "I might be infectious, you see, my precious."

He was standing outside in the snow when his wife came down the stairs. He watched her through the doorway and the arch of the little hall as she walked toward him with the small leather bag in her hand. She came quickly and with her hips swinging, as she'd come to meet him along the path of the medical university where they had first known each other, and later along the platforms of railway stations when his work had taken him away for a time; she walked now, as she had walked then, like a woman hurrying to meet her lover.

He backed away.

"Don't come out. It's cold out here."

She stopped, silhouetted against the warm light of the room, her eyes in shadow, so that he couldn't see them. "Throw it to me," he said, and she hesitated, then swung the leather bag through the falling snow. It fell short and he made a clumsy attempt to catch it, but missed. He picked it up and brushed it off, looking up at her for the last time before he turned away. "I don't want you to worry. I'll keep in touch." His boots crunched over the snow to the place where he kept the car.

CHAPTER TWO

Seven thousand miles away in Arlington, Virginia, a video screen lit up and four men sat watching it.

The picture carried a lot of grain, but they could make out easily enough the slim black object moving in a straight line from the lower left-hand corner toward upper right. At a point not far from the center of the screen it vanished in a cloud of what seemed to be white smoke.

"Vaporized," Jim Forbes said. He was the study leader.

They watched the next picture; the only difference was that the missile looked slightly longer and was vaporized somewhat before the center was reached.

"Are we looking for anything?" asked Bob Shaw.

"No. We're looking *at* something. These are the pictures the CIA took of the Soviet satellite killer being tested. So far, they've vaporized twenty-three missiles in a five-month period."

"Did they miss any?"

"No."

The other three looked at Forbes, who got up and stood sideways to the screen for a moment, his head angled to watch it; then he went to sit at the table in one of the chrome and vinyl chairs.

"Are our shoots as good as that, Jim?" This was Art Powlett, thin, red-haired and at thirty-three the youngest—and, some said, the most brilliant—of the military think-tank staff working

11

for the Institute for Defense Analysis. He wasn't the study leader of the project because Forbes carried seniority and had covered some of the data during earlier research.

"No," Jim Forbes said from the table, "they're not. What we're looking at, though, is simply proof that the Soviets are doing quite well with laser weaponry development. Come and join me when you've seen enough."

They followed him one by one, and Steve Gully switched off the video and limped across to a chair.

"What happened to your other shoe?" Jim asked him.

"It's drying." The rain had left puddles all over the parking lot. "I had one foot out of the car and then one of the top brass monkeys came alongside and threw me a bow wave. Admiral Saunders, no less." This building was opposite the Pentagon.

"Okay," Jim Forbes began, "we have enough data to get this whole thing wrapped up today." He sorted four red folders from the pile of paperwork on the table and handed three of them around, opening his own copy and looking at the contents. "We've pretty well pumped the military and civilian research labs dry, and the industrial contractors are looking for some kind of green light. They won't get one, because what we're meant to be doing, fellers, is this." He looked at them in turn. "We are to advise the White House as to whether the US can convince the Soviets that we have a new and decisive weapon nearing operational readiness."

They became suddenly attentive.

"Is this a PDM?" Steve asked in surprise. Not many Presidential Directive Memoranda came their way; most of their work was done for the Joint Chiefs.

"Yes."

"I'd like to get it absolutely straight, Jim." This was young Powlett, his tone intrigued. "By 'convince the Soviets,' do we mean 'con'?"

Jim Forbes tucked his chin down and doubled it. "I don't know if the President would choose that word."

"Persuade?" Art tried.

"Persuade would be something like it," Forbes nodded.

There was a short silence while everyone looked at the work charts and didn't actually see them. No one got up to lock the door: there'd been a red light burning outside it since they'd come in here. The public paid the Institute for Defense Analysis thirty million dollars a year for "blue sky rumination" and "thinking crazy," and every written sheet of material that went out of here was classified, so that the public would never get to look at it, not only because most of the technical data was top secret but because if the public knew how crazy these people were thinking, it would never sleep.

"And beyond that?" Bob Shaw asked suddenly, and caught them all off balance, trying to remember what had been said before that, because the minds of these young Ph.D.'s took off at the slightest provocation and ranged into the ecosphere and through nuclear wars and out of them in a matter of seconds. That was what they were paid for.

"Beyond that," Jim Forbes said when he'd followed the thought train, "we don't know anything. Ours not to reason why."

Art Powlett kept his red head bent over the sheets on the table, letting his mind deal quickly with what was on it before they had to get down to work. If the US had to "persuade" the Soviets that it possessed a new weapon nearing operational readiness, someone inside the White House was getting edgy about the arms race, and Art didn't want to think about that, because whoever lost it could lose all.

"Let's start with you, Steve," Forbes·nodded.

The man with one shoe off sorted his papers. "I pass," he said. "I picked the laser, and if the Soviets can do that kind of thing all over the video screen, we're not going to scare them. Our people are hitting too many problems: things like atmospheric disturbance, decoys and 'dazzle' from planet-based laser guns; there's been no progress with the idea of a space laser picking out short-range missiles from submarines." He closed his folder, ending three months' trudging through offices and factories and electronic laboratories from New Jersey to San Francisco and back.

"Bob?" said Forbes.

Bob Shaw put out his third cigarette halfway through. "Okay, I spent most of my time with the Livermore lab in California and the Los Alamos people in New Mexico, looking at the rail gun. It works. They've worked it. They've fired very small projectiles at more than twenty thousand miles per hour, which is nearly ten times the muzzle velocity of the most powerful rifle, and that's nothing like the figure the rail gun's likely to achieve farther along the road." He slid two charts across the table toward Jim Forbes. "This is an exciting breakthrough and all the people I've talked to are very warmed up about it. The thing is, they don't yet have electrical power packs big enough to shoot larger projectiles from a mobile unit, because the weight's prohibitive. At the moment it's a single-shot weapon because the explosive strip causes critical damage and it's hellishly expensive to rebuild. So the bottom line isn't any better than Steve's, but for the opposite reason: nobody thinks the rail gun is going into any kind of battlefield—on land or in space—for at least ten years." He pointed a nicotine-stained nail at one of the presentation charts. "The salient figures are in the left-hand column."

The study leader ran his eye down the material as a concession to the prodigious amount of research and analysis and actual writing Bob Shaw had done—the study was two hundred and thirty pages thick. Then he nodded and looked across at Art Powlett, who had become so absorbed in his own worksheets that when Jim spoke to him he swung his head up and looked at Steve instead.

"Excuse me?"

"Let's hear from you," Jim said again.

"Oh. Sure." He pushed three copies of his presentation toward the others. "Particle beam. I think this could be it." He gave them a few minutes to glance over the summary. "I got the wrong idea at first. It's so way out. I mean really exotic. But the people working on this one talk about it like it's the Second Coming. And you can see why."

He gave them some more time, and the silence in the room was broken only by the turning of sheets. About half of the study was composed of illustrations: technical photographs, artists'; projections and graphs, and he wanted this stuff to speak for itself in case his own personal enthusiasm got in the way. They didn't want to make any mistakes today, if this project had been initiated in the Oval Office. Art was still uneasy about that; it was a whole lot of fun making up star wars for real, but Betty was pregnant and they both hoped it was a boy and it would be nice if there was still going to be a world for him to grow up in.

After a while Jim Forbes got up and went over to the coffee machine. "Okay, Art, I see what you mean, but they're talking about six or eight years from now, most of them."

"What I like about the beam," Art Powlett said as he followed along for some caffeine, "is that although it's so incredibly sophisticated, there seem to be fewer problems in the way. I mean like we have with the laser: atmospheric disturbance and things like that. This one just zaps right through all the mundane objections. It's unearthly. I think if we needed it badly, and did a crash program like the Manhattan Project, the beam could be operational inside, say, three or four years. And I think we're looking at something like the invention of gunpowder, or again, the atom bomb. I mean, a breakthrough." He overfilled the paper cup and got coffee on his thumb and waited till the pain went away. "And obviously that isn't just my opinion."

When they'd all been to the machine they came back to the table and loosened their ties and tilted their chairs back and Bob Shaw lit his fifth Benson & Hedges and nobody talked anymore until it was almost noon.

By three o'clock Jim had taken them through the beam study twice, throwing out questions, trying to disillusion them, especially of course Art Powlett, partly because Art was so dizzy with the thing and partly because he didn't want his enthusiasm to affect the other two; in fact the problem with Art Powlett's reputation for blue sky magic was that he tended to swing the votes.

"I'm going to remind you," Forbes said at this stage, "that what we are expected to do is to show there's sufficient *technical* data for the *credibility* of a new and decisive weapon within a year or two from now. Or to show that there isn't."

In a moment Bob Shaw said: "In the eyes of the Soviets?"

Jim tucked his chin in and looked down. "In the eyes of anyone. Including the Chief Executive."

Bob put out his cigarette, half-smoked. "I'll say yes. Given a Manhattan Project–type crash program."

Jim nodded. "Steve?"

" 'A year or two from now' is nice and vague."

"That makes it easier. Right?"

"It makes it damn close. But I'll go with it. Given the crash program."

Forbes looked at Art Powlett. He'd left him till last, to lessen his influence over the other two, though they all knew what he'd vote. Art's freckled hand slapped the file.

"It could be done. That's what the people working on it say."

"I want to hear what you say."

"I say it could be done." He looked down at the file again, a thought flashing through the complexities of the axons and neurons of his brain: *do I think it could be done because if we give it enough credibility they'll order a crash program and we'll win the arms race and there'll be a world for this firstborn of ours to grow up in after all?*

"Thank you," Jim Forbes said, and got up from his chair and dropped his coffee cup into the bin and rubbed his eyes. Bob Shaw followed him with the heaped ashtray, and Steve went over to fetch his shoe where it had been drying in the current of air from the exhaust register.

By 3:25 the room was empty, and the red light over the door outside was no longer burning. Jim and Steve had gone along to the gymnasium to work the long day's lassitude out of their muscles; Art had gone straight to a phone and called up Betty to ask how she was feeling, because she was due in three days now; Bob was trying to dig up a partner for the squash court, convinced that if you tried hard enough you could pump all that tar out of your lungs before it did any damage.

There was nothing to show in the empty room of the narrow black building opposite the Pentagon that today these four reasonable and responsible young men had made their contribution to the alchemy that in less than twelve months would bring all life on the North American continent to the brink of extinction.

CHAPTER THREE

By 9:15 in Moscow the worst of the snowfall was easing off, but for the past two hours the traffic at Sheremetyevo International Airport had been suspended, and the slender Tupolev TU-144 was still in its bay. Twice during this period its passengers—ninety-one members of the Bolshoi Ballet—had been brought off the freezing plane to be offered light refreshments in the freezing VIP lounge, simply because it was larger and they could vent their frustration by moving about.

"Didn't anyone tell them about the weather?"

"Why couldn't we have stayed at the hotel?"

"Don't they have instruments of some kind?"

Pale, sensitive faces froze for an instant in the flashlight as the gentlemen of the press searched for dramatic angles, especially of prima ballerina Novikova, who played instinctively to her audience by turning her body this way and that, so that those who had seen her dance could ignore the dark sable coat and watch that incredible grace as her hips swung and her feet slipped in mesmerizing patterns across the marble floor, seeming never to touch it.

"Do you want us all to crash on takeoff, you idiot? Can't you see the snow?"

"But why did they bring us along here, when they knew we couldn't fly?"

At 9:20 Irina Novikova announced that she was going back to

the hotel and taking the entire troupe with her, a statement that
was immediately effaced from the journalists' notes by the minister of culture's permanent representative to the Bolshoi, the
greater part of whose life was devoted to effacing most of prima
ballerina Novikova's announcements to the press.

A dozen members of the company had already gone flitting
precipitately across to the toilet to be sick, their nerves unequal
to the suspense of the delay, their natural fear of flying and their
increasingly feverish excitement at the thought of their destination: none of this particular troupe had ever been to the United
States of America, and Aeroflot flight 378 was scheduled direct
to New York.

By ten o'clock the salt trucks and work gangs were ordered
clear of the runway, and it was announced that traffic was
shortly to be resumed. Half an hour later the Tupolev with the
red flash at the tail was rolling cautiously past the terminal buildings, its pointed droop-nose casting a crooked shadow along the
tarmac as it passed the string of lights. At the tenth window
from the rear of the cabin sat Nadia Fedotova, a young and
talented soloist who had been promoted from the corps de ballet
just a year ago and was already singled out, at the age of only
nineteen, for the demanding roles of a mature dancer. She was
one of those who had spent most of their time in the toilet.

"Breathe deeply!" the choreographer beside her said again.
"Take deep breaths, darling!"

But Nadia kept forgetting, and sat by the window in the stillness of thraldom, as if posed for a portrait, the luminosity of her
dark eyes defying the shadows and her lips parted in an eternal
and unspoken question: *What was it going to be like?*

She had refused point-blank, six months ago. She wouldn't
leave Russia—ever. It was her home and her world, it was where
the Bolshoi danced, it was where her mother and her sister
and all her friends lived and loved her, and where she loved
them and always knew where to find them. But, the director
had explained, his tones hushed with concern, she must recognize her sacred obligations not only to the Bolshoi but to Soviet

culture, which must be shared with the rest of the world and offered as an example of the creative genius that could flower in the nourishing soil of Socialism. Whether or not she would have finally allowed his arguments to persuade her was proved academic. "Of course you must tour with us, child!" the prima ballerina had told her sharply. "It's your duty!" To please Irina Novikova, the girl sitting transfixed at the window of the Tupolev would have put her head straight into a lion's mouth at feeding time—or even, for that matter, go to America.

Like the rest of the company she'd been required to complete an extensive questionnaire. The first part was easy enough: born Arkhangelsk 1966, single, atheist, father deceased, normal education, entered the Arkhangelsk Junior School of Ballet at age fourteen, joined the Bolshoi 1982. But some of the questions were quite a struggle to answer, because there seemed to be surprising gaps in her "normal" education. *What are your thoughts on Western Imperialism? On the Second World War? On European political thinking? On the United States of America?*

Although she had visited her father in London several times when he had been a consul there, and had found what little she had been able to see of England not altogether unpleasant, she knew better than to say such a thing. England, after all, was a capitalist country! *Mr. Churchill,* she had written in her backward-sloping hand, *was a courageous leader but made a show of smoking large and expensive cigars, which the proletariat could never hope to afford. The wedding of the Prince of Wales was a blatant example of capitalist extravagance, and the pretence that his bride had worked as a schoolteacher was a crude attempt to hoodwink the working classes.* The questions on the United States of America were the most difficult to answer: she could only fall back on the few things she'd read about it. *The city of New York is the center of the narcotics industry, and bands of armed robbers roam the streets at night, crazed by drugs and ready to murder at the slightest provocation. Huge gratings in the roadway are constantly steaming, such is the humidity in the subways.*

This was now her greatest fear, as the brakes of the jetliner were released and the four huge engines reached their maximum thrust: that she was actually going to stay in the city of New York and would have to make the journey from the Lincoln Center to the hotel every night after the performance, but the director had reassured her that the company would be moving about as a group, and that six KGB officers were already on board the plane to escort them wherever they went and would never let them out of their sight.

As the Tupolev lifted at last from the runway and began climbing at a steep angle, Nadia Fedotova opened her eyes and stared from the window at the beautiful city below her, its lights winking like stars against the winter snowscape and gradually beginning to blur as the tears came, springing from a dread sense of foreboding that she would never see it again.

Below in the city, the fluting whistle of the Tupolev 144 faded from the air, overwhelmed by the running of the engines. A score of vehicles stood in a wide ring surrounding the wasteground, their headlights casting an acid radiance across the loose rubble and weeds, silvering them and throwing stark shadow against the drifts of snow. They were vehicles of the militia, the police department, special KGB patrols and fire services, their rotating lamps fanning a red glow across the buildings beyond. Other vehicles were still moving in from the adjacent streets, responding to their radios, and now a gleaming black Zil limousine swerved through the gap left by the police vans and came to a halt alongside the row of three Chaikas. No one got out.

In the center of the ring stood the ambulance.

Movement began again as four engineers left the State Radio vehicle that had pulled up alongside a pile of bricks left behind by a demolition squad. Unwinding their reels of cable, they set up a standard microphone six feet away from the driving door of the ambulance and moved back toward the group of limousines, where they arranged a loudspeaker, standing it on a wooden crate they had found among the rubble. The sound of sirens was still coming in, and an order crackled through the radio network; in a moment the sirens moaned to silence, and there was only the crunching of tires over the snow.

Five minutes ago a newspaper reporter had arrived in his car, showing his credentials to the two militiamen posted by the gap between the vehicles. He had been informed that any journalists in the area would be arrested on sight and that any attempt to bypass the official board of censors with a reference to this incident would cause them to be summarily shot.

The engineers made a signal to someone sitting at the wheel of the militia van that had been the first to arrive and returned to their own vehicle, getting in and slamming the doors; there were now visible only the two guards, who stood facing the street with their repeater-rifles slung at the ready. Exhaust gas crept and gathered across the snow, casting a blue haze in the glare of the headlights.

The four black limousines had been drawn up to face the ambulance at a distance of thirty feet, and the pale blur of faces could be glimpsed behind the reflections on the windscreens.

A voice sounded from the loudspeaker.

"Dr. Lopatkin, you will please show yourself."

In a moment the driver's door of the ambulance came open and a single figure emerged, walking clumsily in its protective clothing. The white face of Lopatkin could be seen behind the heavy plastic visor. He slammed the door of the ambulance shut behind him, and the sound echoed like a gunshot from the buildings. Obviously dazzled by the concerted glare of the headlights, he stumbled over the rubble until he reached the microphone that had been placed there for him. For a moment his visored head swung to look across the ring of vehicles, reminding those who watched him of a wild creature, trapped. It was the feeling they had arranged to give him. They were not pleased with Dr. Lopatkin.

The loudspeaker sounded again, and his head swung toward it.

"Dr. Lopatkin, this is the minister of health speaking to you. Others present are the deputy minister of health, the chairman of the committee for public control, the second deputy chairman of the committee for state security, and the chief of the department of epidemiology. We wish to know, first of all, whether anyone in this area stands the slightest risk of infection."

The figure moved a hand to the microphone, but didn't touch it; colors reflected in the shining polyester suit ran in rivulets until the movement stopped.

"Comrade Minister, no one is at risk. Every precaution was taken."

The suit still reeked of the disinfectant they'd sprayed it with, after he'd put it on in the isolation chamber; he was finding it difficult to speak without choking.

"Very well. Dr. Lopatkin, is it certain that this accident took place at the Gestov-Klinik? We require details."

"Comrade Minister, there was an accident, yes. What we don't know is whether it was contained in time. The staff at the Klinik is still working hard to find out the position. Dr. Pokryshkin and I are the only two technicians who left the Klinik during the critical period and who might have carried the genetically altered bacillus to other people."

To Elena and Ludmila, when they had kissed him. The scene in front of him swayed suddenly through the visor, and he moved one foot to steady himself. It might not have happened. Nothing was certain yet.

"You mean it is possible that either you or Dr. Pokryshkin, or both, inhaled the bacillus during your work with it, and could have passed it on to other people by droplet infection?"

"Yes, Comrade Minister."

"It has occurred before with laboratory technicians?"

"It isn't common, but it happens, yes."

"But in normal circumstances the affected persons can be given appropriate antibiotics?"

"Yes, Comrade Minister."

"But in this case, there are no antibiotics capable of dealing with the infection?"

For a moment the only sound was the crackling of static on

the circuit, and Lopatkin wondered how long he could hold out before he had to answer. But the longer he hesitated, the worse it would sound.

"No. There are no antibiotics."

There was silence again, this time because the minister wished the others in the group of cars to understand the gravity of the situation. The minister, Aleksandr Lopatkin knew, wasn't putting these questions for his own enlightenment; he was a highly qualified physician himself. He wanted the others to understand. And he wanted Lopatkin to understand, also, that there would be no mercy shown to him even if, by chance, disaster was averted. The difference between safety and disaster must not be a matter of chance.

"Could the bacteria have left the laboratory through the drainage system? By material being washed down the sink?"

"They're trying to establish that now, Comrade Minister."

"There was no biological shielding undertaken?"

"We had no suspicion that there might be any danger in using sealed containers and routine precautions."

"Could you have created a mutated strain that was incapable of surviving in a saline environment, such as the human blood, or in the detergents found in sewage systems?"

Aleksandr Lopatkin lifted a gloved hand to wipe the outside of the visor, but only made things worse, leaving smears of disinfectant on the plastic. The interior was steaming up now as the sweat began running down his body. He focused his attention on the big Zil and looked nowhere else; he didn't want to fall down in front of all these watching eyes.

"If we had suspected any danger," he said against the black barrel of the microphone, "we would have stopped the experiment at once." It had been an accident, they must realize that. He'd done nothing deliberately. But he mustn't try to excuse himself; genetic engineering was not yet fully explored in all its subtle ramifications, and he'd known he and his colleagues had been handling potential dynamite. Worse than dynamite. Much worse. Unthinkably worse.

"Dr. Lopatkin, as a highly experienced and gifted scientist, an honored academician, you should surely have realized that the DNA molecules that comprise part of the genes of the dead bacteria can be absorbed by the living cell, in a rare event. Is that not so?"

Lopatkin found that by closing his eyes to a mere slit, he could drain the droplets of sweat along the crow's-feet lines in the skin, and at the same time keep himself focused on the black oblong of glass whose reflections hid the faces of his inquisitors. For that was what they were. These questions could have been put to him over a telephone, and the other officials here could have been told of his answers. But he must be shown up. He must be seen to stand here in the dazzling light and face up to his guilt. To admit it.

"Yes, Comrade Minister. I realized the experiment was dangerous. But many of our experiments—"

"You should also have realized, surely, that even though the prime carrier of a mutated gene is dead, the genetic pattern can still be perpetuated."

The sweat trickled down Lopatkin's face, itching on the skin. His whole body was simmering under the impermeable protective suit, while the cold air streaming through the mouthpiece filter froze the mucus in his nostrils.

"Yes, Comrade Minister, I realized the danger."

Through the slit of his eyelids he thought he saw the big limousine begin moving toward him, roaring silently toward him, to knock him down with its enormous weight and leave him crushed against the snow. But it was only his imagination, because of the heat, and the fatigue, and the torment of not knowing whether at this moment, in his bloodstream, in Elena's, in Ludmila's . . . Oh, they'd do it all right, these people—they'd knock him down and crush him—but they wouldn't do it with their big black cars; he would simply disappear, as Galkin had disappeared from assay 2 a couple of months ago.

Mea culpa.

"Dr. Lopatkin, you would have expected your colleagues to have realized the danger, also. Would you not?"

"They appreciated the need for containment. They took normal precautions. They—"

"But this was not a 'normal' experiment."

"I was in sole charge of it. No one—"

"But your colleagues are as experienced as you."

"I am responsible, Comrade Minister. No one else."

Mea culpa. It was what they had brought him here to tell them. He had told them.

The row of dark windshields filled the slit between his eyelids, looking like the windows of a penitentiary. He began waiting for the voice to sound again from the loudspeaker, and then gradually forgot that he was waiting, or that there was anything to wait for; he was simply a man standing here in a strange disguise, transfixed by the blinding glare, his legs shifting suddenly underneath him as he began slumping and only just caught himself in time.

"Dr. Lopatkin." His eyes opened wide as he regained his senses. "When shall we expect to know for certain whether this accident will lead to a dire emergency?"

"It depends on—" but that was no answer. "My staff is working hard to trace events in retrospect, Comrade Minister, the series of critical events. It could take some hours, yet. It could take till morning."

Another silence, while they talked among themselves. This time he was careful to keep alert, taking slow breaths, savoring the icy air even though the filter was letting through the sickly taint of the exhaust fumes.

The loudspeaker was silent. He went on waiting. Then the sound of a starter motor came, and the engine of the big Zil began running. It moved off almost immediately, turning for the gap and swinging through it as the two militiamen sprang to the salute with their greatcoats flapping. The engines of the three Chaikas were starting up now, and two of them turned to follow the Zil, bumping over the snow.

One Chaika remained, its frontal aspect different from the others because of the license plate and the small PA amplifier mounted below the radiator. This would belong, Lopatkin decided, to the deputy minister for state security, the second highest KGB officer in Moscow. The minister of health had warned him that he was present.

Static broke from the amplifier, followed by a sharp metallic voice.

"Aleksandr Leonidovich Lopatkin, you are under arrest."

CHAPTER FOUR

At 8:25 Eastern Standard Time, Aeroflot flight 378 from Moscow signaled the control tower at Kennedy International Airport and was given permission to land. Seven minutes later the slim supersonic TU-144 lowered through the faint night haze covering New York City and touched down on the runway. It was a fine winter's night, with only a slight amount of ground frost beginning to form under a clear, starlit sky.

Two hundred miles to the south, a helicopter of the US Air Force Special Services squadron was drifting low across the Potomac, and twenty minutes later a sealed file was signed for and handed over to the senior communications clerk on duty at the White House. This was the feasibility study that had been under final discussion throughout the day by Jim Forbes and his think-tank team at the Institute for Defense Analysis; the classification code on the sealed envelope indicated it was for the president's eyes only.

At this time President Hartridge was at dinner, spooning his Peach Mousse Cardinal and wearing a dark blue business suit instead of black tie, as a gesture of courtesy to the guest of honor, President Janos Lazar, who disliked formal attire as much as he disliked shellfish, which was why the entrée for this evening had been Supreme of Royal Squab Veronique, flown in two days earlier from New York.

Hartridge would not see the sealed IDA file until the morning; there had been no instructions for him to receive it earlier.

At 10:21 the doors of the Oval Office were closed for the third time that morning, and those present were invited to seat themselves. They were the chief of staff, the deputy chief of staff, the secretary of defense, the secretary of state and the director of the CIA.

Alex Dynan, State, and Bob Perrins, Defense, took two of the wingback chairs near the fireplace, where the coals had brightened to a glow as the cold morning breeze tugged at the chimney draught. The others arranged themselves along the two facing sofas, while President Hartridge stayed in the swivel chair behind his desk, pulling open the bottom drawer and crossing his feet on it.

On the desk was the red file.

"You've all had time to go through it, gentlemen?"

One or two of them nodded. No one was expected to say *no*, since their priority instructions earlier this morning had been to read the file while the Chief Executive was at breakfast in the State Dining Room with forty-five Democratic lawmakers who had come out in support of his budget. He himself had read it three hours ago, as soon as the telephone operator had given him his wake-up call, and he had already made up his mind.

"I think I'm going to ask for a show of hands."

Secretary of State Dynan was slightly shocked. This was going to be a pretty important decision, and it ought not to be rushed. But maybe the Chief had already made it, and this meeting was not much more than a concession to protocol.

Hartridge looked around at them. Four hands were in the air. Admiral Walsh, head of the CIA, wasn't expected to vote anyway; he wasn't part of the decision making.

"Mike, let's hear from you." Mike Simpson, deputy chief of staff, was on one of the sofas, and began playing with his transparent plastic-framed glasses. "I'm in favor, Mr. President, but with certain reservations. Certainly I believe it might be ex-

tremely profitable in our negotiations for SALT III to 'leak'—
quote unquote—the information to the Soviets that we are in
the final development stages of a new superweapon. But if we
fail to do it with guaranteed success, if in other words the leak
were seen to be deliberate, it would either be monumentally
embarrassing for us in our relationship with the Soviets, or a
great deal worse."

President Hartridge made a steeple with his fingers and put
them to his lips, watching nobody, his studious, crumpled-looking face contemplative and his gray eyes calm. During the rest
of the day he would preside over eleven meetings, deliver five
speeches and greet close to four hundred official visitors, but
that was no reason to hurry the project in hand; the schedule
on his briefing sheet allowed them another fourteen minutes
and they could steal another sixteen if they had to, and they
could reconvene after dinner this evening and spend half the
night on it, if necessary, though he didn't think it would be: he
had a good feeling about this project and was only going to allow
Mike's characteristic caution a limited amount of rope.

The president crossed his feet the other way on the edge of
the drawer, and gave Bartlett a chance to field Mike's reserva-
tion.

"No, we can't guarantee success," the CIA director said comfortably, "but we understand the size of this thing, and so far
our special action group hasn't ever fumbled the ball." He
watched Mike Simpson with a cool stare.

"Okay," Mike said, turning from the CIA man to the Chief
Executive, "but just the same I'd be a lot happier if we considered the consequences of actual failure. They could be very
grave."

Hartridge let them argue for another ten minutes, inviting a
freewheeling discussion, then he decided to sum things up.

"Okay, gentlemen, the schedule on this project has reached
thirty-nine hours and nobody can say we haven't given it
enough thought. I think we should look hard at the risk-benefit
factor, and to me the proportion seems overwhelming. The risk

of our fumbling the ball seems very slight, while the benefit of success would be far-reaching. The Soviets have been stonewalling on the SALT III talks for too long now. They're not impressed by the increase we've made in the defense budget, and it could well be that in the four or even five years it's going to take us to catch up with them in advanced strategic weaponry, they'll be tempted to call a showdown. And I mean militarily."

He looked at them in turn, but they knew he wasn't inviting comment; he wanted them to hear the echoes of that last sentence. "It's my plain duty to take every conceivable step to prevent such a disaster; and it's now my opinion, which I've reached by virtue of the intensive thinking you've all given this thing, that we should do all we can to persuade the Soviets that we have a new and potentially devastating particle-beam weapon nearing completion, and that it behooves them to go to the conference table for the SALT III talks and reach an agreement on strategic arms limitation before it's too late—for them." He looked at his watch, then across at the CIA director. "How soon can you make the move, Gordon?"

Admiral Walsh got up from the sofa. The others would be leaving now, and he would be asked to remain. "We're ready to go, Mr. President. The initial leak can be made before midnight."

Medina came through Washington National Airport from Los Angeles at 9:25 on the evening of the same day, taking a taxi as far as Georgetown, walking three blocks and taking another taxi on M Street. He told the driver to pull in to the curb when they reached 21st Street.

"We're picking up a friend of mine, okay?"

"Sure. Right here?"

"Outside the hotel."

There was no one waiting on the sidewalk. Medina looked at his watch. "What time d'you have?"

"Twenty after ten, give or take some grit in the hairspring."

Medina sat back again, his left hand on the briefcase. "You want to wait?"

"Where to next?"

"The Smithsonian."

"I can wait."

In five minutes a man in a herringbone overcoat came down the steps of the hotel, looking along the street and lighting a cigarette with a match. Medina snapped the rear door open, took a sharper look at him and was satisfied.

"Did your watch stop, Niki?"

The man dropped his cigarette in the gutter and climbed into the cab, resting his worn black briefcase next to Medina's.

"The Smith?" the driver asked.

"Right."

Medina slammed the door shut and Nikolay turned his head to look through the rear window as they started away from the curb.

"Fantastic town," Medina said. "You can see the buildings."

The driver glanced into the mirror. "You in from LA?"

"Right."

"I got a sister there."

"She's choking to death."

At the Smithsonian Medina paid off the driver and stood with Nikolay in the parking lot until the cab had turned into the traffic stream along Independence Avenue, then both men walked across to the dark blue Pontiac, Nikolay looking around him before they got into the rear and shut the doors.

"How are things with you, Niki?"

"Things are very well." His accent was almost a speech defect, thought Medina.

"Very good, Niki. Things are very good. Got it?"

"You are in a superlative mood," Nikolay said.

"Christ, where did you pick that one up? No one ever says it. But you could say I'm in a fantastic mood, Niki. Fantastic would be a good word." He slipped the looped chain off his left wrist and opened the briefcase and took out a single file, dropping it onto the Russian's knees. "This is it. The whole bit. Everything you asked for—including worksheets and diagrams."

Nikolay opened the file and Medina gave him ten minutes and then stopped him. "Seen enough?"

"The light is not good here."

"It's good enough. You can see the diagrams. You can have the whole thing for five hundred thousand." He pulled the file from the other man's knees and closed it, slipping it into his briefcase.

"The price agreed was two hundred."

"Not for this, Niki. This is the whole works. I didn't expect to get it." He took a cigarette and lit up, his fingers shaking as he offered the pack. Nikolay took one and Medina flicked his lighter again, watching the man's face, watching his eyes.

"I can pay you two hundred thousand," Nikolay said flatly. "I bring only two hundred."

"That's okay. I trust you people. I can get more where this came from—you'll need bringing up to date as the work progresses. Right?"

"I must take the material and look in better light. I—"

"*Shit*," said Medina through his teeth and hit the door open and got out, throwing his cigarette onto the floor carpet and swinging the door shut against the other man's arm as he tried to keep it open. "You know what's wrong with you fucking Reds? You want everything for nothing." Medina's face was tight with rage as he stared into the car at Nikolay. "I had to kill a man to get this stuff, you know that? It was close, you know what I'm saying, you fucking Bolshie? This stuff's worth a million to you bastards—ten million, I don't know, it depends what you do with it. And you're acting like it was a patent for a fucking mousetrap!" He dragged the door wide open and swung it viciously against the Russian, who caught it and came out of the car so fast that Medina jerked out of his reach and had his right hand on the mace canister before Nikolay said:

"We will talk more. Come back inside car."

"Two hundred," Medina said. "Cash. Now. And three

hundred more in a week, same time, same place. Or this is all you'll ever get."

"Very good. Two hundred now. But inside car." He looked beyond Medina, his heavy face worried. "Somebody see us, if we stand out here."

"No tricks. Or by Christ I'll—"

"Of course, no tricks. You trust, and will be okay."

They caught the man known to Medina as Nikolay on Belmont Road in Northwest Washington, ten minutes after he had dropped Medina outside a small hotel. He had parked the dark blue Pontiac five minutes later in an all-night garage and was on foot halfway along the 2400 block when four men of the CIA's counterespionage section pulled up at the curb and got out and stopped him. He didn't give any trouble; he stood there in the lamplight looking as if he were in shock. He probably was: since he had driven away from the parking lot at the Smithsonian he had made a dozen feints and loops through the streets to make sure he was in the clear.

Inside the car they looked at his papers and gave them back to him. They looked at the file he'd been carrying in his worn black briefcase. As the car started off, they asked him:

"Where did you get this?"

"I found it." Perspiration was dripping from his chin, and he was too preoccupied to wipe it off, even to notice it. He sat leaning forward between two of the men, in the rear of the car, his squat hands dangling.

"Where were you taking it?"

"To the lost property place. It looks valuable."

"To the lost property place at 1825 Phelps Place?" It was the address of the Soviet Embassy.

Nikolay Kostandov—it was the name on his papers—said nothing.

The car turned south on Virginia.

"You probably know," one of the CIA men told him, "that we

can make things an awful lot easier for you if you'll give us the name of the contact. The name of the man who passed you the file." He had to say it again before Nikolay Kostandov answered.

"I find it."

"The name?"

"No. Not name. I find this thing, I tell you."

This was routine. They knew it. He knew it.

"Just remember," the CIA man told him, "that you'll have an easier time, a *much* easier time—I mean by ten or twenty years —if you'll give us the man's name. We want him, more than we want you. We want him badly. Do you understand what I'm saying, Kostandov?"

"There was no man."

"Okay. There was no man. But if you'll give us his name when we start interrogating you, you can save an awful lot of your skin."

Nikolay Kostandov said nothing. He was still sitting with his elbows on his knees and his hands dangling when the other car hit them and slewed them around in a half-circle as a tire burst with the sound of a gunshot and the driver fought with the wheel and hit the brakes, ending up with the front fender smashing across a lamp pole before the car slammed broadside against a fire hydrant, a rear door springing open.

The five men were tumbled together and Kostandov was the first to pull himself off the floor at the rear. There was only one man between him and the open door, and Kostandov used a heel-palm against his face, thrusting him backward and lurching onto the sidewalk and breaking into a run while the others began shouting. One of them fired seven shots, and Kostandov could hear the shells ringing against the iron railings at the intersection as he reached it and vanished.

The man at the desk listened to the voice on the telephone, interrupting only once.

"Okay, but what were the precise instructions?" He listened

again, gazing at the photograph of President Hartridge that was on the wall over the filing cabinets, an informal picture taken on board a yacht in Long Island Sound.

"We were told to give him time to look at the file. Medina said he gave him ten minutes, in the car. Then—"

"Medina's been debriefed?"

"We're debriefing him now. Then we were told to take Kostandov before he could reach the Soviet Embassy—or a copying machine."

"Where did you get him?"

"On Phelps Place, in the seventeen hundreds. Then we turned south and waited for the contact. We were to be hit by another car—a hit and run scenario. That went off as arranged, and we let Kostandov run clear."

"Without the file."

"Without the file."

The man at the desk considered. "Okay. Do you feel Kostandov was convinced?"

"Medina says he threw a tantrum, to make it look authentic. He's satisfied with his end."

"And are you?"

"Yes, sir. Kostandov was sweating badly, white to the gills. I fired a few shots when he took off, and he ran like a professional; he's dodged gunfire before."

"Fair enough. When you've finished debriefing Medina, tell him I want to see him."

"Yes, sir."

The man at the desk looked at the brass ship's chronometer on the wall. "Change that. He's done enough for today. I'll see him in the morning. There are five more leak actions to set up. Tell Medina he's on one of them. And tell him I said good night."

CHAPTER FIVE

They moved the switch and Lopatkin jerked into the semblance of life again, pitching backward off the chair and catching his leg in one of the cables before he hit the bare linoleum, his breath shuddering out of his lungs.

"Get the straps," a voice said. "Strap him in."

Hands reached for Lopatkin, dragging him off the floor and pushing him onto the metal chair again. He sat there with his eyes red hollows under the blinding light, his mouth hanging open. There was the smell of burning flesh in the room from the metal clamps on his wrists.

They strapped him in.

He had been there for three days and two full nights. This was the third night, just beginning, and he had still not slept. He had begun losing consciousness recently, but that wasn't sleep. He could still think clearly sometimes, and he knew where he was: at the Serbsky Institute of Forensic Psychiatry, where political cases were brought and treated for their condition, which was usually a tendency to stray from the Party line.

They moved the switch and the lightning bolt crashed through his body again. After a long time he heard the voice, the same one, Ligachev's. Ligachev was not a psychiatrist, the man in the chair knew by now. He sounded more like a KGB officer of high rank. There had also been a general here; Lopatkin had listened to them talking when they'd thought he was unconscious, or dead.

"Don't you want to see your family again?"

That was the voice of Ligachev, coming from the far side of the light, where they were busy driving him toward madness, and death. *If only death would come, before the lightning struck again!*

"Don't you want to see your wife again? Elena?"

They'd brought her to see him, yesterday, whenever yesterday was, the day before the lightning began. They'd let him talk to her and ask how she was, while she stared into his face with the clear knowledge in her eyes that she wouldn't see him again, that this was the last time, the last kiss.

"Answer me!"

Yes, quick, otherwise he'll—"I would like to see her again, yes. But I can't do what you're asking. I'm a healer. I'm in medical research. I want to cure sickness, not kill people by the thousands—"

"Stop saying that! All we're asking you to do is run the same experiment again, create the same organism. That is *all*. It's nothing to do with you what anyone else does after that. You are a servant of the State. You must obey the State. Are you going to obey the State, Lopatkin?"

He tried to answer, but couldn't seem to make his tongue move. All he could do was wait for the next shock so that it couldn't take him unawares, when he wasn't ready. The sweat was drying on his face under the heat of the great lamp, itching on his skin. His mouth was a husk, and he couldn't remember the taste of water, the feel of it, because it had been so long since he'd held his mouth under the rusted faucet in the cell, catching each drip as it came, at intervals of fifteen minutes or so.

He felt the heat of the lamp inside his mouth, but didn't let it worry him. The only thing that worried him was that when the lightning came again he would disintegrate, like the fragments of a bomb. There was no way—

Shock and the light burst and he was flung through whirling fires as the thunder boomed and broke his skull and left him hanging from the straps with his ribs working like bellows for oxygen, a strange voice crying, his own.

"So . . . Lopatkin . . . lucky . . ." from the other side of the explosion. "Hear me . . . can you hear me?"

"*Ess . . . Yes . . .*"

"Then listen to me. So far, you've been lucky. There was no harm done, after the accident. You remember that, don't you?"

"Yes." The minister, with his hard bright eyes, *No one knows better than you, Lopatkin, what the consequences would have been, for all of us, as a result of your unpardonable mistake.*

No mercy. Well, he'd expected that.

"My instructions," said the man behind the light, "are to offer you the alternatives. You can go straight into the camps with a sentence of hard labor for life, while your wife and your children will follow you, so that every day you will be reminded by their suffering that you disobeyed the State. Or you can continue the life you were leading before the accident, working in your laboratory and going home at night to your family. Not a bad life, with your privileges as an academician, and I know which I'd prefer. But this is your last chance, do you understand?"

Images swam inside Lopatkin's head, of Elena, staggering under the weight of firewood . . . of Ludmila, her hands monstrous with raw chilblains as she broke the ice in the buckets . . . of Petr, reeling under the blows of a brutal guard . . .

"*Do you understand?*"

Quick—"Yes, yes, I understand. But you don't realize what you're asking me to do. You know the precautions we had to take, when—"

"We *know* the organism is deadly! We are not fools! We are not children!"

Then another voice came. "Colonel, let me talk to him." It was a modulated voice, its tone reasonable. "Dr. Lopatkin, I am a scientist, like you. I understand your point of view, and indeed I commend your regard for ethics. But all you are asked to do is the same as you have done before, but this time under the most strictly controlled conditions, so that there can be no question of another accident. What puzzles us is your reluctance to trust in the good sense and humanity of our leaders. They fully appreciate the potential danger and are more than capable of avoiding it. Trust them, my dear Lopatkin, and trust me."

He straightened a little on the metal chair, calmed by the man's voice. "But they'll use it for war, don't you know that? And they won't be able to confine it, however capable you think they are. And even if they could, I am not going to see one man die because of the thing I created. Not one, do you hear?"

"It's for the State to decide whether—"

"This is for me to decide. For me. A man has a soul. And a conscience."

He thought he heard a sigh. "Siberia is full of people with consciences, I'm afraid."

"And they're better than yours. And so is mine."

"Your colleagues aren't of the same mind. We've talked to them, for a long time. They won't be staying here; they're to be released in the morning."

This was Lopatkin's worst fear. Vladimir and Gregor and the others could duplicate the procedure, using the logs and their own memory. It might take them longer, because his work with the liquid chromatography was more sensitive, more intuitive. But if they wanted to—*if they were forced to*—they could do it.

"I can only pray they have a conscience," he heard himself saying quietly. Vladimir? Yes, without a doubt. But Gregor? He was a Party member.

"Lopatkin, I'm going to make a last appeal to you, as a scientist and an academician. You—"

"That means nothing. You've got to appeal to me as a human being."

But it was no good. He'd been listening to his own voice, the words slurred and thick as he forced his dry lump of a tongue to move in the parched hollow of his mouth. He sounded like a drunk, like an imbecile.

"Doctor," he heard the KGB man saying quietly, "this is the only way, you know."

In a moment the other man said reluctantly: "Very well. I'll come back later."

Lopatkin braced himself but was too late, and the lightning broke along his nerves again and sent him jerking to the dance of the mad.

At the Gestov-Klinik they had worked for three days nonstop, with Gregor and Vladimir sleeping at the laboratory in shifts and their two assistants confined to the same quarters and isolated from the rest of the staff.

They had followed the logs, using human white blood cells for the structural information in the form of messenger-RNA molecules; using the RNA as a template they had synthesized double-strand molecules of copy DNA and inserted it by recombination into the Kushevat Forest bacterium. As Lopatkin had done, they had cleaved the restriction enzyme and inserted the DNA into the gapped plasmid circle, now deliberately repeating the error by their choice of enzyme.

At the end of the third day they exposed a selected assay batch of the white Ukrainian rats, using the same number of controls. Before midnight the first of the rats began dying.

They called Director Smirnov to the laboratory.

"This is a precise duplication of the first experiment?"

"Yes."

Gregor showed him the DNA hybrids on the filter, using autoradiography and revealing the dark spots across the film. He showed him the microscope slide, and Smirnov kept his eye at the lens for almost a minute without moving, fascinated and at the same time repelled. The bacterium was unusually long, like an undulating worm with extremely fine filaments at both ends, not unlike *Spirillum minus*, but with a greenish tinge.

He straightened up at last from the microscope as Vladimir came toward them from the *in vivo* cubicle.

"Two more," he said.

"Dying?"

"Dead. And others dying."

Smirnov followed him to the cubicle. "What process is it?"

"The nervous system is attacked. Invaded, more accurately, through the myelin sheath."

Smirnov waited a few minutes longer, watching one of the rats as it began twitching with a regular series of spasms, running—as they always did—to the familiar locus of the nest for reassurance. Within ten seconds it was dead, the legs stiff and the black eyes still open.

Smirnov took them into the little office at the end of the lab section and, after locking the inner door, spoke to them quietly. Watching his eyes, neither of the two biologists could define the expression in them, partly because he looked away from them most of the time, guarding his own secrets. Did he feel, as they did, a sense of fear, or more precisely, foreboding? Was there any doubt in him that they should be doing this, even at the orders of the ministry? Was there even a hint of pride, that in the Gestov-Klinik was vested some kind of dramatic and far-reaching future for them all? They could not tell. Vladimir, for the most part, felt a sense of profound relief, of deliverance. *If the experiment can be duplicated*, the representative of the minister had told them, *you will be relieved of censure and given special status as your work progresses*.

Vladimir also thought of Lopatkin.

"Let me tell you," Director Smirnov said in his confiding tones, "what is to happen here at the Klinik, according to the information given to me personally by the minister. We ourselves will be confined here for a certain period and will be allowed to leave only under escort, and then only when essential to the work on hand. Our families will be permitted to move into the residential quarters, provided they will accept the same conditions. All the staff not now engaged in this experiment will be dispersed among the other clinics in Moscow, and you will be given a new corps of technician-assistants who will be designated Gene-K9 in the logs, since that is the assay number. The *cordon sanitaire* will remain in place, isolating the Klinik and protecting us from intrusion."

He noticed that Vladimir Dobrynin was looking apprehensive. He had committed himself to immediate and unswerving obedience to the State and to the minister when they had begun interviewing him at the Serbsky Institute three days ago; he had a stable and devoted family background—as Lopatkin used to have—and wished for nothing more than that his family should abide in peace and perpetuate. "I am instructed to tell you," Director Smirnov said to him, "that all these security measures are for our own protection and well-being; we are by no means prisoners here. On the contrary, we are to consider ourselves privileged."

Vladimir felt his relief returning, but again thought of his friend and colleague Aleksandr. "Have you any news of Lopatkin?" he asked the director cautiously.

Smirnov looked away. "We won't, unfortunately, see Lopatkin again. But then it was his own fault. There is no place among the scientific elite for counterrevolutionary tendencies."

The assay cubicle was in partial darkness. At some time after the director had left for his quarters, an assistant had switched off the lights, and now there was only the glow of the street lamps entering the narrow stretch of windows high on the east wall and reflecting from the glass assay tanks.

There was no longer any movement inside. The last rat to die had tried to reach the nest, but had not been able to make it; it lay on its back like the others, its legs stiff and its once bright eyes dulled to a dusty black.

Like the men who had caused their death, the rats too were privileged in a certain sense. They were among the first creatures on the planet to succumb to an organism that had never before existed, a new life form against which man was powerless to fight, either by inoculation, vaccination or any means known to medical science. It swarmed still in the droplets of culture medium that remained on the floor of the glass tanks, and in the blood of the dead white rats.

CHAPTER SIX

Nadia Fedotova stood staring through the huge window of the store, while behind her the sleek, polished traffic of New York flowed opulently through the chasm of Fifth Avenue, its lights and the glow of the Christmas decorations spreading the appearance of warmth between the buildings and keeping away the chill of the winter sky.

The young ballerina's attitude—her dark head tilted, her small gloved hands reaching out a little toward the window—made her seem frozen in time, as perfectly still as the life-sized figures beyond the glass. The tableau they composed was very different from the scenes she'd observed from the special bus that took the Bolshoi company from the hotel to Lincoln Center and back. This Father Christmas wasn't red-nosed and overweight and comical, like the others; he looked more like a winter god from the Norselands, the frost clinging to his gilded coat and casting a glow of soft light against his silvered face as he held the reins of the swift, leaping deer that dashed through the snows, their jeweled harness sparkling under the stars. On the painted sleigh the boxes and packages were piled high, their rainbow colors glowing against the background of white-mantled firs. The window was a stage, and Nadia's imagination took a breath and sent her leaping through the glass and onto the backs of the reindeer, her feet flying to pirouette and fall and leap again, her slight body weightless as the sleigh team bore her through the snows to the jingling of their magic bells.

Then the reflection of a man moved suddenly onto the window glass close beside her, and she whirled around with a scream starting in her throat. They stared at each other. He wasn't so close as he'd seemed in the reflection: he was behind her, toward the edge of the sidewalk, an ordinary-looking man in a shabby coat, hands thrust into his pockets against the cold, his eyes watery as he watched her, his mouth opened a little in surprise.

"You okay, lady?"

The breath was still blocked in her throat, and she couldn't answer, but simply went on staring, her whole body beginning to tremble now as her taut muscles relaxed. It was all right; he hadn't attacked her; she was still alive. The man took one hand from his pocket and made a brief gesture toward the window. "Cute," he said, "huh?" His smile was forced and embarrassed. When Nadia managed to nod in reply, he turned away and walked on, his eyes slanting downward quickly, in the manner one glances away from a lunatic.

She felt ashamed. This was her third day in New York, and by now she should be adjusting her beliefs about it, losing some of her fears and learning the realities of this alien city. On the first night here she'd had nothing to go on, except for hearsay in faraway Moscow. As Madame Olga had shepherded them up the steps of their hotel three nights ago, Nadia had glanced behind her fearfully, remembering the stories of armed and drug-crazed robbers that held this city in a reign of terror. The hotel was their only shelter, but even inside it, safe from the streets, an assault of a different kind was launched on their senses. The deep pile carpeting, the opulent furnishings and the brightly lit window displays proclaimed what these people were. This city was the very heart of capitalist materialism.

As some of them stopped to look at the windows, Madame Olga had spoken sharply. "Do you know how many citizens of this country can afford such baubles? Perhaps one percent. Perhaps even fewer. Now come along—we don't want them to imagine we're admiring their vulgar rubbish!"

Nadia had hurried toward the elevators with the rest of them.

"Did you see that dress?" Irina had whispered to her. "The gold one?"

"Yes," Nadia told her. "Quite appalling. The typical ostentation of the bourgeoisie."

"I thought it was beautiful!"

"Then you'd better not let Madame Olga hear you!"

That first night, Nadia had cried herself to sleep. It was true, then. All you could hear in the streets was the screaming of the police sirens as the robbers seized their victims; and wherever you looked you saw nothing but the displays of costly merchandise that branded this society for what it was: a worshipper at the shrine of the "Yankee dollar."

"Are you all right?" Irina had whispered from the next bed.

"I want to go home," Nadia had said.

The next day they'd talked of nothing but *Christmas*—a word for which there was no satisfactory translation in Russian. The word, with the other words, "Happy" and "Merry," appeared in almost every window along the street, and was displayed on banners and in colored lights against some of the buildings.

"It would be more acceptable," Madame Olga had instructed them acidly, "if these people were truly celebrating the birth of a mythical and benign figure—that would be harmless enough. But the bourgeois factory owners and merchants have long since turned it into a blatant excuse for extracting money from the working class, playing on their sentimentality and urging them to squander their meager earnings on so-called 'gifts' that nobody really needs. Indeed, the major stores offer to exchange these items of merchandise at a later date so that the recipients aren't forever saddled with things they've no earthly use for, and of course the stores profit once again, since the merchandise must be exchanged for something *at least* as expensive—and usually, of course, somewhat more."

Nadia listened to these brief lectures with the feeling that they protected her from the cultural contamination to which they were all exposed in this city, and this was probably the intention, since she sometimes noticed Madame Olga reading from half-concealed notes. It was just as well, with girls as young as Irina in the company—a mere seventeen.

But on the second day, Nadia's fears melted a little. Backstage at the theater, she noticed that these Americans had a habit of holding doors open for each other, instead of letting them slam as was the custom in Moscow; it had happened to her more than once, and she was curiously touched. And after the first rehearsals, the theater manager made a short speech of welcome in halting but rather charming Russian, explaining that he'd spent a "memorable" year in their "beautiful" city by invitation of the Cultural Exchange Committee for the Arts. He was a tall, stooping man with a ruff of white feathery hair and a smile that brought one's defenses down immediately—also there had been no signs of his having been robbed and beaten in the street on his way there.

By the third day Nadia had felt a certain turmoil beginning inside her, the more she saw of this city and mingled with its people. Though most of them were presumably working-class, they were rather well-clothed and looked cheerful enough, many of them carrying colored paper bags and packages—the "gifts" about which Madame Olga had lectured them—and Nadia found herself wondering what they were, and whom they were going to, and whether they'd like them.

This afternoon she had finally decided to do something so outrageous that she would probably have to pay for it very dearly. As she stood at the fringe of the throng at the Museum of Modern Art, where Madame Olga and three of their security guards had taken them after first rehearsals, she had felt the urge to walk quietly away and leave them there, and explore this interesting city on her own and without the accompanying lectures. And this is what she had done. There'd been a moment of panic as she'd reached the outer doors and walked into the street, and she'd almost turned back, but her curiosity prevailed, and an hour later she was standing here gazing into the window where the reindeer raced through the snows.

Apart from the incident with the man who'd appeared, she'd felt a certain sense of elation during her escapade, a sense of freedom. After moving constantly in a group shepherded by Madame Olga and the guards, she felt as if she had dived from a ship to swim alone in the open sea, and with the promise of distant islands where she could make discoveries. (At school, she had run away from the classes dozens of times, when there was a circus in town or a parade going on, and today it felt a little like that.)

Turning away at last from the scene in the window, she looked upward and let her imagination float among the tall glittering buildings, seeing them as crystal castles thrusting their towers into the night sky, each reflecting the others' perfect symmetry. It was perhaps at this moment in time when Nadia Fedotova fell in love with New York City, for the world was still full of wonder for the young ballerina in this, the nineteenth and last year of her life.

CHAPTER SEVEN

"These days," said Boytsov, "they simply push a scalpel up the inside of the penis till they reach the prostate, then they cut it away from there."

The polished black Zil with its smoked-glass windows and gray curtains swung out of the Kremlin through Spassky Gate and turned left into Red Square, and the traffic light in the archway turned from green to red again. Ahead of it, a buzzer sounded at the Granovsky Street intersection, and the policeman waved the cross traffic to a halt. In the front seat of the limousine, next to the chauffeur, the uniformed escort used his radio-telephone to alert other police along the route to the green-belt area.

"It sounds painful," Koslev said, his thin body sunk into the soft leather seat, finding comfort where he could get it.

"With the anesthetic," Boytsov said, spreading his hands in an appeal to reason, "it's nothing. You won't feel it. Get Dr. Strautmanis to do it, at the Klinik; he's American-trained."

The third man in the rear of the limousine sat silent with his own thoughts. He was Mikhail Rudenko, chairman of the council of ministers, his face heavily lined but his hair still dark, his London-styled suit showing two inches of white linen at the cuff, his single gold ring matching the gold cuff links and the pin in the French silk tie. Those who did not know him called him a dandy. Those who knew him better called it his sense of elegance. Those who knew him well were aware that these were simply the correct trappings of power, in the eyes of Rudenko himself. He was a man who knew his place, and his place was close to the leadership of the Soviet Union. Within a year, if his strategies proved effective, he would be voted into the seat of the chairman of the Presidium of the Supreme Soviet, to become one of the two most powerful men on earth, equal in rank with the president of the United States of America.

He was not thinking about that now. He was thinking about the dead white rats.

When they reached his apartment, he surfaced from his thoughts.

"I should have asked if you had other plans for this evening," he said to his colleagues as the escort snapped open the door. "But then, you would have told me in any case."

"Of course," Boytsov nodded quickly, deceiving none of them. When Mikhail Rudenko asked them to confer with him in private at his apartment, any other plans for the evening must be canceled at once, discreetly. He was not their boss in the hierarchy, they ranked equally, but he was the accepted leader of the *troika* they had formed during the past year or two; these three men, each of them ranking only below the chairman of the Presidium himself, had become drawn together by instinct, each either finding or fulfilling a need in the others. But if one thing had brought them together more than any other, it was Rudenko's personal aura of power. He was more than ruthless when ruthlessness was demanded; he was more than shrewd, intelligent, formidable as an in-party adversary and loyal as a friend. Sharaf Boytsov and Viktor Koslev sensed something in him quite beyond the qualities of leadership and long experience in government. He was a visionary.

Mikhail Rudenko's apartment occupied the whole of the third floor of a solid, red-brick building in Lenin Hills, its white-framed windows overlooking the city from across the Moscow River. The floor below was the town residence of Ivan Rusakov, chief of the KGB.

Rudenko's apartment was elegant, functional and quiet. One

would not have known there were servants in the place, though there were five. They themselves were privileged, by edict of the *Upravleniye Del*, the administration of affairs committee that regulated, by its secret budget, the status and awards of those whose service to the State was considered valuable. A greater part of the privileges enjoyed by Rudenko's servants was due to their having signed a sworn statement avowing that they would never reveal the conduct or behavior of their master's private life.

The only servant who appeared this evening was Tatyana Brekhova, a young woman whose severe hairstyle and black satin uniform barely disguised her dark, vibrant sensuality. She moved about the salon in perfect silence as she served the meal for Rudenko and his two guests, except when the crystal dish of caviar touched a porcelain bowl, or a wine glass rang musically against its neighbor. Though she had no one to help her—this was her preference—she conveyed the impression that if one of the guests dropped a fork it would be back in his hand before it could touch the floor.

Visitors to the Rudenko apartment had no doubts that a good measure of Tatyana's duties concerned the private needs of her master after hours; his wife had died three years ago and he had no taste for the comings and goings of mistresses; this young woman of the smouldering eyes was more than capable of satisfying his demands, which—as in most men of great power—were frequent, urgent and immediate.

This evening Rudenko gave the girl no more than a passing glance; he was in a mood, thought Boytsov, that presaged some kind of announcement, even revelation. Sharaf Boytsov, first secretary of the Communist Party of the Soviet Union, probably knew Rudenko better than any other man, simply because he had put his mind to it. Boytsov was no toady—he didn't attempt to ape his distinguished comrade's manner or behavior; he didn't bathe in his light. Boytsov had light of his own. As secretary of the CPSU he wielded great power and influence; as a gatherer of information—especially of information that was none of his business—he was without equal, and in his round, polished head was stored enough information to blow apart the whole of the Kremlin, ramparts and all, if he chose to use it, since he had long known that the most indispensable information is the kind of information that is none of your business to know.

Boytsov was also a man of intense energy, of the brand that rekindles its own fires instead of bringing exhaustion; portly, pink-faced and always seeming freshly shaven, he bustled along the corridors of power with unflagging zeal, his round, innocent-looking eyes missing nothing. But he was not a noisy man; his energies had the smoothness of a well-oiled machine, and he disturbed no one if it could be avoided; only when people were undisturbed, he had learned during his thirty-year career, could you come upon their strengths and weaknesses, while they were disarmed. These qualities had put him well ahead of the game that was played within the Kremlin walls. As a comrade of his had once put it, "If a fire breaks out, don't waste time looking for the extinguisher—it'll be in Boytsov's hand." His companion had nodded in agreement. "Yes, unless of course the fire's to his own advantage; then you'll know where the matches are."

This evening, the tip of Boytsov's tongue chased a remnant of caviar from behind a wisdom tooth as he watched the dark-eyed Tatyana clearing the dishes away, her breasts moving tautly beneath her black satin uniform. It would be quite enjoyable, he thought abstractedly, to bundle up with that buxom wench under the eiderdown, if he could get her there. On the other hand, if Mikhail ever found out, he'd finish his career breaking rocks in the frozen Gulag, and no mistake. There were other plums in this town you could lick the bloom off without losing your lollipop.

Sitting opposite him at the polished mahogany table, Viktor Koslev, his fellow guest, was occupied with much the same area but with distinctly less pleasure; it was all very well Boytsov's saying that some good anesthetic plus the American-trained Dr.

Strautmanis would fix would fix his little problem, but the very idea of a razor-sharp scalpel (a *scalpel*-sharp scalpel!) working its way up his urethra until it reached . . . His thin, long-fingered hand sought the balloon-glass again, and he stifled his thoughts in the fumes of the Remy Martin *fine Champagne*. That man Boytsov was so damned healthy!

Koslev was not always in such an anxious mood—anxiety has never taken any man to the heights of success; it had rather been Koslev's courage, and his cold, scientific mind. His looks didn't belie him: tall, thin, even donnish, his sparse hair silvered as if by the light of knowledge shining beneath his skull, he looked—as a friend had once remarked—"a pushover for the Nobel Prize for scientific endeavor." But the actual material Viktor Koslev had used for his tireless research was not chemical or biological, save in the sense that a human being is of both components. His studies were devoted to human beings as thinking creatures, and to the social environment in which they flourished, failed or found their individual equilibrium.

Where Boytsov could often tell when someone's mistake offered immediate and bountiful profit to someone else (usually to himself) simply by instinct and shrewd divination, Koslev could deduce its advantage on graph paper, drawing upon the historical patterns and trends of human behavior. He would have made a successful stockbroker.

He watched Comrade Rudenko as the servant removed his coffee cup, having to steer it past his outstretched arms as they rested on the table; he didn't notice her. Koslev had never seen his host so deeply preoccupied: He hadn't called them here tonight to discuss the state of the weather—it must be to do with the new American weapon, nothing less.

This, indeed, came into the conversation as Mikhail Rudenko led his guests into the room adjoining the salon and asked them to be seated while he paced the floor, unable himself to sit still. This was the place he called his study, though it more resembled a boardroom, with a long polished table running down the middle with twelve chairs on either side and one at each end. The décor was somber, with its heavy oak paneling and black marble fireplace and the thick velvet curtains that were now drawn against the distant lights of the city. At one end of the room hung a portrait of Lenin, at the other, Karl Marx.

"We know about this new weapon the Americans appear to have in production," he told his comrades after a brief preamble. "We *all* know about it." They knew that by "all" he meant the twelve members of the Presidium, including its chairman, Dimitri Vladychenko, the general secretary and chief of state. "And we shall continue to deliberate this rather dismaying issue in our normal course of procedure within the Kremlin. The last word I had from Comrade Vladychenko, at a little later than four o'clock this afternoon when he was getting into his car, was that there seemed to be the possibility that the Americans might conceivably be 'leaking' this information through covert CIA channels so as to push us into the SALT III talks and reach an agreement. However, Comrade Vladychenko added that even if this were true, we're not going to risk an assumption. It's far more conceivable that it is indeed true, since the CIA would have to be very clever to conceal a leak—and the CIA is not usually very clever."

Good thinking, nodded Koslev to himself. Historical behavior patterns.

"So we are faced," Rudenko went on, "with two hazardous choices. We allow ourselves to be pushed into a SALT III agreement before we're ready, or we dig our heels in and let the Americans deploy their new weapon at their leisure."

We've been over this already, Boytsov thought as he lit one of his host's Havana's. I don't like this much. He doesn't normally waste time in preamble.

"That is the background," Rudenko said, "to the proposal I shall now make." Halfway between Lenin and Karl Marx he stopped pacing and looked at his comrades in turn. His tone became lower. "And my proposal is for your ears only. You must understand that. I am not even informing Comrade Chairman Vladychenko. My proposal is far-reaching in its scope. It would demand a full meeting of the Presidium—*without secre-*

taries present—even to present a brief outline, as I shall do here tonight." In the glow of the chandeliers his eyes seemed darker than ever as he focused his attention on the two men in turn, the hushed intensity of his voice causing them to straighten in their chairs. "Do you understand what it means for me *not* to inform Vladychenko before we have talked of this proposal ourselves, in private? Of course you do. It could be seen as treason."

In the silence, ash fell from Boytsov's cigar; he didn't notice. "So, comrades," Rudenko told them, "you have the opportunity of leaving this room before I take the matter further. Think well. Your careers will depend on your decision. Perhaps your lives."

They watched his face. He's got older in the last two minutes, Koslev thought absurdly. It was a trick of the light. Boytsov stared up at Rudenko, his eyes round with wonder.

"Why won't you be informing our Comrade Chairman of this?" he asked softly.

"Because I don't think he would ever countenance what I propose. And I think it should be countenanced. I think it should be implemented, and finally carried out."

"Without his knowledge?" Koslev asked drily.

"Without his ability to object."

Boytsov snatched a quick breath.

What precisely, thought Koslev, is he talking about? The chief of state's resignation? Or his death? Yes, this might not be a bad time to walk out of here, and find somewhere safe to hide out. With Rudenko in this mood, there was going to be a lot of fallout, if he . . . *Was that it?* Fallout? The real thing?

"To implement my proposal," Rudenko said, "would first require the removal of our Comrade Chairman. So you will understand my invitation for you to leave here now. I shan't think the less of you, my friends."

"You mean—" Koslev began.

"There's no compromise?" Boytsov was quicker. "We can't have a chance to look at your proposal, and decide whether we want any part of it?"

"No chance, no. Because once you know what I propose,

you're not going to sleep too well. This can only be shared if we are to act together."

"Simply to hear your proposal," Koslev asked him carefully, "is to commit us irrevocably to joining you in carrying it out?"

"A hard bargain," nodded their host, "I agree. But these are hard times." He leaned over the table to bring his gaze directly into Koslev's. "You see, Viktor Viktorovich, anyone with this knowledge in his head must ally himself with me totally and unreservedly. Otherwise he might be a danger."

Koslev held his gaze for a moment, then looked down. According to his accurately plotted analysis of Rudenko's character, anyone who proved a danger to him would have to be removed. Even if he were the chief of state. Or Viktor Viktorovich, for that matter.

"I'm sorry to have to put it like that," Rudenko said as he straightened up, his glance taking in Boytsov too. "But a very great deal is at stake, you see. And there is—" with a shrug of his hand "—the door." He went to the end of the room and bent to fetch a magnum of mineral water from a cupboard in the huge sideboard, and brought it to the table with three cut-glass tumblers, part of a set of Waterford presented to him by the British ambassador last spring. As he filled them, he waited for one of his comrades to move, or both. But he didn't think they would, either of them, or he wouldn't have brought them here tonight. These were the only two men in the whole of the Presidium—in the whole of Soviet Russia—whom he could trust. And they were probably the only two men who had the intelligence, and the nerve, and the courage, and the endurance to go with him in his plans: the endurance that must somehow let them sleep at night, and greet their comrades each day as if all were still normal, and finally face each other and themselves when the moment came to act.

As the water splashed into the third tumbler, Sharaf Boytsov got up slowly from his chair and walked to the door, taking his time. Rudenko screwed the cap back on the water bottle and took it to the end of the table, setting it down quietly. Koslev sat

very still, listening to Boytsov's movement across the carpet, his
eyes angled down as if to see behind him. He didn't look around.
From the other side of the room there came the delicate vibra-
tion of a windowpane behind the heavy curtains as a jet airliner
took off from Sheremetyevo airport.

Boytsov reached the door and took the massive bronze handle, turning it, then coming back to the table. "Just making sure
it's locked," he said innocently. He liked little jokes.

Yes, Rudenko thought, he'll have the endurance.

"And is it?" asked Koslev, looking around at last.

"Yes."

"Then that's all right."

And so will he, thought Rudenko.

"Very well," he said abruptly. "Of course you may try to dis-
suade me in this project, and you may succeed. It's not certain
that we'll decide, finally, to go ahead. I need advice, and that's
what you're here for. But I believe you'll find this opportunity
irresistible . . . as I do." He began pacing again, and the images
came back to him, the images of that man's tortured face—
Academician Lopatkin's, in the psychiatric hospital—and of the
dead white rats in the laboratory. He'd spoken to no one—*to no
one*—of what he planned, and it was going to be difficult to
express an idea so monstrous in mere words. It had come to
him for the first time in the laboratory itself, not earlier when
he'd watched Lopatkin from behind the windshield of the Zil in
that floodlit wasteground. But once the idea had taken hold of
him, there'd been no stopping it.

There is no defense against this organism? he had asked the
group of biologists on his visit to the laboratory. Through the
visor of his protective suit he saw them shake their heads.

None, Comrade Chairman.

Their voices sounded metallic over the intercom that linked
them.

*There is no antibiotic? No antidote? Nothing in all medical
science?*

The robot voices came again.

Nothing, Comrade Chairman.

Nothing.

Nothing.

His plan had started then, and since then had grown with the strength and urgency of a seed in fertile ground.

Turning again under the portrait of Karl Marx, he paced back the length of the room. "Very well. I believe we are agreed that sooner or later the already prolonged contest of ideologies between East and West must be fought to a decisive conclusion. It already endangers the motherland, as the United States prepares to lay waste to our farms and pulverize our cities and decimate our peoples, denying us our last chance of proving that Communism, and Communism alone, is the only form of government and social congress that can bring the peoples of the world a life of peace, harmony and progress. Until a few weeks ago, the balance of power—the balance of potential mutual destruction—was such that neither side could make a decisive move without also destroying itself. Now that has changed. *Or can be changed.*"

Inside the narrow academic head of Viktor Koslev there was a sudden flurry of activity as several billion signals flashed in rapid exchange between his nerve synapses, and within a few milliseconds the result was presented as a semiverbal, semivisual readout in the privacy of his mind. *Until a few weeks ago?* Was that really what Rudenko had actually said? Yes. They were the precise words, he'd been listening very carefully, as he always listened to Mikhail Rudenko. *Then what had happened a few weeks ago?*

On the other side of the table, Sharaf Boytsov was drawing a slow, quiet breath as he watched the face of Rudenko, reading in it something of what Koslev was busy inferring in a different way. Koslev was assessing facts, drawing implications; Boytsov was watching the set of a man's face, the light in his eyes, and seeing great tension, a spirit in turmoil, a conflict of emotions that Rudenko was forced to damp down, to contain its fires, to present his thoughts as an expression of logic, of ordered concepts, as from a man certain of himself and of his destiny.

Boytsov had seen this degree of strain in the faces of his comrades within the Presidium at times when grave issues were beleaguering their loyalties, forcing them to take sides, demanding of them their last spiritual strength in a bid, sometimes, to save themselves, and sometimes from public disgrace and a career breaking away from under them as the shadows of extinction drew close. But tonight the strain he saw in this man's face and in this man's eyes was of a different kind, and Boytsov identified it with absolute precision. Rudenko was fighting the most ferocious battle that any man could fight: the battle against himself.

His voice was barely under control. "The conflict between East and West can now be resolved, and for all time. The cost will be high—that much cannot be escaped—but it will be less high than if both sides embarked on the ultimate insanity of nuclear war." He stopped pacing, and stood with his hands behind his back and his head raised a little to face the heavy curtains, as if placing himself under the judgment of his private and unseen gods. "To carry out my plans, it would be necessary to sacrifice the population of the United States of America, to do it within a short time—a matter of weeks from the outset—and to do it without contamination of the rest of the planet. After which the peoples of Soviet Russia can wake to the day when there'll be no war, nor any talk of war, ever again in the future of mankind."

Listening to him, Viktor Koslev felt his mind stumble like a runner and then shut down, leaving him numbed.

Rudenko turned to look at them at last. "We now have the means for this. It can be done."

Between the fingers of Sharaf Boytsov's hand the cigar had gone out; below it on the polished table the soft gray cylinder of ash was cold. He felt himself flinch as Rudenko's voice came again.

"It can be done."

CHAPTER EIGHT

President John G. Hartridge missed his step slightly, but corrected it well.

"Excuse me."

The wisp of a girl in his arms flashed him a brilliant smile.

"It is nothing."

"I guess I didn't have so much training as you."

"But you dance well," the ballerina said.

"You should see my *entrechat*. It's terrible."

She laughed again, more than politely. Her eyes were as brilliant as her smile, and she felt like a bird he'd captured, her slight body vibrant as they moved together across the dance floor. Was she always this way? Probably. They lived on their nerves, these people. Or it could be the champagne.

"Your English is excellent," he told her, tripping slightly again and thinking *shit*. He decided not to apologize again: it'd occupy the whole of the conversation.

"My father was consul," she said, "in London. He say it was good that I learn English. He like London very much."

"That's great. Maybe we could fit him in over here sometime."

"Is dead, now."

"I'm sorry." He steered her inexpertly toward the edge of the floor; his aide had told him he'd have one minute twenty seconds with each ballerina, two minutes with each soloist and three with the prima before his feet gave out. They must have calculated at what precise time his feet gave out by watching him on previous occasions in the state ballroom; they ought to go and work a goddamned computer on the stock exchange. "You know something?" he told his exquisite partner, "this does my heart good. I'm looking around me and half the people in this room are Russian nationals, and they're my honored and welcome guests. Now wouldn't it be nice if we could have all the members of your government over here like this, so we could talk everything out with them? Be a whole new world, wouldn't it?" He smiled down into the huge liquid eyes. "Tell them I said so, when you get back, will you? I just made you my Plenipotentiary Extraordinary, how about that!"

At the edge of the floor he bowed courteously and switched to the next ballerina, who smelled faintly of garlic.

Nadia Fedotova found herself in the immediate company of three elegant-looking men, as if passed deftly like a ball from the president to his staff.

"May I have the pleasure?" He was the youngest, though his hair was thinning and he had slight bags under the eyes. A liveried waiter was beside him, offering her his tray of champagne, but she shook her head.

"I have too much," she said a little breathlessly to the man in the tuxedo, and stifled a nervous laugh.

"Goes to the head," he nodded, turning on a rueful smile. "Shall we dance?"

"No. I must sit, please."

"Okay." He summed her up expertly: at first glance she seemed, sure, a little high on the champagne; but there was something more to the brilliant eyes and the nervous laughter; maybe it was just being where she was—not too many Russians got into the White House. And the four weeks the Bolshoi had done at Lincoln Center hadn't drawn the notices they must have hoped for; most of the critics had given praise where praise had been due, but the consensus had been that the repertoire was "tired," "predictable" and "the same thing over again." One writer had given the actual score: since the Bolshoi had first started touring the US, its American audiences had seen eleven *Nutcracker Suites*, nine *Swan Lakes*, seven *Don Quixotes* and five *Giselles*. "The distinguished company itself," Richard Le-Jeune had reported in the *New York Times*, "appeared to be bored with the repetition of work it must presumably have performed several hundred times already." So maybe this girl, thought the man in the tuxedo, had been drinking her troubles away. But she'd danced well, he remembered; she was one of the soloists.

"I'm Bruce Paget," he said easily, "a presidential aide."

"Fedotova," she said.

"Of course. I remember your exquisite pas de deux in *Giselle*. The *Times* said you didn't seem aware of the audience, remember? I thought it was inspired." The home team here had been ordered to bone up on details of the Bolshoi's performances after watching every one of them, but he enjoyed ballet in any case and he really did remember this slight and enchanting soloist on the Lincoln Center stage.

"You see me dance?" she asked in surprise.

"The whole of New York saw you dance." Not strictly true: for the first week there'd been full houses, then the numbers had fallen off, for the first time in history. He led her gently to one of the silk brocade chairs near the orchestra, glancing around to check where the president was. He was okay. taking time off to talk to the prima ballerina while he rested his feet. Two of the security guys were within ten paces of him, with four more nearer the walls. The First Lady was talking to the deputy director of the ensemble, looking like she was enjoying herself. "So you leave tomorrow," he said to the little soloist. "You must be pretty homesick by now."

"That mean—?"

"Uh, you must be missing your folks. Uh, your family."

She looked suddenly haunted, and he wondered what he'd said. "Yes," she said, looking down quickly. "Yes. But you see

—" She shook her head. "I would like champagne now, please." The request sounded almost urgent.

"Sure. Coming right up." He signaled the nearest waiter.

"Your president," she said hesitantly, "seem a nice man, I think." But it was a question, and she was looking up at him with those enormous liquid eyes. "Like a father," she added strangely.

"Absolutely. That's just what he's like." And you should just be here, he thought privately, when he's bawling us out.

She was still watching him intently. "You say you are president—" she looked for help.

"Presidential aide." The waiter had come up now with his tray, but the girl seemed too engrossed with what she was saying.

"You are important man, then." Her eyes never left his face.

"Uh, well, I'm kind of close to the president, sure." He took a glass of champagne for her, but suddenly she was standing right up close against him and gripping his arms, her voice hushed but urgent.

"*I wish to stay in America, please. You understand this?*"

Her small hands were shaking him, the fingers digging in. His thoughts did a quick swerve, then got back on track.

"Do you mean," he asked carefully, "you want to defect?"

Her fingers dug harder still as she nodded vehemently. "Yes, to defect. Help me, please. *Tell what I must do.*"

"It's crazy," Patolichev had told them yesterday, sitting cross-legged on the stool at the café, his loose shirt knotted at the waist, the great, the notorious Patolichev. "I don't know how you stand it over there!"

He meant in Moscow. It sounded strange, Nadia had thought, to talk of home as "over there." She sat between Novikova, the prima ballerina, and Irina, her friend and fellow soloist. No one knew they were here at the Café Russe—"no one" meaning Madame Olga, the deputy director of the troupe and the five KGB men. "There'll be trouble," Novikova had told them with a defiant laugh, "but are we going to leave New York without seeing Patolichev?" She'd smuggled Nadia and the other soloists into the café by the side door, having told Patolichev they'd meet him here.

"*Giselle*," he was saying, his arms sweeping the air, "*Nutcracker . . . Sleeping Beauty . . .* oh, my God!"

Strange, too, to hear these greatest of the classics ridiculed.

"You know what we've been doing?" He leaned forward dramatically, his shadowed cheekbones moving into the light. "*Eugene Onegin! The Ave Verum Corpus* or the rest of *Mozartiana! The Garden of the Lilacs!* And a dozen other modern American works, experimental, innovative, breaking new ground!"

Nadia had come away with her head reeling. "How subversive the man is!" the prima ballerina had laughed, trying to sound correctly scandalized, as she'd led them out of the café. "But what he says is true, you know. The ballet in Moscow is dying."

Nadia and the others said very little, but listened a lot. It didn't do to try *discussing* these things with Novikova; one was expected simply to pay attention, thinking what one chose to think but not putting it into words. "Isn't it exactly what Gayevski said in his book? We've been stuck in the mire of false traditionalism for the last fifty years, with not a Balanchine or a Béjart to our name!"

They'd seen she was deeply disturbed by her meeting with Patolichev, and understandably: he had defected only a few months after Nureyev and was now the director of the New York Ballet. Talking of it feverishly in their hotel room that night, Nadia, Irina and three of their closest friends still felt under the spell of Patolichev's flamboyant personality. There'd been trouble, of course, as Novikova had predicted, but she'd taken full responsibility for visiting the Café Russe with the soloists, whom she'd warned to say not a word of their actual meeting with the great defector—that would have been an offense that even the prima ballerina would have found it hard to make light of.

Nadia's earlier escapade had cost her dearly, and after an exhaustive interrogation by Madame Olga, the deputy director and the five KGB guards she'd fled to her room in tears. Why had she chosen to "defy the most inflexible rules" and "fly in the face of authority" like that? Had she encountered any American or other non-Russian? Had there been an arrangement made to meet anyone? Why hadn't she telephoned *immediately* to the Soviet Embassy to report that she was lost? Where had she been for almost two hours, alone?

She could only repeat her story, even though each of them had tried hard to break her down. She'd seen another room in the gallery they hadn't visited, and thought simply to go there herself and wait for them to catch up. Lost in the crowd, she became too scared to approach an American and ask for help, since she'd heard the most fearful stories of crime in the streets. Finally she had sat in a café drinking cup after cup of tea, trying to muster the courage to telephone the hotel and risk some American's knowing she was lost and helpless—and at anyone's mercy. At the beginning, she'd been ready to admit she'd simply taken time off alone to enjoy herself, but the sight of the KGB men's faces had made her switch her story at once, and for the first time in her life she had realized something that she'd heard rumored so many times in whispered conversation: that Soviet Russia was a "police state"—an expression she'd always thought to mean simply that it was well policed and therefore orderly. The revelation had chilled her, and the interrogation that followed had frightened her beyond any expectation; what she had seen as a mischievous escapade had been turned into an unforgivable crime.

There was also, in the eyes of this sensitive, vulnerable teenage artist, something even worse than fright that she had been made to suffer, and this was humiliation. Old enough to dance as a soloist, old enough to go with a man and bear a child, she had been castigated for simply walking in the open streets of a city she was beginning to love. *Her own people had treated her like an escaped prisoner.*

It was this thought that had come crashing into her head with an almost physical impact, and she remembered half-falling as she reached for the nearest chair. Two of her friends were in the room with her at the time, and were worried about her, but she simply told them the interrogation had left her dizzy, and let them fetch her some water. But it was this thought, with all its terrifying implications, that had kept her sleepless for most of that night, and by morning she had reached a decision.

For God's sake, thought Bruce Paget as the ballerina clung to him at the edge of the dance floor, *couldn't she have just walked into a police station instead of choosing the White House?*

"There's no problem," he told her calmly, and looked around him, lifting a hand. "Bob," he told the man who came up, "the lady would like to dance."

"My pleasure."

Bruce gently pried her fingers from his arms. "I'll go and set things up," he smiled cheerfully. "Then we'll wait till your party starts leaving, in around an hour from now. At that time I'll be right beside you, and there'll be no problem. Okay?" Turning, he murmured to the other man: "Don't let her out of your sight, and don't let her leave the room. Priority."

"Yes, sir."

But the girl gripped his arm again. "I cannot wait for that. I am afraid. It must be now. Please."

Bruce raised his eyes a fraction and focused on the people behind her in the middle distance, under the main chandelier. Of the men in tuxedos, two were Soviet "escorts," and they were watching the girl. Beyond them, slowly on the move to keep close to the president, were four or five White House security men. They couldn't help him; "Potus"—their name for the president—was their sole concern. Across the dance floor, "Flotus" —the First Lady—had her own discreet entourage.

Bruce Paget looked down at the girl; she was near tears and her slight body was shaking. Right, she wasn't going to hold out for another hour. "Have you given your security guards any trouble while you've been in New York?"

She hesitated, then said, "Yes."

That was why they were watching her like this, among the fifty other dancers they were here to "escort." It wasn't going to make things any easier. There was no question of his not being able to get this girl across; the problem was how to do it without ruffling the surface of a gala evening in the presence of the Chief Executive.

"Okay," he told her with a fixed smile. "Bob here is going to dance with you for just a couple of minutes, and he'll lead you slowly across the floor to the other side. When you get there I'll be waiting for you. Do you understand?"

She stared up at him with her eyes glistening, her face deathly pale. "Yes, yes. You will help me?"

"Of course." For an instant he felt moved by her appeal, by her naked vulnerability. "Just do everything we tell you and you'll be fine." He gave the other man a casual glance. "Stick to the orders."

"Yes, sir." By the time Bob had taken the girl in his arms, Bruce was moving steadily around the edge of the floor, his bright smile beginning to ache on his face.

"Bruce," someone said, "I'd like you to meet—"

"Busy."

He moved on, pausing to shake hands with Senator McBridie from Idaho. "Well, Bruce, it's been a long—"

"Excuse me, Senator."

From the tail of his eye he saw the men who'd been standing behind the ballerina; one was still watching her, the other was watching Bruce himself. *Shit.* It was an even choice now: either he waited until the girl's nerve broke and she became hysterical, or he kept on going and risked a scuffle, not just in public but in the White House; not just in the White House, in front of the president.

Let the chips fall where they may.

By the time the girl had reached the other side of the dance floor he'd gotten hold of three of the Secret Service men and briefed them, and as she left the arms of her partner Bruce took over smoothly and walked with her toward the tall double doors;

at this moment they were wide open and flanked by two liveried footmen.

"Don't let anyone through," he told one of them as he took the girl's hand, and then everything happened at once. Two of the escorts had moved in on them the instant they saw the girl heading for the doorway, and one of them broke into a run as the Secret Service people came in from each side to cut him off and one of the footmen came forward to block his path. But the escort wanted to tough it out with them and get to the girl, and it took three of them to trip him and put a single-arm hold on him from the rear as he began shouting for his own people to help him. The orchestra missed a couple of beats and the presidential bodyguards closed in on their charge like a drill team, getting between his body and the scuffle going on by the doors. Conversation dropped in sound volume as if someone had turned a switch, and for a moment there was near silence except for a stream of Russian oaths from the captive escort; then he was hustled outside and the doors were swung shut and the orchestra picked up the beat and things returned to normal.

In the anteroom where Bruce Paget had taken the ballerina, he was thinking *Jee-sus, that was pretty crude and the Old Man's going to have my balls off.* Then he picked up a telephone.

"I want Immigration." As he talked he shot a smile or two for the girl, who was leaning her back to the wall and holding her shaking body with her arms folded, her huge eyes watching him. "I know their office is closed, but I want two of their people here right away. What? I don't care where you get them from—the airport, the harbor, wherever, just get them. Yes, supervisors with special-situations rank, and it's your ass if you don't move it."

CHAPTER NINE

There were not too many people on the beach. Of those who had come down from the hotel at the sand's edge, most had formed groups and sat talking and smoking under the sunshades, while others lay supine on straw mats, looking as if they had been washed ashore among the debris of driftwood and tin cans and food wrappings that lay everywhere. Quite a few were swimming, for even now, in early February, the temperature of the water was 18°C, according to the scribbled figures on the piece of paper on the bulletin board at the hotel. That wasn't bad for the Black Sea in winter.

Some of the people lying on the straw mats had brought their clothes down with them from the hotel. Even at Sochi, a resort for the official elite, one wasn't quite sure of finding one's clothes again in the dressing room: the staff was notoriously light-fingered, since a waiter, for instance, would need to work for six months to afford a good woolen suit like the one lying folded near Terebilov, a member of the Secretariat and a voting member of the Politburo.

Arvid Terebilov had come down from the hotel a half hour ago, alone, with his bundle of clothes and his straw mat, and had lain on his back with his eyes shielded from the pale sun's glare by a handkerchief folded across them. Sometimes he became aware of people talking near him, and of the waves falling along the shore, and the cry of gulls; then he would hear the voices again, as he had heard them before.

The danger, you must understand, is that we should think of this matter too parochially, too locally. I quite appreciate that the bare idea of sacrificing the population of the United States of America in order to establish Communism globally, at last and for all time, and put an end to the bitter and senseless struggle that plagues the world, is shocking to contemplate. But we must steel ourselves to look beyond that, beyond the planet where man at present makes his home.

Mikhail Rudenko. Logical, reasonable, convincing.

The doors of the anteroom had been locked, and the Kremlin guards ordered away from them. Even then, they had kept their voices low: Rudenko, Boytsov, Koslev and Arvid Terebilov, who now lay here on the littered sand with his handkerchief over his eyes and a terror in his mind that had not left him in peace for weeks.

Technology has advanced with breakneck speed, almost as if man realizes the need to transcend his present social and geographical limitations. Whether he is alone in the universe is a question less important than whether he is eventually to populate the stars himself. He is already on the threshold of his momentous odyssey, and at the crossroads of his destiny. There must come a time when we shall ask: is he to take his petty wars out there into the firmament, and spread the ideological conflict that maintains its stranglehold on his true endeavors here on earth? Can he never change? If he .can change, when should he begin?

The waves lapped at the seashore.

A good orator, your Chairman Rudenko. You couldn't help listening to the man. Even though it cost you your sleep for thirty nights, and your wife's patience, and your appetite for food, and your comfortable impression that the world had not gone stark staring mad, you had to listen to him, and keep on listening.

I believe man can indeed change. And I believe he should begin now. So what we have to do, my good comrades, is to wrench our minds to encompass not only a world scene, but a cosmic scene. We must realize that we may be alone in the universe. If we are, our responsibility to our species—to the very history of our species—is almost unimaginably great. Let us stand back and get our perspective, and see beyond—far beyond —this one small satellite that circles one small star. If we are to leave it, we must go as a species that has come to grips with its early beginnings, that has reached a maturity that has decreed the cessation, for all time, of mutual and suicidal aggression, terror and enmity. Man must seek his new horizons as a brotherhood, in which the insane cost of armaments today can be vested in the grand design that will tomorrow open the gates to his universe. And there is only one form of true brotherhood that can save man from the eternal strife of egotism and materialism. We must ensure, with all the power and with all the spirit and with all the determination we can find within us, that the man who reaches out to the glittering panorama of his new worlds is Communist man, a social creature able to forge his tools for the immense tasks that lie ahead of him, secure in the knowledge that he forges them in peace, and for the perpetuation of everlasting peace across the distances of his boundless domain.

A small boat met the sand's edge and was heaved ashore with much grunting from the crew. A woman laughed, a lilting sound that for an instant brought hope to Arvid Terebilov that all might not be fearful, and insane, and unthinkable; then this one pure note of music died away to leave him with his nightmare.

And if there is life only on this one small planet, by a freak chance of chemistry, then we are today the custodians of all civilization throughout the universe. Are we to stand and do nothing? Are we to cringe at the awesome challenge that evolution has thrown down to us? Or are we to recognize within ourselves our true role as the saviors of mankind, as the architects of the grand design that will grant mankind its place in cosmic history?

Oratory, yes. But Rudenko knew what he was doing. The last bit, about their "true role," had been added for the edification

of Boytsov, as an appeal to his vanity. And there was truth in it.
If they undertook this appalling mission, and brought about
global Communism, they would go down in history with names
greater than Napoleon's, Alexander's, Caesar's. That would
please Boytsov, yes.

His fingers digging restlessly at the coarse sand, Terebilov
tried to shut out the voices of the nightmare, but in vain. He
had not come here to Sochi to forget, but to decide.

I need time, Mikhail, to think.

Of course you do. Take a little vacation. Go to the sea.

The others, he supposed, were still meeting surreptitiously at
Rudenko's place, talking behind locked doors in the Kremlin
and in the privacy of the limousines—though in the limousines
they would need to speak almost in code, choosing words with
double meanings. What were they saying? Nothing that gave
Arvid Terebilov much hope: the others had already been
brought around to consider carrying out this hideous project,
and if they could consider it, they could launch it.

They'd called him in because they needed him. They needed
his experience of the checks and balances that maintained the
equilibrium of power within the Politburo; they needed him as
a shield against Chairman of the Presidium Vladychenko, who
must not be told a word of what they planned; and they would
later need his friends, to help them finalize their planning. And
from the moment they had called him in, he had scarcely slept.

They had called others in: three nameless men whom Rudenko had introduced as "trusted experts in their field." At this
time the oratory had given place to facts and figures.

The dissemination of sufficient quantity of the "activator" to
decimate the population of the United States could be carried
out by fewer than a hundred agents, each of them sent in to the
main target areas simultaneously. The "process" would then
accelerate of its own energy.

A hundred men? Terebilov had asked. *To "deal with" two
hundred million?* (He had been careful to use neutral terms, as
they did, to express the inexpressible. He hadn't said "to wipe

out." He had known very early that he must appear sympathetic to their cause, once he was privy to it: he owed a duty to himself, to keep his head in place.)

The Americans stopped World War II, Rudenko had pointed out calmly, *with a couple of bomber crews.*

The "process," one of the nameless experts had reported, would require between two and three months for total contamination to be reached. After that, thirty days would be required before any outsider could cross the borders of the United States of America in safety.

A *lifeless America?* This had been Sharaf Boytsov, his eyes round with wonder to conceal his ability to grasp instantly the implications of what was being proposed.

By this time, yes, the expert had said. The man had smelled faintly of a hospital, or a laboratory, and Terebilov could have believed he'd left his white linen coat outside the door. And a briefcase with the skull and crossbones on it.

But how would the contamination be contained, Viktor Koslev had wanted to know, *within those borders?*

By what Rudenko called a "trigger mechanism," which he then explained, calling upon another of his experts to present the facts and figures. The United States of America would be persuaded to close its own borders, its own seaports and airports, before the main phase of the project was launched.

The fingers of Arvid Terebilov dug into the sand, while sunlight penetrated a gap between his handkerchief and his brow, blinding him in one eye. He brushed sand from his right hand, and rearranged the handkerchief. Listening to the slow leap and fall of the waves, he pictured himself lying on the shore of a different continent, the last of its denizens to succumb to the Soviet project. So, behind him, they were all dead? From coast to coast, from each point of the compass to its opposite, on hill and in valley, in every street and every building and every room of every city . . . *dead?* Every man, woman and child? The citizenry of two nations, *dead?* So, once there had been Americans and Canadians, and now there is only America and Canada—

Soviet America and Soviet Canada? *Is that what you mean, Comrade Rudenko?*

Questions like these had come to his head and lodged there like quiet maggots to nibble at his brain in the dark of the night, in the silence of the night, *Can't you sleep, Arvid?* his wife had asked him a hundred times, *Can't you sleep, my love? I'll make you some broth; you ate almost nothing for supper.*

The waves leaped and fell. All *dead?*

And to repopulate America, Koslev had asked the architect of the grand design, *to put it into production again? How would that be done?*

Trust Koslev, with his reptilian-cold, scientific mind, to pass over the little matter of annihilating the population of a continent and inquire as to its rehabitation.

With the Chinese, Rudenko had replied, ready for the question. Their good neighbor would see clearly enough the necessity of complying with any demand made upon her, and her people—though not at present capable of understanding much more than the workings of a bicycle—could be trained to operate machinery and plow the land under the supervision of European experts. Within a year at the most, the productive capability of the United States of America would be in gear again.

As if nothing had happened.

A fly settled on the cheek of Arvid Terebilov, and for a time he didn't notice it. *As if nothing at all had happened.*

Where would they put all the corpses?

No one had asked about that.

And the death notices, the obituaries—where would they be printed? For two hundred and fifty million people?

One could go mad, and ask mad questions, if one thought about this thing long enough. What would they do with the Statue of Liberty? Cut it down at the base with jackhammers, like a tree? That would make a splash. And what would happen to the White House? It wasn't nearly big enough for a totalitarian seat of power: Soviet America would be governed from the

Pentagon. They could use the White House as a museum. Or a morgue.

The last meeting Rudenko had convened was held in Koslev's *dacha*, in the green belt beyond the hubbub of the city, where they could talk quietly. By that time Rudenko had begun exuding a mood of dark and terrible jubilation, and it was Terebilov's feeling that the chairman of the council of ministers had come to realize that already he had carried his argument to the point where none of them could deter him from his project. Perhaps he had underestimated their readiness to see in him a visionary whom they must follow in blind faith to his new world order, or perhaps, thought Terebilov, he had simply underestimated their total ruthlessness.

The final argument Rudenko had put to them, the day before Terebilov had left Moscow for the coast, had sounded ominously conclusive.

If we fail to proceed with this project, I am not sure what the consequences will be to Soviet Russia and her allies, in view of the new weapon the Americans appear to be developing. But I am sure we have no other answer to it, other than a decision to embark on global nuclear holocaust. Yet, even leaving aside the threat of the American weapon, let us look at where we are. Triangle diplomacy is very real. We now face the risk of a joint assault by the United States, China and Japan. Again, our only answer would be in nuclear retaliation and, subsequently, the extinction of life on earth. If we attempted to remove the risk of invasion along our western borders, by launching a limited war upon Europe, we should let China and Japan in by the back door, aided by American resources. To launch a limited—in a nonnuclear sense—a limited war against the United States, we would need first to align South America politically, and secure massive military support and the availability of established bases. And again, we should expose our eastern borders to assault by China and Japan at a time when our own forces would be depleted.

Rudenko had stopped his incessant pacing to stand facing

them with his feet neatly together and his hands clasped behind him, his attitude a deliberate understatement of the gravity of his words. *My comrades, let there be no doubt. Even without the threat of the new American weapon, the situation of our mother country is so perilous at this time that we have no choice but to proceed with our project, and without further delay.*

By "proceed," Terebilov assumed, Rudenko meant to call in other people, especially other "experts in their field," and undertake a more elaborate feasibility study, before the final political moves that would oust General Secretary Vladychenko and surround Rudenko's *troika* with a loyal and determined group with the power to set *Wasteland* in motion. (That was the name someone had given the project, and already it had stuck. It was, in Terebilov's present thinking, the most horrifying word in the dictionary.)

Above all else was his growing certainty, as he reviewed the situation again and again, that it was already too late to prevent this thing from happening. Rudenko had already convinced two of the most powerful members of the Presidium of the Supreme Soviet that there was no choice; he would convince more, and finally there would come the day when they would wake in the light of the new dawn, and shave, and eat breakfast, and convene in the privacy of the Kremlin chamber and say, yes, we will now do this thing. And the orders would go out, encoded and by secret courier.

Wasteland.

We always think, Rudenko had told them, *that the world can never change, that all the great changes in the history of mankind have already been made. But there was once a date on the calendar—the sixth of August, 1945—that seemed without significance the day before Hiroshima was laid waste and conventional warfare was suddenly a thing of the past. There was once a day—the twelfth of April, 1961—when a man named Yuri Gagarin became the first human being among untold future millions to leave the planet and relegate the life of earthbound man*

*to ancient history. What we now plan to bring about is no more
momentous than that. And no more difficult.*

Wasteland.

Sand fell from the hands of Arvid Terebilov as he sat up
slowly and for a while remained with his arms across his knees
and his head resting on his arms, his eyes closed and his temples
throbbing, his mind butting at the impasse like a fenced goat, as
it did so often and without relief. He wanted no part of *Wasteland*: that was not the question. The question was what he
should do about it.

Lifting his head, he surveyed the expanse of the blue and
untroubled sea, and for a while let his eyes rest there, until he
was sure. Then he turned to the little group of people nearby.

"Would you watch my clothes for a bit?"

A man said: "We're going in half an hour."

"I'll be back before then."

As he went forward across the hard ribs of the sand and into
the shallows, he recognized the chief of the organizational Party
work department, a huge man with black hair on his chest and
a long string of mucus hanging from one nostril as he waded
through the waves; Terebilov wondered vaguely whether he
should point it out to him. Then he was in deeper water, feeling
the cool shock of it around his thighs and then his chest as he
went on moving into the smooth and undemanding sea. At last
he reached forward with his hands, and began swimming slowly
away from the shore.

Someone reported later that he thought he noticed the swimmer lift a hand from the distant water, but believed he was
simply waving to his friends on the beach.

CHAPTER TEN

"It's a question of values," Braithwaite said as he watched the waiter pour the Beaune. "On the one hand the environmentalists decry the killing and eating of birds, while on the other hand the London County Council is at its wit's end trying to get rid of the pigeons all over the place." He swirled the wine in his glass. "Now I ask you, if they're regarded as not much better than airborne vermin—which is a pretty fair description, since they spend their entire lives dropping pigeon-shit all over the windowsills—then why is it considered such terribly bad form to shoot them, pluck them, rub them carefully with a half lemon, stuff parsley into their bellies and braise them in hot fat?"

Watching his host, George Vickers didn't make the mistake of answering. Instead, he observed the lean looks of the man opposite him at the table—the perfectly groomed silver hair, the long-fingered hands, the ice blue eyes and the dinner jacket whose dark nap was now showing just the correct amount of shine at the shoulders—and thought that if anyone came in here looking for the chief of the British Secret Service he'd pass immediately over this pedantic, pigeon-loving intellectual simply because he looked exactly the part. A good spy, surely, should try to look like a stockbroker, or someone equally harmless—given, of course, a dull market.

"So what we come down to," said Braithwaite, spreading the pâté de foie gras to cover his toast completely, "is an inexcusable defamation of the pigeon. The plucking, braising and eating of the bird is a process of ennoblement, don't you see. Once a common creature regarded as vermin, now a welcome visitor to the stomach of a higher organism, with an obituary seen to grace the most splendid menus in London." He leaned forward to fix his guest with that notorious ice blue gaze. "Now which epitaph would you rather have, George? One that stands as a lasting reminder that the best you could do in life was to leave birdlime on Nelson's hat, or one that lauds you for having brought grace and gastronomic enjoyment to some of the greatest names in history?"

He allowed his gaze to linger for precisely five seconds and then removed it. He knew George was here to talk about the problem he was having with the new computers in Codes and Ciphers, but the hallowed dining room of the Savage Club was no place for that, so they were going to talk about pigeons.

"I see what you mean," said George Vickers flatly. He was damned if he were going to turn this into an actual conversation.

"I doubt if you do, but I shall proceed to elaborate." He glanced up as the headwaiter came to stand near.

"If you'll excuse me, Sir James . . ."

"What is it, Willy?"

"A telephone call, sir. A Mr. Conway."

Sitting opposite him, George Vickers saw not the slightest reaction in the chief's eyes, hands or attitude, though his own heartbeat began thudding under his rib cage. There was no member of the British Secret Service named Conway, but if anyone at all had occasion to telephone the chief on a matter of the highest possible urgency, that would be the name he'd use to signal the urgency itself.

"How very tiresome," Braithwaite said thinly, and used his napkin. "Tell him I'm coming, please, Willy."

Twenty minutes later Braithwaite was at his desk in the office overlooking the Houses of Parliament, and Vickers was taking direct calls from Codes, Operations and Movement. A short man with a bald head and a totally deadpan face, he spoke very quietly on the phone, as if desperate to preserve the atmosphere of cathedral calm in the long carpeted room; it was the kind of silence, he thought vaguely, where a discreet cough would sound like a nervous breakdown.

"It hardly seems conceivable," Farleigh said again. He was chief of Operations, as thin as Braithwaite but not nearly so distinguished-looking, tending rather to an absentminded seediness even at the best of times. Tonight—and it was now nearly twelve o'clock—he was wearing a hastily donned overcoat with the legs of his striped pajamas showing beneath it and above his rain-spattered galoshes. He'd been fast asleep in bed when the call had come. "Did they ask for confirmation?"

"Twice," Braithwaite said, and adjusted the silver figurine on his desk, turning it precisely to face him. It was in the form of a goddess, beautifully sculpted, her hands held forward one above the other and palms upward, presenting herself to whomever watched. It had been a gift from Mildred, his dead wife of so many years ago that he hardly remembered much about her, except as a woman who had given him this figurine. Though he'd never married again.

"Is the Company in on this?" asked Farleigh. He meant the CIA.

"Not so far. We'd have heard."

"You bet we'd have heard," the untidy man nodded. "They'd burn up the ether."

His chief glanced up sharply. "I hope not. It isn't a case for that." He didn't like Farleigh's lingering distrust of the Company; it was just that the Americans thought that everything should be aboveboard so that nobody would get sued, even for dusting Castro's shoes with cyanide.

"Would we tell them?" Farleigh asked, deliberately casual.

"If we have to." Braithwaite turned the little figurine again. "Or at least as much as we have to. But you'll have to get that drip off your nose, Farleigh. *They* haven't trusted *us* since Philby took off. And he wasn't the only one."

"Right, sir." Admonition acknowledged. But it was an interesting thought: Kim Philby had been in his own mind just now, because tonight's news was having just as much impact, and by the morning this whole place would be galvanized. "Where did it first come from?" he asked Braithwaite.

"Our consulate in Yambol, Bulgaria. With onward transmission to the embassy in Turkey." He began feeling the onset of indigestion, surprising after such excellent pigeon, but not surprising after such stupefying news. This was big trouble, a big hoax or a big disaster, and only one thing was at this moment certain: whichever it was, it was big. "George," he called suddenly, having made up his mind, "I'd like you to get Clay for me."

George Vickers put a hand over the mouthpiece of the phone he was using. "Who, sir?"

"Clay. Get him."

Vickers said quietly into the phone, "Hold everything." He looked at his chief again. "He's gone under, sir."

"Where?"

"I don't know."

"What's he working on?"

"Bill-Baker-3."

"Which is?"

"The Exocet missile deal with Pakistan."

"Try Paris, then."

Vickers unblocked the mouthpiece and began talking into the phone again as one of the three on Braithwaite's desk gave two rings and stopped. He lifted the receiver.

"Yes?"

"The prime minister's due back at any time now, sir."

"At Checkers?"

"Yes, sir."

"Find out when she arrives and keep a line clear for me." He hung up.

"We're telling the PM?" asked Farleigh from the window where he was standing.

"We have to."

"She won't like it."

"Like it?"

"She'll want all the details."

"Well?"

"We haven't got any." Farleigh gazed through the rain-soaked windows at the Houses of Parliament. He could feel the flu coming on and would very much like to have spent the next day in bed, but of course he'd be here all night and most of tomorrow trying to make sense of all this.

"We can't get details," his chief said sharply, "until we've got the man across. We're certainly not going to risk exposure in either Yambol or Istanbul by exchanging signals."

"No, sir." It was clearly a warning.

George Vickers was blocking the phone again. "Yes, sir, he's in Paris but not at his hotel at the moment."

"For God's sake, where's his control?"

"They're together, I suppose."

Braithwaite let a brief silence go by, then broke it. "George, this is what I want done. I want Clay located and I want him to telephone me personally, overriding all other traffic, the instant he's found. I want you to put three highest-echelon debriefing officers—I suggest MacDonald and Blythe for two of them— onto an air force plane, destination Istanbul. You can brief them in the helicopter on your way to Kenley. And meanwhile I want the tightest blackout on this operation you have ever heard of in your entire career. Is that understood?"

"Yes, sir." He picked up a different telephone.

From the window Farleigh asked gloomily, "Can I slip over to Piccadilly for some Serocalcin?"

A phone rang on Braithwaite's desk. "Send someone for it," he said and picked up the receiver. "Yes?"

"The prime minister's just got in, sir."

"Please tell her I'm on the line."

Somebody once said of Charles Clay that he seemed like a man who might one day go into the bathroom and shoot himself. If this could be called a description of him, it wasn't a bad one. What they were talking about was his general air of distraction, his faraway look, his tilted head, his appearance of listening not to what you were saying but to a sound so faint, so distant, that only he could hear it: the sound, perhaps, of muffled drums, or a night bird, or a woman's cruel laughter.

At first meeting you would recognize him as a pleasant enough fellow, almost nondescript: medium height, thinnish, with mouse-colored hair and moustache, and eyes that had so little expression in them that you'd wonder for an instant if he were blind, and being clever enough to conceal it; then your recognition would change to doubts, to puzzlement, even to suspicion—not that you might be wrong, after all, but that he intended you to be wrong. It would seem as if he might say to you, if only he could stop listening to that distant sound, *If you're trying to get to know me, I wouldn't bother. It'd be a waste of your time, and even dangerous. But don't worry, there's no chance.*

There was involved, the psychiatrist had said, an identity crisis, not uncommon, but not, for all that, easy to deal with. This was at Tonbridge, quite a long time ago, when the headmaster had come into his study to find Clay there with a service revolver held to his temple. It hadn't gone off, and in any case wasn't loaded, but the incident of course supported the later impression on the part of acquaintances (Clay had no friends) that he might one day shut himself in a bathroom and shoot himself. It could still happen.

At Tonbridge there'd been an older boy, Ashton Major, who was quite a character. He was a prefect, and older than Clay by a couple of years—quite a gap, between sixteen and eighteen—but Clay saw a lot of him because they were in the same House. Ashton Major was mostly an enigma. He owned a second-hand Alvis, and roared through the school gates in it with his cap on and a woolen scarf flying out in the slipstream. There was talk of girls and drinking, though with no real evidence; it was just that the other boys had to find some sort of explanation for

Ashton's mysterious comings and goings. He was often seen waiting outside the headmaster's study, obviously summoned there; this alone marked him as something of a scoundrel, fresh from deeds begging for punishment.

He'd laughed a lot, Ashton, but even at his young age Clay had recognized it as the sound of desperation in disguise; it had the ring of piratical laughter flung into the teeth of the storm when the ship was sinking and there was nothing else to be done save scorn the gods. But young Clay took to him, and more, much more: he worshipped him, less perhaps as a folk hero than a folk villain, a dark and mysterious creature who lived half his life in some sinister world where all was truth, if you could only face it.

On one momentous occasion, Clay had actually walked up to Ashton Major and made an outrageous request. "Do you—do you think you could take me for a quick run in your Alvis one day?"

And that laugh had come, breathless and narrow-eyed. "My God, you don't want to go where I'm going . . ." And that was that. To the reasonable mind, it had simply been a way of refusing a younger kid's company without being unkind; to Charles Clay it of course put the seal on things: the place where Ashton was going was that other, sinister and tantalizing world where half his life was spent, and where he could only go alone. It had reminded Clay of a few lines he'd seen somewhere: *Of all the Rakes in this fair Town, None can go so far to Hell on Half-a-Crown as I . . . for I know the Way.*

Then one day, Ashton Major left the school. No one knew why, though rumor was abundant. Most agreed he'd been sacked, and for some appalling deed; the headmaster's daughter was mentioned, though mostly by boys who were going through the time when sex demanded their total attention. Others had it that Ashton had smashed his car up trying to get away—though no one was quite sure from what. No official reason was ever given, though eyes hot with drama searched the notice boards for weeks. The effect upon young Clay was startling. He retired at once into a shell, and was twice found wandering along the banks of the Medway with bare feet on a winter day. Then he was discovered with that gun to his head, and the psychiatrist was called in. Most of the school knew that the headmaster kept a revolver in his study, in case of burglars—or such was his excuse; in fact he'd seen service in the war, and his gun was probably a memento. The probability was that Clay had been left alone for a moment in the head's study and had opened a few drawers: No one really knew (and here it could be seen, had any been watching, that he was already taking on the mysterious character of Ashton Major).

The psychiatrist dredged up a lot of stuff about Clay's parents, who'd been on the brink of divorce throughout most of his youth; and there'd been other things—though symptoms rather than causes—like his enjoyment in risking his neck by climbing the main hall tower and other places, without even a rope. There was the theory that he missed Ashton Major so grievously that it would actually have come to suicide if that gun had been loaded. What happened in fact was that he did exactly what Ashton had done: he got himself sacked from the school. Someone said it was for taking money, though the truth was never made official; as with Ashton, there was talk of wild nights with girls, and secret drinking parties. Anyone who knew him at all knew he didn't have to pinch money: his people were frightfully rich.

The truth, in the clouded stillness of young Clay's mind, was that he not only missed Ashton Major unbearably, but was terrified that if he didn't leave school himself, he'd never catch up with him, wherever he was "out there." It was pretty clumsy, getting himself sacked for stealing, of all things, but then he was young and had never heard, as he did later, of a good "cover story." The thing was, he was out of school, and the search had begun then. It wasn't possible to trace Ashton Major, because he was someone who never left a trace: His people lived in India, and no reply had come to the one letter Clay had written. But he felt he would one day find him, if he could only "think himself" into Ashton's mind. Ashton was still somewhere in the world, and all Clay had to do was to pick up his scent. He began by getting a job as a junior clerk at the Hong Kong Tourist Association a year after leaving school. "Why on earth Hong Kong?" his father had asked, without getting a real answer: It was simply one of those sinister, exotic places where Ashton was likely to go. After that there was Rangoon, and Tahiti, and Algiers, as Charles Clay acted out what he now thought of as the "Ashton Syndrome," a spiritual quest that drove him around the world as day by day, year after year, he tried to get into Ashton's mind and divine where he was, knowing with the intuition of the deviant that when at last he found Ashton he would find himself.

A year in the Caribbean, working as a shipping clerk; then six months in the embassy at Bangkok; then London, and the Foreign Office, developing his flair for languages and learning Russian for the sake of promotion; and finally two years in "that place across the street" where the spooks were recruited and trained; then trips abroad again, often into Soviet Russia and out soon afterward, with satisfactory debriefings. Moscow, Tashkent, Odessa . . . and tonight in the bleak winter chill of the Bulgarian border, waiting to help Terebilov across.

CHAPTER ELEVEN

He needs me."

"Okay." Laura Paget waved a flour-covered wooden spoon in the air. "He needs you." Then she went on stirring the béchamel.

It was worse, Bruce thought, than if she just blew up. If he ever had to give grounds for leaving his young, attractive and very intelligent wife, he would have to say it was her absolute calm. It was like a wall. But then, it was her absolute sense of calm that had always intrigued him; he still remembered leading her across to the group near the buffet and saying, "I'd like you to meet the president." Her reaction had been perfect: pleased surprise, the precisely appropriate inclination of her head in the European style and the disarming, "Mr. President, how nice. And you're so much younger than I'd thought." Since that time—and at that time he'd only met the president twice himself, as a White House staff rookie— he'd seen hundreds, thousands of people greeting the most powerful man in the world, and maybe one percent of the women had known how to acknowledge him also as a man, and as a male.

"It's the job, Laura," he told her now.

"Of course," she said. "I understand." He leaned in the kitchen doorway watching the spoon make its meaningless gyrations in the pan, but visually aware of her as an act of memory:

tall, Junoesque—maybe a little too Junoesque of late, but then seventeen years didn't thin anybody down—her head down to watch what she was doing, pretending with him that the smoothness of the béchamel sauce was the most important thing in their lives, her cool eyes contemplative, her whole attitude designed—and successfully, expressively—to shut him out, to keep him this side of the wall.

"It's Nicaragua," he said, trying to get a note of importance into his voice. "Everything's blowing up, you know that."

"Of course. As you say, it's the job." With an untypical concession to the need for communication she added—but still not looking at him—"It's hard for some men to understand that some women—probably most—would secretly prefer that it was another woman. To have a *job* as a rival is so bloodless."

Lamely he said, "It's bad luck for you, Laura. You didn't know what it'd be like, married to a presidential aide."

"No." The spoon circled. "But I know what it's like being married to a presidential aide who's married to his job."

They went into the hotel by a side door, along a green-painted passage and past double doors with steamed-up windows in them, then into the lobby and across to the elevators. For Bruce it was almost routine: as a close member of the presidential party on so many public occasions he was used to being smuggled in past the kitchens of big hotels.

For Nadia it was simply intriguing. On the first two occasions she had tried to feel guilt, or at least shame, because of his wife, but it was only a sham, a gesture. In the harsh, rigorous years of her training she'd learned that if you were to succeed you must find your place, and if someone else were in it, you must get them out. There had been times, many times, when she'd watched a more mature dancer performing better than she did, and thought of giving up; then she'd called forth her reserves and danced better than she'd ever believed she could—and better than her rival. Now she was dancing better than this man's wife.

They made love almost at once, without washing first—which Laura always insisted upon, approaching the matter with calm premeditation. Here in the hotel room Nadia simply threw herself across the silk coverlet of the bed and spread her legs, arching her back so that her skirt fell into folds around her thighs, revealing the smoky fringe of hair that escaped her briefs. The first time she had done this it had shocked Bruce a little; it was a favorite trick of tarts, to ape abandonment, but today he simply fell on the slight, ivory-skinned body and pulled at the briefs, nestling his hand in the strong thick hair, profuse and animal and surprising on a girl so young and so tiny. She had no breasts —or they were no fuller than a boy's—but this was typical of an athlete—he'd always noticed it at the Olympics (my God, they're all like sticks! Laura had often said, strangely offended). This too was part of Nadia Fedotova: her resemblance to a hermaphrodite was an aspect of her strangeness, of her novelty for Bruce. Used as he was to the middle-class Washington matron with her formal codes of hygiene and her devotion to deodorants and depilatory lotions, he discovered something overpoweringly attractive in this wild, nubile creature from the far Russian snows who clawed and nibbled at him, pulling him into her with a fierce insistence that brought words from her that he didn't understand yet understood, their accents rushing and whispering on her heated breath and conjuring images for him of sleighs running through forests bright with frost under the northern stars, to the sound of bells tolling from golden domes and the scent of woodsmoke and frankincense, until she reached her first orgasm and his name was on her breath, in the way she pronounced it . . . *Brutze* . . . *Brutze* . . . *Brutze* . . . again and again while she threshed under him with her dark head jerking from side to side on the green silk coverlet and he felt her tears flying against his face.

"I feel such guilt," she said later, sitting at the dressing table and staring with her huge dark eyes into the mirror, as if she wondered who she was and what she was doing here.

"You don't have to." He was thinking of Laura, who would

notice the scratches on him, and the tiny toothmarks, and maybe change her mind and wish she only had the bloodlessness of a job to compete with. "She likes you."

The eyes in the mirror moved to his. "Who?"

"Laura."

"Oh." She glanced down. "I don't think so. I expect she knows what we do. No?"

"You don't have to feel guilty," he said evasively, "about anything at all." Because he realized now that her guilt had nothing to do with Laura. "You can always go back, if you want to."

"No. They would punish me badly. I would go back to be with my mother and my sister, but not to the Bolshoi."

"It's not what it's cracked up to be?" He leaned with his head against the silk upholstery, feeling sated and ashamed, as he always did, not so much because of Laura but because he hadn't risen above the routine Washington rut of the easy lay and the easy lie that the ambiance of politics engendered.

"What is that, please?"

"Huh? Oh. The Bolshoi isn't—uh—so good as everybody thinks?"

With a quick sigh she left the dressing table and took three exquisite steps across the carpet, making him catch his breath. "It is not possible to stretch," she said, "in the Bolshoi, to stretch your art." He noticed she was picking up the American idiom of the ballet from the New York company where she was now training. "The reper—reperty? I—"

"Repertory."

"So. Repertory is too restrained. Is that—?"

"Constrained, maybe." He loved her childlike appeals for his help with the language.

"Yes. The company is so big, you see, that you dance not very often. You have to take your turns. And it will be all your life, also, with nothing else, and when you are old, by forty years and so, there is nothing left but pension." She lifted her thin, ivory-colored arms and let them fall, her small hands describing the flight of a bird through the air while he watched enchanted.

"And so you become bored and do not care so much, and you eat more, and grow weight; there is not inspiration in that. No, the Bolshoi is not so crack up, like you tell me." She moved suddenly to the bed and knelt with her arms on it and her head down, letting him stroke her hair. "But I feel such guilt about my country—" she pronounced it *cowntree*, with a slight trill to the *tr*, which he found beguiling, like everything else about her —"because they will hate me for leaving there."

"It doesn't have to be forever, Nadia, unless you want it to be." Stroking her soft dark hair he was surprised at the tenderness she'd evoked in him; at age forty-seven you don't expect to have your heart turned over by a girl of nineteen. Was it because of Sally? Sally had been three years old when the leukemia had been discovered, and four when they'd watched the tiny coffin slide through the blue velvet curtains into the furnace. Sally would have been seventeen now, almost Nadia's age. Was this dark head the Sally part of her, and the lovemaking another? A woman was all things to a man; the permutations were endless.

"You do not think so?" she asked, her voice muffled against the coverlet.

He had to bring his thoughts back. "Of course not. In the West, we think of the world as somewhere to explore, so we can find out what other people are really thinking and really doing —because you can never tell from the media. That brings understanding, and a desire for peace." Jesus, what a trite platitude! He felt the warmth of the small dark head under his hand; what thoughts had possessed it to bring her all this way?

"You will take care with me, Brutze." She lifted her face and he saw her eyes were bright with tears.

"Sure. I'll take care of you." Part of her guilt—most of it, maybe—was fear. Moscow had made the most of her defection with a formal protest in Washington from the Soviet ambassador, Mr. Boris Lein, and a bitter tirade in *Pravda*. *On an occasion such as the visit of the Bolshoi Ballet Ensemble to the United States of America, which was made in order to afford American audiences the enjoyment of high Soviet culture, it surely would have been expected that in the White House, the very seat of government and custodian of diplomatic protocol, the good manners and integrity of international relations might have been observed. Instead, the world was to learn of the most blatant breach of faith in the virtual kidnapping of this young and talented dancer under the eyes of President Hartridge himself, who made no attempt to bring order to the humiliating scene where actual scuffling broke out among the security guards. It remains to be questioned whether the United States of America should in future be accorded similar visits of Soviet artists to its shores.*

Alexander Pershing, American ambassador to Russia, was called to an hour-long meeting with the Soviet foreign minister in Moscow, and received an exhaustive and well-publicized drubbing.

"I only have you," Nadia said, the tears brimming over now to streak her cheeks. "Everyone else hate me."

"No," he said, "they don't. But a lot of people envy you. You're the sixth member of the Bolshoi to stay behind in the States in the last four years. Doesn't that tell you anything?"

"It tell me I need you." It was all she could think about.

"Okay. We'll settle for that."

"Something new?"

"Yes. Koslev's due for a prostate operation."

"Oh, Jesus . . ." the chief of the NSA unit gave a gusty laugh. "Is that all you've got?"

"They got onto us long ago," Stacey told him, "you know that. What do you think they're going to talk about inside the limos? Classified stuff?"

In the days of Gamma Guppy it had been very exciting. The embassy unit had been catching vibrations from some of the Kremlin windows and from some of the Zils, and they'd got a whole lot of sensitive material; then one of their moles in Sacramento had picked up the echoes, and since then the Politburo chiefs hadn't discussed anything inside their cars more interesting than the weather.

"We can only hope for peripheral stuff," the chief told Stacey. "It'll help us find patterns." He glanced along the beeping console, looking for movement, but it was pretty scarce: at this time it was midnight in Moscow.

"We've been getting a pattern for you," nodded the man beside Stacey. "It'll be coming through in the printout. In the past few weeks—we can't put an exact time on when it started—the chairman of the council of ministers, the secretary of the Communist Party and the chairman of the Party control committee have been holding what looks like special meetings." He shrugged. "You know, for special read secret or discreet or whatever: What we're getting as a pattern, after distilling a few thousand signals, is that these three seem to be meeting more often, and on their own. They're—"

"That's Rudenko, Boytsov and Rusakov, right?"

"Close. Not Rusakov—Koslev. Viktor Koslev."

"The guy with the prostate."

"Right," Stacey said with a grin. "We tend to remember all the useless stuff too."

"Nothing's useless, Bob. Remember the patterns."

"Okay. Now, these meetings have been—" he broke off as a phone rang, and picked it up. "Yes?" He listened a moment. "Why don't you bring it in? Don's right here."

In half a minute a small man with a troglodyte pallor and untamed hair came shuffling around the corner from the analysis room with a paper in his hand. "Hi, Don. Okay, this is coming in on unit five. Rudenko, Koslev and Boytsov have been forming what looks like a *troika* between themselves, with Rudenko in charge. They're—"

"Okay," Stacey said. "We already have that." He glanced at his chief. "I'd say you're ready to spread this."

"Sure. We'll forward to Georgetown."

The small man combed his hair back with nicotine-stained

fingers. "Okay. Second item is, we've coalesced a very definite signal from a whole morass of stuff they've been picking up from the windows of Koslev's *dacha*, where they've held three of their meetings already." He looked up at the other two men to make sure they were attending. "The phrase 'the new American weapon' has been picked up seven times to date."

His chief looked suddenly deadpan. "Jesus," he said softly, "*that* is for the White House."

CHAPTER TWELVE

There was moonlight.

Clay had told them about this.

On the line from Paris he'd said: "We'll have to wait for three days. Then we'll have three hours of darkness to work with before moonrise. I can't work with less than that; it's forest terrain and under snow."

Braithwaite himself had been on the London end of the line.

"We want him brought across as soon as he gets there, and as soon as you get there. You'll have rendezvous briefing when you reach Edirne on the Turkish side. I want you to leave for there now; is that understood?"

"Under moonlight, sir, there are risks. Can't we get him across somewhere else?"

"I would very much like to. Unfortunately he is now on a train between Svilengrad and the Turkish border and in less than first-class physical condition. The moment you get him to our consulate in Istanbul he'll need medical attention, if not earlier, in Edirne. That will be for you to decide."

The line had been crackling with static, and a Frenchwoman's voice in the background had kept cutting in, faint but strident, some tart bawling out her pimp. Why couldn't they use the embassy signals room, for Christ's sake? There wasn't time for him to get there, Braithwaite had told him. You couldn't argue with Braithwaite, but you could give him the score.

"Sir, it's going to be hellishly difficult under moonlight."

"That is why I chose you."

Clay shifted his feet again, his back to a lightning-shattered pine whose blackened skeleton gave better camouflage for his dark parka. It was two hours since he'd come here, and his vision was starting to worry him. For two hours he'd moved his head from one side to the other and back a couple of hundred times, sweeping the line of trees that stood dark against the snow under the moonlight, and by now his eye-brain system was feeling the effects of monotony. Two or three times he'd seen a man's figure coming through the trees; then it had vanished like a mirage.

The first time he'd got a man across there'd been a floodlit deathstrip of raked sand with trip flares and mines and an electrified fence and watchtowers, but that hadn't been too difficult because his team had used drugs on the guards and blown three major fuses in the nearest village, and he'd had a ground plan of the mines. Here it was less dramatic but more difficult: All along the Iron Curtain, from the Baltic Sea to the Turkish border, there was the same equation: the fewer mines and flares and floodlights and machine-gun posts, the more soldiery. Through those trees there were guards on the move, keeping warm by patroling the fence that ran a hundred and forty-nine miles from the Aegean to the Black Sea. There was no way of getting through the fence without triggering the watchtower alarms, and no way of finding a gap, in any case, between the moving patrols.

Terebilov would be coming through immediately ahead of where Clay stood now, but Clay kept moving his head from side to side in case they'd got it wrong by a few hundred yards.

It would have been a bloody sight easier if the man could have gone farther west and made for the Greek border, where there was a maze of tunnels and catacombs—the relic of the old Metaxas Line against the Germans in World War II—and enough running cover for a whole platoon to get lost in. But the

chief had talked about "less than first-class physical condition."
Maybe Terebilov couldn't run.

Arvid Terebilov, secretary of the Communist Party of the
Soviet Union and a voting member of the Politburo . . . fourth,
according to the last analysis, in the hierarchy of the Moscow
power structure. It didn't bear thinking about. *That is why I
chose you.*

That would have been fair enough, except for this fucking
moonlight. It could be a killer.

The flash of the first explosion was blinding, and he shut his
eyes, seeing the light of the second and third bombs through his
eyelids. When he opened them he saw that the trees were in
flames and the glare reached as far as the foothills; the night was
loud with the screaming of animals, and an owl flew straight
past him in its panic, a wing tip brushing his face. There were
men screaming now; they'd be Bulgarians: The Turks had been
ordered to draw back from the border fence for half a mile on
each side of the target point.

Smoke began drifting on the fringe of the air blast, a pall of
black across the orange glare of the blaze; a dozen pines had
caught, and stood with their branches bearing the flames aloft
like decorations. A lot of shouting broke out now, and Clay
could see figures moving on the far side of the trees. He watched
them for a long time, not prepared to believe that Terebilov
would ever get through that inferno. Nor was he prepared to
believe that he'd fail to get Terebilov to Istanbul and then to
London. Braithwaite himself was running this operation, which
meant it must have prime ministerial authority; this wasn't a
simple border bust to bring a rookie spook across, covered in
shit and with nothing to show for it but the plans of the new
sewage plant in Trashgrad; this was a priority-one directive with
Christ knew what behind it on a cold-war hotline level.

One of the guards had started running through the trees to
the left, where the smoke was drifting; he stopped once and
shouted something, looking behind him, and then ran on. Clay
lost him in the smoke and then saw him again, a little taller

now, a little closer, running with his hands flung out in front of him and his uniform coat flapping open, his boots kicking up snow that fell like candy floss in the ruddled light of the flames.

Clay watched him. Some of the guards would have been killed outright by the explosions; others would have caught the shock waves and been knocked out; others would have stayed on their feet but would now be disoriented, staggering around and trying to find their direction. At this distance it wasn't possible to tell who they were, or who this one man was as he ran closer, stumbling and picking himself up again, lurching through the snowdrifts like a drunk.

He'll be wearing a Bulgarian guard's uniform, the briefing signal had specified.

It was the only possible image he could present in this situation: there wasn't anyone within miles of this place who wasn't a border guard in uniform. But it made identification difficult.

The running man came on.

Clay watched him, and in a minute or two started moving forward from tree to tree in the pattern he'd worked out, using the maximum available cover. He could hear the man's breath now, in soft snatches of sound against the crackling of the trees. Clay reached inside his parka and brought out the gun and thumbed the catch off and held it close to his side, moving forward steadily and watching the running man; his silhouette against the flames was puppetlike, jerking and lurching, half-falling and straightening again with its hands held forward all the time as if he'd been blinded by the explosions or the smoke; but he could see, all right: he say Clay now, and slowed suddenly.

Clay brought the gun up, and waited. The man was still not much more than a silhouette, and all Clay had to work with was a meager degree of backwash reflected from the blaze by the snows behind him; he needed to identify one feature of the man: his age. All the border guards would be young.

The man came on, his hands lifted higher now because he'd seen the gun. *"Rachmaninov . . . Rachmaninov . . ."*

Clay didn't move. The face under the military fur hat was
catching more light now, and he saw the loose flesh below the
eyes, the shadowed lines from the nose to the mouth, and the
pendulous skin of the neck above the uniform collar. *"Rachmaninov . . ."* the voice came again, desperately.

Clay lowered the gun. *"Stravinsky,"* he said, and caught the
man as he tripped and began falling. In Russian he told him,
"We can't stop. Try and keep going. Come on." But Terebilov
seemed to think he was home and dry—either that or the run
from the border fence had burned him out. *Less than first-class
physical condition* . . . and you could say that again; the man's
bulk leaned on Clay as they started hobbling together—you
couldn't call it running—through the trees toward the road
where Clay had left the car. Terebilov's breath came painfully,
and once he dragged Clay to a halt and they stood swaying while
the man's head sank onto his chest and his breath made a sawing
sound as the windpipe was constricted; Clay jerked his head up
and pulled him forward again as the first shot sang past them
and smacked into a pine tree: Clay saw the chip of white suddenly there as the bark came away.

"Hurry," he said.

"I can't go any—"

"Come on, damn you!" The second shot was closer and he
went into a crouching lope, dragging Terebilov with him. The
guards wouldn't know who he was: they'd just seen he was running in the wrong direction, that was all; of the several hundred
defectors who'd crossed to the West since the Wall was built,
quite a few had been actual guards, smarting from the discipline
or tempted by stories of the treasures over there: rock and roll
and blue jeans and jazz and Volkswagens for all.

Another close shot and Clay drove his ski boots into the loose
snow, dragging his load, cursing the man in his own tongue and
meaning it: there were two lives here to be lost, not just one.

"Come on, fuck you! You want to get shot?"

He could see the car now, a dark hump at the edge of the
road; a half dozen men stood near it, doing nothing, watching

them trying to run. They were on higher ground and out of range from the guns. They were the Turkish patrols who'd been drawn away from the border fence, with orders not to return fire if any broke out.

"*Come on, for Christ's sake, keep going!*" The man was a dead weight now, and when Clay tripped on a buried rock he couldn't get moving again: Terebilov's head was down and his arms hung loosely, the hands limp and the fingers open, with a trickle of blood showing black in the moonlight.

"*Terebilov!*" He felt the man's back, and found the coat sticky below one shoulder. "Can you hear me, Terebilov?"

A sound came from the man's throat, and Clay turned, staring across at the car. "*Richard!*"

"Yes?"

"Get the ambulance!"

"Okay!"

Clay began dragging the Russian backward across the snow.

Sir James Braithwaite was stirring the lemon into his whiskey grog when the phone at his bedside began ringing. He picked it up.

"Yes?"

"Signals, sir. Sorry to disturb you."

"I wasn't asleep." The illuminated twenty-four–hour clock on the wall was at 1:15.

"Istanbul, sir."

"Very well." He waited, allowing himself a slight feeling of elation. Clay wouldn't have failed.

"Sir?" This time there was a lot of static in the background.

"I'm here." He watched the lemon juice form spirals of iridescence on the surface of the Scotch. There was a pause on the line, but he waited patiently.

"We lost him, sir."

The iridescence went on spreading across the surface of the liquor, touching the glass at last and circling it. Braithwaite could hear his wife, still brushing her teeth in her bathroom with the tap full on. She always took longer than he did, he thought abstractedly.

"Lost?" he said into the telephone.

"There was shooting, sir. He died soon afterward."

The coup of a lifetime, George Vickers had said to him at the office this evening. Yes, quite right. If it had come off.

"You're sure of the identity?" He asked quietly. He'd learned long ago that grasping at straws would never save you; but it had its uses as a defense mechanism, allowing you to go on hoping while the shock was eased into your consciousness. "It was in fact Terebilov?"

"Yes, sir. He had papers sewn into his coat."

"I see. Where is the body now?"

"In a hospital in Edirne, sir."

"Very well. I'll signal the embassy in Ankara." Almost as an afterthought: "Is Clay all right?"

"Yes, sir. He's here with us now."

"Debrief him."

Blythe put the phone down in the consulate in Istanbul and crossed to the soiled easy chair and dropped into it on the other side of the table from Clay. MacDonald started the tape recorder again.

"How much did he tell you? Anything?"

"Not much." Clay sat perfectly straight at the table, to a kind of attention, trying to find refuge in formality, in what remained from the shambles. "I got a few things out of him while I was dragging him to the ambulance, but nothing vital; then in the ambulance, he seemed to think he could trust me, or that there wasn't going to be time to do anything else." His voice was a monotone.

"Don't blame yourself, old boy." Jack Blythe watched him carefully, lolling back in the armchair at his ease, chubby, smooth-faced, soft of voice, one of the service's most brilliant debriefers, known for having kept even a dying agent talking. "It was an unlucky shot, you know that. We knew there was a risk—"

"*It was that fucking moonlight.*" A fierce whisper.

"You warned London about that, and they decided to go ahead. Can't possibly blame you, old boy. You could have got shot dead yourself, and no thanks to them."

MacDonald passed Clay the cigarettes, but he looked down at the packet and away again. "He couldn't run fast enough."

Blythe waited for a moment, then asked gently: "How did he cover his tracks?"

"What?" Clay's blank eyes rested on him for an instant. "Oh. From what I could gather—it was all pretty disjointed—he swam as far as he could out to sea, leaving his clothes on the beach, then turned and swam along the coast and came ashore farther along, where he'd left some other clothes beforehand. Then he started heading for our consulate in Svilengrad."

"So we're to expect," Blythe nodded comfortably, "a report in *Tass* that he's presumably drowned while on holiday at Sochi?"

"What else can they think?" Rather sharply.

"Quite so." Blythe made a note.

"The main thing," Clay said, toneless again, "was about Rudenko. And something they've got in the works."

"In the—?"

"A project of some sort. He used the word *appalling* several times. He said—look, you can't expect me to give this to you as it came out. You—"

"I don't, old boy. The man was dying. I understand."

"Yes." He wished Blythe weren't so fucking amiable: it would be good to blast his head off about something, to get relief; but that would need provocation. "Yes, he was dying." He remembered the heavy, muscular body under the greatcoat, the chest heaving as the words came out in grunts and murmurs, while Clay went on dragging him backward; then later in the ambulance, with the Russian's eyes coming open sometimes and filling with fear. "*America . . . they want to . . .*" and there'd been whole minutes of unconsciousness. *"Rudenko . . . he has an appalling project for . . ."* It had seemed to Clay that in the mind of the dying man there was a huge struggle going on as he tried to think intelligently, to decide whether to tell this agent everything he could, or whether to try hanging on to life and letting them debrief him at their mission. Some of the words had been no more than a whisper, and Clay had bent his head to lay his ear against the man's mouth. Twice Terebilov had surfaced to sudden and total consciousness and gripped Clay's wrist with surprising strength, forcing out a whole string of words before the blood had come springing from his lungs and the words had turned into gurgles, the sound of a man drowning. *"Lay waste America . . ."* was the last Clay had heard.

"Putting it together," he told Blythe, "he was saying that Rudenko has planned some kind of frontal attack on the United States, though he didn't mention arms, nuclear or otherwise. The phrase *laying waste* came more than once, and I think *wasteland*, or translated alternatives like barren land, empty terrain, or wilderness, along those lines."

Blythe got himself a cigarette. "A wasteland *in* the States?" His tone terribly helpful. "Desert land? An American desert?"

"No." Clay shook his head quickly. "America *was* the desert. The wasteland."

"Jesus," MacDonald murmured at the tape recorder.

Blythe shot him a look to mean shut up. "Any idea," he asked Clay gently, "about time?"

"What? Nothing definite." With another flash of impatience he said, "I'm trying to tell you, what I was getting was not so much coherent phrases, but a *sense* of what he was saying." He remembered not jumping back from the stretcher in the ambulance when the first gushing of blood had come from the man's mouth; he remembered just sitting there and not moving, letting it pour over his hand and his knees.

"Of course, old boy." Blythe made more notes. "Any *sense* of time, then?"

In a moment Clay nodded. "Yes. Soon. There were words

like *progress, development,* and one phrase that sounded like *no going back.*" He said in a kind of controlled fury—"Look, I got about thirty or forty words, and about half of those were totally unintelligible and about a quarter had some kind of meaning but out of context and the rest gave me the picture I'm giving you, d'you understand that?"

"Of course, old boy."

"I tried to put questions, you see—what *kind* of attack and would it be nuclear and what kind of forces would it involve, military, naval, air force and so on—but what was happening, you know—" he turned his whole body to face Blythe now— "was that the poor bastard was having other things to worry him, like who I was and if he could trust me with this, you know? And probably even wondering where the hell he was and what he was doing there anyway. The man was *dying . . .*"

In a moment Blythe said with a friendly blink, "Right you are, old boy, I know exactly what you mean, and I'm quite sure you managed to get more out of him than anyone else could have got. You—"

"If you'd only put some *blame* on me," Clay told him with his eyes shining, "it'd be such a fucking *relief.*"

"Doesn't need two of us, old boy." He waited until Clay looked away and put his thin elbows on the table and buried his face in his hands. "What we've got, then, is that Rudenko is planning some kind of assault on the States, possibly with a new kind of weapon, and time could be running out. Something like that?"

Clay wasn't even listening. There was a sob in his voice as he said, *"If only to Christ it hadn't been moonlight . . ."*

CHAPTER THIRTEEN

Three thousand kilometers northeast of Istanbul the train came to a halt in the freight yards of the station in Tobolsk, in the Siberian lowlands of Soviet Russia.

The march began from there.

In summer the little railway station looked quite pretty, with its painted wood panels and window boxes; the water of the marshes supported bird life, and some wild flowers grew on higher ground; but now it was winter, and night, with a temperature of 15° below zero; and all that could be seen of the station were the rusting lamps on the poles alongside the single track, casting a greenish gaslight across the metals as the people were ordered out of the train and told to start marching.

It was more a shuffle, really. Some of the men wore sackcloth around their feet, since broken chilblains made the wearing of boots or clogs too painful; others lurched, a few of them singing until a guard clouted them: their song had sounded too like a hymnal. Some of the women were holding hands, partly for the comfort of another human's touch and partly to help each other along and keep pace with the men. They wore rags.

Toward dawn they reached the compound. It was a hundred yards along each side, and square, with nothing inside the barbed wire: nothing at all; no huts of any kind, no form of shelter, nothing. It looked like a big cage, put down here on the frozen marshland to catch something. Floodlamps shone inward at each corner, lighting nothing.

Outside, by the dirt road with its potholes and ice-filled ruts, was a single hut, long and low and standing out against the night in the glare of more floodlamps. Beyond the hut and the cage there was no road to be seen; it stopped here.

"Halt!"

They shuffled to a stop and stood swaying, their breath steaming in the bright light, their eyes looking around them, some frightened, some with the disinterest of despair. They were from the labor camps in the north, and used to being treated like cattle; but a few of them—having been driven half mad by the guards up there, by the iron clamp of winter around their skulls, and by sickness—a few of them had believed they were being moved farther south, where it was less cold, and where the work might have been less onerous. Now they stood staring around them at the cage and the hut and the group of military vehicles parked at the edge of the marsh.

"Where are we?" a man asked, breaking off an icicle of frozen saliva that had drooled from his mouth because he couldn't feel it.

"No talking!"

There was movement around the main doors of the hut, and a guard came out and gave a signal. "Bring them in! One at a time!"

The line began moving. Inside the hut there were men who showed authority but who were not military or camp police; when they began speaking, the prisoners knew who they were: it explained the red cross markings on two of the vehicles outside.

"Name?"

"Demichev, Yefim."

"Age?"

"Forty-six."

"Diseases?"

The man blinked and said nothing; frost melted from his tangled beard, for the stove in here gave off warmth.

"Speak up! Diseases?"

They were doctors, these people.

The big man didn't know what to say; for the last six months he'd spent half his waking life in the latrines and the other half in a fever from dysentery; his skin was raw from the bites of fleas and his lungs were rotten with tuberculosis; his left leg was half paralyzed after a blow from a guard's cudgel, and two of his friends had needed to drag him here to this place; his sight had gone in one eye because of a cataract, and if he ever took more than a spoonful of camp stew he brought it up again.

"No diseases," he said. "I am a fit man."

If you admitted to anything wrong with you, then you were dead. Those not fit for work were left in the snow when the gangs were driven back from detail. It saved food.

The doctor shuffled his papers contemptuously. "Take him for an exam," he told his assistant. "We'll have to find out somehow."

Others in the line had the idea they were here for medical treatment, and trotted out their whole history. The line moved faster, for them.

"Name?"

"Lopatkin, Aleksandr." A tall man, he stood swaying like a tree in the wind, his head held down to one side because of his dislocated spine.

The doctor shuffled his papers again. "*Doctor* Lopatkin? The academician?"

The man became still for a moment, as if the question had stirred his memory; then he frowned, because the effort was too much for him. "Lopatkin," he said, swaying again now. "Lopatkin, Aleksandr."

"Age?"

"Forty years."

"Diseases?"

"No diseases."

"Take him for exam. Next!"

It took four hours to process the entire group of one hundred prisoners. A hundred and twenty had originally left the camp in the north, since some were expected not to survive the journey. Fourteen had never reached here; the shuffling of boots through the snow on the march here from Tobolsk had been accompanied by the crying of wolves behind them. Six men had been removed from the group on arrival, so that the exact number should enter the compound; if any died before then, they could be replaced, up to a total of six.

"Next?"

The hut smelled of woodsmoke, and sweat, and coffee, and urine. On the long march there had been only three stops; if you didn't time it right you had to do it into your boots.

"Diseases?"

A pale sun had risen from the horizon to the east, and hung in the sky like a lamp keeping deathwatch.

"Take him away."

An orderly sprayed the hut with disinfectant when the last of the prisoners had gone. For an hour they were kept standing in close order between the hut and the huge barbed-wire cage. Two men and three women fell to the ground during this time, and were dragged away, to be replaced from the six reserves.

Soon after noon the medical teams closed the hut and boarded their vehicles. The ten guards herded the prisoners into the cage through a narrow gap, which was then closed with chains and a padlock. The Jews among their number began singing quietly, and this time no one stopped them.

At 1239 the guards went to their vehicles and boarded them, turning to follow the medical teams along the frozen dirt road. Two men stayed behind, sitting in the last remaining vehicle— an armored car fitted with special equipment—chain-smoking and talking desultorily for the next hour, when at 1339 precisely a call came through on their mobile radio. They responded and helped each other into their protective clothing; then one took the wheel and drove the vehicle slowly around the four sides of the barbed-wire cage while the other manned the equipment and sent a spray of liquid hissing from a black nozzle through the wire and among the prisoners.

It took less than five minutes; then the vehicle returned to the dirt road with drips still falling from the nozzle that projected from the side. After two miles it passed within a hundred yards of some stunted bushes, from behind which a Mark VI flamethrower engulfed the armored car, halting it and turning it into a funeral pyre, its black smoke rising under the pale winter sun.

In the management committee chamber of the Isolation Hospital for Rare Diseases in Zagorsk, seventy-one kilometers northeast of Moscow, Chairman of the Council of Ministers Rudenko nodded to the man on his left.

"Your report, please, Comrade Inspector."

Karpov stood up, taking his papers from the desk. "Comrade Chairman . . . Comrade Secretary . . . Comrades . . . Here is my updated report on the procedures outlined in the referendum, some of which have now taken place."

Secretary of the Communist Party of the Soviet Union Boytsov watched him attentively. In the three months since Rudenko had first proposed his project, Sharaf Boytsov had found himself living in two worlds: the one in which life in general went on in accordance with the established and familiar routine of eating, sleeping, working and womanizing; and the one in which he was invited to look forward and see the United States of America laid waste and the Soviet Union not only freed at last from her gnawing fears of invasion and subjugation, but raised to the position of total dominance over the rest of the planet, with himself elevated to an eminence unattained by any other man in the history of the world, including Julius Caesar. Alongside, of course, Rudenko and Koslev.

It was a scenario of such magnitude that even Boytsov, with his ability to encompass momentous events in political life, had the feeling that he was on board some huge leviathan, such as the *Titanic*, whose course across the dark sea had become unstoppable, undeviable and irreversible. Once Rudenko had found they were ready not only to listen but to aid him at the highest level, he had proceeded with the development of *Waste-*

land with an almost appalling energy, calling in the scientific resources necessary to the project, bringing closer to him those of the Secretariat and the Politburo whom he knew would prove his allies, and quietly initiating steps toward the dismissal or overthrow of those whom he knew would prove his enemies. General Secretary Vladychenko, of course, must be left where he was at the head of government, until the time was ripe for his removal. To attempt his removal now would spread alarm and suspicion throughout the hierarchy. Vladychenko's doctors, in any case, had been visiting him more often of late, and had yesterday asked him to visit the clinic for tests; the rumor was that his kidneys were giving out. He'd be seventy-six next week and already it had been announced that the celebrations were to be strictly private. The amount of vodka, thought Boytsov as he watched the medical inspector, that had passed through the chairman of the Supreme Soviet's kidneys in the past half century must have left them pickled—not that Vladychenkov was a drunk; he'd simply got through an awful lot of state occasions. Boytsov himself, though not sixty yet, had started knocking it off a bit lately; he wanted to enjoy his coming elevation to world eminence for a long time.

Look at Koslev. By the clock on the wall he was now lying on a table with a miniature scalpel poked up his urethra, cutting away his prostate. You had to take care of yourself.

And look at Terebilov. *Tass* had reported his "tragic and accidental demise" at Sochi, "almost within sight of so many vacationing citizens who would have swum to his aid had they realized his mortal predicament." Though past sixty, *Pravda* had pointed out, the late voting member had been of strong physique and a notable swimmer, and it was often the case that such men overtaxed their strength.

No one had mentioned suicide, of course. Rudenko had been depressed for a few days, then had snapped out of it and gone on with the project. Terebilov hadn't been able to stand the strain, that was all. He'd lacked the vision, the ability to realize that to achieve great change there must often be great sacrifice.

"The compound was then contaminated," Medical Inspector Karpov was saying, "and the operators were removed from the scene and placed under conditions of quarantine."

Bloody liar, thought Boytsov. They were killed outright. But then there'd been no alternative. The whole vehicle had been contaminated, and they couldn't have left it there and walked; nor could anyone have picked them up. Besides, they'd had a story to tell, which no one must hear. There had to be sacrifices all along the line.

He watched Medical Inspector Karpov: a thin raw-skinned man with gristly ears and cold eyes and rimless spectacles, no older than thirty-five but brilliant and already an academician. Rudenko had put him in sole charge of the medical work for *Wasteland*. Karpov lived his life in the laboratories and the isolation wards and the decontamination chambers of the experimental biology clinics, eating there and sleeping there and spending his days and many of his nights casting his cold eyes across charts, printouts and monitor screens as the microbes wriggled on the glass slides and the antibodies waged their miniscule wars and the rats lived or the rats died and became a cipher, their white upturned bellies a contribution to the results of another experiment.

Medical Inspector Karpov, thought Boytsov, was the perfect choice for the man responsible for the implementation of Rudenko's grand design; energized by the missionary zeal of the true scientist and by his devotion to the sacred ideologies of Marxist-Leninism, Karpov was a man capable of contemplating the megadeath of an entire nation, his faith in its necessity unshaken by any thought of individual human life. This man was to the American people as Adolf Hitler was to the Jews.

"Remote observation," he was saying, "showed that after three days there was no sign of life inside the compound."

Three days, thought epidemiologist Antonov. In comparison to the incubation period of most organisms, this was a bolt of lightning; this L-9 microbe hit the nervous system, destroying the myelin sheath.

There were ten other men at the long table, each of them an eminent specialist in his field: immunology, microbiology, epidemiology and rare-disease medicine. There were also among their number three agents of the KGB, the highest-ranking terrorism specialists in that organization. Their task would be to ensure the dissemination of what was known in *Wasteland* terminology as the "active material" throughout the United States of America.

"Tests were then made," Medical Inspector Karpov said, "at the end of a further two weeks, which is to say seventeen days after the first contamination of the subjects. Fifty labor camp inmates were entrained to Tobolsk and marched to the compound, and during the past sixteen days have lived there in isolation, in normal conditions of adequate food, shelter, warmth and exercise, and in the constant presence of the infected cadavers." He lowered his papers and looked along the table. "All have survived and have passed medical tests which show no trace of any infection or the presence of the L-9 microorganism in the bloodstream. Similarly, postmortem examination of the cadavers has shown that the L-9 organism had ceased activity."

"You mean it was dead?" someone asked.

"What? Yes. Dead."

"And therefore harmless."

"Of course." He gazed at the questioner as if he were a rat who'd escaped its cage and would have to be put back. "It is a characteristic of L-9 that it survives only for a few hours in a cold host body."

"We're to understand, Comrade Inspector"—this was Sharaf Boytsov—"that on a large scale, then, the population of a given area would succumb to the contamination within three days, and that two weeks afterward it would be possible for military and other units to enter the area in absolute safety?"

Karpov scraped the side of his raw nose with a gristly finger. "The *contaminated* portion of a given population would succumb, Comrade Secretary. There's a matter of—"

"Dissemination," nodded an epidemiologist. "It's like starting a forest fire. All of the trees don't burn at once."

"I see." It couldn't, Boytsov thought, have been more clearly put.

Medical Inspector Karpov spent a further thirty minutes reading his papers and replying to specific questions, then for the next three hours reports were read by five of the other specialists, and by the first creeping of dusk across the minarets of the town the overall picture of the operation was substantially outlined.

"On the one hand," epidemiologist Antonov pointed out, "the population of the United States of America is extremely mobile in its intraday activities; long distances are traveled on the intercity highways. Also the major cities are highly populous; the area of Manhattan Island, for instance, is the most vulnerable on the entire surface of the earth. These factors, peculiar to the continent, are to our advantage."

"The characteristics of L-9," a colleague said, "include high potency, even in comparison with anthrax. In specific studies it has been found that one ounce of the L-9 agent, introduced into the air-conditioning system of an enclosed sports stadium, is capable of infecting fifty thousand persons in the space of thirty minutes. This is partly due to the fact that there is no indication of the infectious process until the damage to the nerve sheath is irreversible."

"It must be borne in mind," Medical Inspector Karpov added, "that it wouldn't be necessary to infect the entire population in order to incapacitate it. The medical-care problems resulting from even a low degree of partial contamination would be enormous. The transport and communication systems would break down rapidly; food supplies would be cut off from the cities. There would of course be widespread panic."

Secretary Boytsov left his chair and helped himself to a glass of water from the dispenser, but paused before he took the first sip; somewhere among all the figures he remembered having seen that one milligram of the agent L-9 in a glass of water would be sufficient to exterminate fifty persons. Taking slow sips, he felt the chill of the water reach his stomach, where the sharp knot of pain had been coming and going over the past few weeks; it was probably an ulcer. Heinrich Himmler had felt agonizing pains in his stomach, he remembered, caused—according to his doctor's diagnosis—by guilt feelings over the extermination of the Jews.

As the overhead lights were turned on, three more reports were read and discussed. Shortly before ten o'clock the three KGB agents took their leave after briefly acknowledging Chairman Rudenko. Others followed them from the room until only Boytsov, Marshal Klauson and Rudenko remained.

"For all its immense complexity," Rudenko said with a trace of awe in his tone, "the project seems less difficult than we'd imagined. Was that your impression, comrades?"

Before Boytsov could speak, Marshal Klauson said brusquely, "On paper, Comrade Chairman, things always seem easier than in practice." A big man with square jowls and a frame—even while approaching seventy—that looked as if it were bursting out of his military uniform, Boris Klauson always commanded respect at meetings such as this had been; most of the questions had come from him; short and uncompromising questions about the physical problems in disposing of two hundred million corpses before sanitation procedures could allay the outbreak of typhoid and similar diseases; about the risk of wholesale conflagration in cities where fire precautions could no longer be observed by a dying populace—including fire-fighting personnel; about the difficulty of total containment of the spread of the contagion. Some of his questions had received answers that he found satisfactory; others had not.

"You have misgivings, Comrade Marshal?"

"On technical matters, yes." He reached across the table for his peaked cap and took a pair of smoked glasses from his dispatch case—he had affected these, rumor had it, since he'd noticed how exotic General MacArthur had always looked in them. "But hopefully your experts will be coming up with the necessary answers."

Rudenko noticed how the man always referred to "your" experts and "your" project, and so on; and he wasn't quite sure whether it was to acknowledge Rudenko's role as the architect of the grand design, or subtly to warn him that if it turned out a disaster it was going to be his fault.

"Your technical objections are valuable," Rudenko told him with an impatience he didn't wish to hide, "but we must remember that problems are made to be overcome; your own successful career attests to that." He was referring deliberately to the incident seven years ago involving Marshal Klauson in a scandal that had seen the dismissal of a dozen minor functionaries and two ministers from their government posts; it wasn't so much that a brothel was involved, as that its considerable finances were being plundered by those who trod the corridors of power.

"If any of your problems require the experience and skills of the Red Army," the Marshal nodded, "you'll know they'll be dealt with promptly."

He closed the door with a slight slam.

"Do you think it was a mistake," Boytsov asked the Chairman of the Council of Ministers, "to let him in on *Wasteland?*"

"We couldn't do it without him. The experience and skills of the Red Army are going to be called in to deal with the salvage operations."

"I think that's what's worrying him," Boytsov said in a low tone; people had been known to listen at doors, even army marshals. "That man's a born soldier, Mikhail. He came out of the shambles of Stalingrad a full major at the age of twenty-six, and he hasn't had a decent war on his hands since 1947." He moved closer to Rudenko, full of persuasion. "I have an idea that he doesn't like *Wasteland* because it won't require any soldiering: no strategical planning, no campaigns, no brilliant and surprising tactics to execute. And in the end, no glory."

Mikhail Rudenko stood perfectly still with his polished shoes together and his hands behind him, reminding Boytsov of the portrait of Lenin in the chairman's apartment; perhaps he'd adopted the pose consciously, mindful that one day his own portrait too would be seen everywhere, on the wall of every room in every building in every city, not only in Russia but the entire Soviet world.

"Klauson has a job to do," he said impatiently, "and if he's looking for glory instead of the satisfaction of having devoted his talents to the greatest cause in the history of man, then we'll replace him."

"I think in the meantime he should be *watched*." Boytsov felt the slight pain gnawing at his stomach, like a mouse by night. He'd see Dr. Strautmanis about it, go on a milk diet, give up the vodka altogether; he'd got bigger things to worry about. "Something else was made clear during the meeting," he said more cheerfully, "as I'm sure you saw yourself. We don't need to eliminate the whole population of the United States." He waited for Rudenko to respond, but nothing happened. "Considering the breakdown in transport and communications that's going to occur, and the widespread panic, we don't have to knock out more than perhaps twenty-five percent of the populace; the survivors wouldn't be in any condition to offer resistance to our salvage teams when they went in."

Rudenko took a neat step sideways, a neat step back. "That would appeal to me too, Sharaf. I want you to understand that only against the infinitely larger background of humankind's cosmic destiny can I contemplate the idea of mass slaughter. Unfortunately there are two reasons why we must eliminate all life in the United States of America. One is that there'd be no feasible way of restricting the L-9 epidemic—I spoke to Antonov about this yesterday—to a specific section of the population, without actually isolating certain cities by issuing orders through the radio and television networks or by grounding all aircraft and demolishing selected highways; and that would only add to the immense problems ahead of us." He looked down for a moment. "To put it bluntly, my good comrade, a dead body will be far easier to deal with than a live one."

"You mean two hundred million dead bodies," said Boytsov heavily. "I was just hoping we might be able to—"

"The second reason," Rudenko cut him short, "is that we've

already seen how difficult it is to persuade the people of our satellite states that they are under our beneficent protection. In Poland, Hungary and Czechoslovakia, the parochial sentiments of national pride are permanently tying up a considerable proportion of our armed forces. Do you believe we could afford to leave a few million—even a few thousand—citizens alive, knowing perfectly well that they'd go underground and harass our operations? The Americans are not to be underestimated; their own national pride would guarantee the most onerous problems for us. We have to eliminate the population in its totality: that is the very essence of our project. Until the last citizen has succumbed to the effects of the agent L-9, the vanguard of our salvage units can't be sent in without the hazard of contamination. Until the last American has been sacrificed for the greater good of mankind, the forces we shall send in would be exposed to the risk of a bullet in the back of the head, at any time and in any place. We are not going to *invade* that country; we are going to remove it from the political map, as the sanctum of capitalist imperialism."

"I take your point," Boytsov said reluctantly. "I'm less of a visionary than you, Mikhail. The cosmic view doesn't come so easily."

Stepping close to him the chairman of the council of ministers took his arm. "Let me ask you a question, Sharaf. If you were certain that a nuclear strike against the Americans could destroy them without any risk of retaliation, would you order it?"

Boytsov distrusted rhetoric; it had a nasty way of taking your mind off logic. A rhetorical question was designed to embrace its answer. "Bearing in mind the new American weapon," he said helplessly, "yes, I would order a nuclear strike if an overkill were out of the question."

"Of course. But we can't risk it, because an attempt at an overkill would be certain. With the agent L-9 there is no risk, and no overkill. For the first time we have a weapon whose infinite potential for destruction can be contained, and we must use it, my good comrade, and we must use it before they use theirs—because they will, you know, as soon as they're ready. So whose lives are we to consider: theirs or ours?"

"You always make things sound so simple," said Boytsov, while the little mouse went on gnawing under his blue serge suit.

It was snowing again as the limousine with its curtained windows entered Moscow from the northeast, moving at a fast clip along Gorky Street with Chairman Rudenko and Secretary Boytsov in the rear. Talking in low voices with their heads together in the soft plush privacy of the Zil, they had no interest in pulling the curtains back to look at the view—Moscow in March was uninspiring, with its leafless trees and the banks of dirty snow half-blocking the gutters.

They were therefore unaware of the two men who stood looking at one of the newsboards where Gorky Street ran into Karl Marx Prospekt, under the tall streetlamps. The shorter man with the crumpled-looking face and the red eyes was Sergey Talyzin, an out-of-work electronics engineer; the other was Charles Clay.

CHAPTER FOURTEEN

Don Schwarz, chief of the A group COMSAT special-liaison unit in National Security Agency's two-story underground building in Sugar Grove, West Virginia, drove his low-slung Corvette through the final check gate and looked around at the new green leaves of this early summer day and thought, "My God, what I'd like to do would be to drive right on past the building into those deep green meadows and lie there flat on my back with the sky in my eyes and think of *nothing* except the hum of the bees and the wind across the grass."

Instead of which he turned into the parking lot outside the windowless concrete Linn Operations Building and got out of the car and slammed the door and plodded across the tarmac. It hadn't been a good day, so far. The plumbing had gone clean out of whack and flooded the ground floor of the house; Jimmie had come home from school with a diplomatic headache and refused to go back; and Linda had left a note in the bathroom on top of his shaver an hour before he'd even been awake, to the effect that if he ever wanted to see her again he could reach her via American Express in Kansas City, where her parents lived. (This was why Jimmie, always a too-sensitive kid, had come home from school: he'd smelled big trouble.)

"Hi, Don!"

"Uh? Oh, hi." He went through the last security check and into the ops room.

As long ago as 1956, Sugar Grove was featured in the law decreed by the West Virginia state legislature which provided for a one-hundred-square-mile National Radio Quiet Zone to protect the area from the electromagnetic interference of normal urban zones. Since then, it has been forbidden for aircraft to overfly the region and for trucks and buses—heavy vehicles creating electronic "buzz"—to move along the roads. In the 1950s the cover story was that the six-hundred-foot dish was for purposes of radio astronomy and deep-space exploration. In 1980 a white one-hundred-five-foot dish was added to the pre-existing array of antennae, and could be seen only from the heavily patrolled access roads leading to the complex of micro-wave-interception units.

When Don Schwarz had joined A Group (targeted on Soviet Russia) three years ago, all the technical problems involved in long distance sensitive listening had already been solved, simply by embassy-based agents in Moscow discovering the necessary station locations, frequencies, directional azimuths and the radio-telephone equipment bands. Cable telephone interception was still made by going through the embassy or one of the ultrasecret listening posts operated by the CIA on the outskirts of Moscow.

"What's new?" asked Don as he walked into the ops room.

"We're getting those patterns for you."

"Which patterns?" He ought to call Jimmie, to say he'd arrived. Until something could be sorted out, Jimmied had only one parent left.

"You said if we couldn't get anything specific from the local traffic—"

"Oh, sure. Sure. Those patterns."

"Right." Pat Steigman ran his fingers through his ruff of thin, undernourished hair that went with his cave-dweller's pallor. "Okay, we have a lot of conversation going on over there that's kind of new in tone. Most of it's routine stuff between the townhouses and the *dachas* and the Kremlin itself, but we've been getting some good material from calls made by those same three in the *troika*—Rudenko, Boytsov and Koslev, with a few others thrown in, all of them very high-echelon people like Marshal Klauson, and some of them nonpolitical people like health officials and public safety officers. Take a look, Don."

His chief took the printouts and perched on one of the stools at the main console, finding his glasses. It was funny: he'd been so worried about what Linda would think of him in his new glasses, while all the time she was planning to quit on him anyway. Had she left him because he looked like Woody Allen? He started concentrating.

I can't call you tomorrow. It will have to be today . . . He'll be at the meeting, but we should discuss it before that . . . I think that's much too soon, because of the weather conditions . . . Don flipped through the ring-bound sheets, already picking up vibes from this stuff and forgetting about what was happening back home. There were no names ever mentioned. The calls were very short, as if they'd been necessary but made reluctantly; there was quite a bit of impatience from Chairman of the Council of Ministers Rudenko: *I made that quite clear. He is not to be informed until things are more advanced. . . . You shouldn't have called me at this place . . .*

Some of their actual identities weren't certain—the voices of the members of what was now referred to as "the *troika*" were of course well known and carried their unique electronic patterns—they'd recognized Arvid Terebilov, who'd come into the picture only a few weeks before his suicide; and Marshal Klauson had been easy enough to recognize from the military signals traffic between Red Army Headquarters and the Defense Ministry.

Our chief concern is to avoid delay. If this requires extreme measures regarding the person in question, those measures must be taken.

That was Rudenko again, laying down the law. By the time Don finished reading, he knew what Pat had meant about the patterns. They even indicated unusual movement among the top Kremlin officials: there'd been five meetings of the *troika*

and several other people—including Marshal Klauson, chief of
the Red Army—at the Isolation Hospital for Rare Diseases in
Zagorsk, northeast of Moscow. Nothing of what was said at
these meetings had been picked up, but a dozen or so telephone
calls arranging the rendezvous had been noted; and Don was
now concentrating enough to catch a very interesting thing: *all
the arrangements had been made by the principals, not by their
secretaries or staff.*

"What the hell," he asked Steigman, "is going on?"

"Good question."

Don made a note in the margin against the reference to the
Isolation Hospital. *Subject of these meetings: germ warfare?*

In Georgetown University, Washington, D.C., three men sat
late over a tray of coffee and doughnuts and watched the sun
go down over the trees of the campus.

"I'd say it's a power struggle."

"But with a difference."

"You mean Rudenko's timing?"

"Right."

A telephone rang and one of them picked it up. "Who? No.
This isn't Oriental Cookery." He hung up.

"But close," someone said, and they all laughed. They were
specialists in Foreign Studies, or less formally, Kremlinologists.
Drawing their information from the NSA, the CIA and fifty
other sources of news, they tried to find out what it meant, for
instance, when the chairman of the Communist Party of the
Soviet Union sneezed, not otolaryngologically but politically.

"You mean what the hell's Rudenko formed a power clique
for at this time?"

"Rather than wait, yes. If Vladychenko has these kidney problems, there might not be anything Rudenko has to do but wait
till he's hospitalized or hits the hearse."

One of them stood up and stretched, standing for a minute
at the windows to see the blood-red rim of the sun throw the
tops of the cedars into black lacework. "I don't see why those

three guys want to get Vladychenko out and Rudenko in, unless they're trying to do something they know he wouldn't let them do."

"Okay. He's not hot war——or even very cold war——oriented, right? So if the note we had from Sugar Grove about a possible germ warfare connection is on target, it could tie in. While Vladychenko's looking to spread his peace-among-men thing all over the globe—"

"Which I think is smart, Joe—"

"Oh sure, sure, I agree it's smart; he's winning the war in a lot of places, even in England and Germany, where the housewives are coming out of the kitchen to sit down outside the missile sites. Sure, he's winning pretty nicely. But while he's doing that, the Rudenko *troika*'s convening secret meetings at isolation hospitals and clinics and places like that—"

"With military commanders and epidemiologists sitting around the table together, if you can imagine such a thing—"

"I'd rather not," said the man standing at the windows, and turned around to face the others. "I really would rather *not* imagine such a thing."

There was a short silence.

"Jesus," said someone softly.

"Hell, Joe, germ warfare isn't practical, you know that."

"Okay. So maybe those guys are trying to *make* it practical?"

There was another silence, this time longer.

"Shit. You really think so?"

"I'm not thinking anything, Barney. We're just asking some questions, right?"

"Then try this one." He dropped his plastic cup into the bin. "What's their hurry? Why now?"

"Because we're putting pressure on them."

"What pressure?"

"Let me put it this way." As the sundown burned along the horizon to the dying of the day, the man at the window became a dark silhouette. "When we leaked the idea that the United States was developing a decisive new weapon, we thought it was

pretty smart. But was it? Or was it, in fact, appallingly dangerous?"

"Okay," Claude said, "I'd like to see the *pas de chat* again. But
take your time over it; there's no hurry."

Nadia made the spring, bending her right knee, then her left,
landing neatly enough. "I think I'm—"

"You're not turned completely face on, darling, that's all; the
rest's fine, but I want to see you do it the way Balanchine suggested—it's a big jump, nearly a leap. With your speed you'll be
okay." He squatted on his haunches, his pointed elf's face intent
on her body as she jumped again, this time higher, "Yes, darling. Yes, yes and yes. Very nice."

He worked her for another hour, getting her still higher, until
she felt something of the elation in it; whatever Balanchine created, elation became a part of it, after all the bone-breaking
work.

Later Claude rehearsed her for the ballet she would be doing
in two weeks' time: *Stars and Stripes*. "Okay, after the *pas de
chat* on the left side, you move downstage between Beryl and
Marie, then you start the *jetés élancés*. Just follow Marie—she's
very good; but give yourself room—it takes so much *space*, darling."

He worked her for yet another hour, going through the whole
sequence, until the sweat was soaking into her leg warmers and
trickling on her neck; by this time her whole body was on fire,
but not aching yet; that would come later. Claude ran people
into the ground.

The man was in the narrow, poorly lit corridor when she left
the studio; it was the pianist who said, "Oh, Nadia, this is
Mr.—" then she looked helpless.

"Tarasov, Nikolay." He gave a warm smile, his eyes resting on
her steadily. "A great admirer, I assure you."

"Thank you." She spoke in Russian, as he had.

"I was watching you," he said.

"They let you into the studio?" Claude never allowed anyone
near the place when he was working.

The man's smile came again. "There is a crack in the doorway
to the other corridor"—he pointed behind Nadia—"where one
can peep a little. I thought you were brilliant, my child."

She thanked him again, trying to sum him up; there'd been
quite a few Russians coming to her or telephoning their admi-
ration since she had joined the company; so far, she'd received
flattering reviews. But there was something different about this
short, diffident man in the worn gray suit, his thinning hair
catching the light from the bulb overhead, his eyes watching
her own attentively. "It would be a privilege, Ballerina Fedotova, if you'd join me for some coffee next door."

"I'm very—"

"What am I saying?" His smile turned to a quick soft laugh. "I
mean a great dish of borscht—you must be starving after all that
work!"

"I'm hungry, yes." He spoke like someone who knew what it
meant to dance; he also spoke her mother tongue, and its soft
cadences reminded her of home. "Thank you," she said on im-
pulse. "That would be nice."

They were halfway through their meal when he said, his careful fingers breaking a piece of crust from the loaf between them,
"I have news of your mother, and your sister."

Nadia caught her breath. "Who are you?"

It was the characteristic question of the defector: not "How
do you know?" but "Who are you?"

"They are quite well," he said quickly to reassure her. "Quite
well." His eyes were a faded blue, but had the light of interest
in them; he'd hardly looked away from her since they'd come
into the little café. "But of course—" he shrugged reluctantly
"—their lives have changed a little."

"Changed?" But she knew what he meant; she'd been trying
not to know it all these months. She'd written a letter to them
every week, telling them about New York, about America, asking how they were, whether they hated her for leaving them,
begging them to write just one short letter so that she'd know
they were all right, and didn't hate her too much, only a little.
There'd been no answer.

"You are a dancer," Nikolay Tarasov said softly, confidentially. "I understand that." With a wistful smile—"I was a dancer once, myself, though many years ago, of course; but I still know what it means for young artists like you to dance: it's not just something you decided to do for a living—it's your life. So I understand why you left your country and why you are here now." He shrugged again. "But that isn't so well understood in Moscow. They—"

"Is my mother being . . . maltreated?" She said it fearfully; it had been a recurring nightmare for so long, induced—a psychiatrist had said—by guilt.

"No. Not—" he lifted a hand and let it fall again "—not physically. But her friends, and your sister's friends, don't speak to them very much now; it wouldn't look too good, you can appreciate that. And the officers of the *Komitet* . . . have their duty to do, and their duty is to make it clear that the relatives of citizens who betray their country are not to be treated like heroes. Of course—"

"What are they doing to my mother?" She was suddenly gripping his hand, but he showed no surprise; he would have been expecting this outbreak of fear.

"They have not harmed your family, Nadia. They are not thugs, you know. Your family is still distinguished, in artistic circles: they had a relative in the Bolshoi . . . once." He put his other hand on hers. "But what you did in coming to America has naturally outweighed all other considerations."

"But what *are* they doing?"

His slight shrug came. "The *Komitet* require your mother and your sister to report to their nearest office every week, for questioning. They—"

"What questioning?" She gripped his hand until her fingers were bloodless. The nightmares were coming true at last, as she should have known they would; the total absence of any letters from home should have warned her. "What questions are they asking?" She had never fallen foul of the KGB, but like other citizens of Moscow had witnessed ugly scenes in the streets when someone had been summarily arrested and bundled into a car, and had often heard that an acquaintance had "disappeared"—usually, in her world, a student or an artist who'd said or written something critical of the State. Now her own mother and sister were being made to suffer, and for something they'd not even done themselves. "What questions? You must tell me!"

Nikolay Tarasov shrugged. "How would I know, my child? The questions themselves aren't important, anyway; it's just that your mother is being taught a lesson; after all, she played a big part in your upbringing, so who knows that she didn't put a few subversive ideas into your head that finally led you to abandon your true culture for another?"

Nadia took her hand away from his, and slowly pushed her unfinished plate of pasta aside, no longer hungry. He'd forgotten to smile, she noticed. "How do you know about my mother?" she asked him in a moment.

"I sometimes get news from Moscow."

"About my mother?"

"About a lot of people."

"How do you mean?" she asked impatiently.

He didn't answer, but went on watching her with that damned smile of his coming back, but with a different message this time. He wasn't answering her because he knew it wasn't necessary.

"You're in the *Komitet* yourself," she said at last.

"Of course."

She felt her body collapsing on itself as the strength suddenly went out of it and she sat slumped on the chair as if she'd been doped; the lactic acid began burning in her muscles now as they relaxed. The whole of her daring and impulsive escapade was replayed in her mind during the next few timeless seconds, in a medley of kaleidoscopic scenes—the Christmas window displays and the Bolshoi's opening night and the meeting in the Café Russe with the great defector Patolichev and the ballroom of the White House and Bruce with his arms around her in the rooms of so many New York hotels—and now this, the last scene, the real one where she was being made to wake up and face the truth: that she'd betrayed her mother and her sister and exposed them to suffering and humiliation at the hands of the dreaded *Komitet Gosudarstvennoy Bezopasnosti*, who had no mercy on people they did not approve of.

Staring at the man in the shabby gray suit across from her at the table, she saw the whole room swing suddenly around him, and then there was a sharp pain in her thigh as she got to her feet and knocked against the table's edge and lurched between chairs and other tables to the dark passage and the women's room, the door slamming shut behind her on its spring as she stumbled into a cubicle and stood there swaying until the churning of her stomach reached its climax and she squeezed her eyes shut because this had always frightened her since the first time as a child when she'd believed the whole of her stomach was coming out and she was going to die.

When it was over she rinsed her face and dried it with a paper towel from the rickety dispenser and then stood staring at it in the mirror, hating her face, hating herself more—much more —than even her mother or Klavdya could have hated her when they heard the news of what she had done to them. Someone came in to the room and said *hi*, and she said *hi* back, coming away from the mirror at last and shaking her hair from her face and looking for the door. *You okay?* the woman asked her.

Yes, yes thank you.

The man was still there when she went back to the table.

"I am going home," she said.

"Home?"

"To Russia."

He looked concerned; in the mirror her face had been white and her eyes feverish. "Sit down," he said.

She found the chair as the waitress came up. "You okay, honey?"

"Yes. I—"

"Bring you anything else?" she asked the man.

"You have vodka? Or cognac?"

"Sure don't, we're not licensed."

"Some tea, then. Very strong."

I must call Bruce, Nadia thought. But that idea, too, was frightening. How would she say good-bye? *I want never to leave you,* she'd told him only yesterday. *Then you don't have to,* he'd said.

"When are you going to Moscow?" she asked the man.

"Next year." He seemed surprised. "I'm at the Soviet embassy here."

"I see. Then you can't take me."

"To Moscow?"

"Yes. To help me explain to them. You say you understand why I came here. You say you were a dancer, once. I'm asking you to help me." She sat shivering in the warmth of the café, the cooking smells nauseous now, while a short time ago they'd been so appetizing. "Will you help me? Will you take me to the embassy, and help me explain? I don't want them to put me into prison when I go back."

He was watching her pensively, his head on one side, his faded blue eyes intent, not smiling. The girl came with the pot of tea and poured it for them. "I brought you these extra bags," she said, "you wanted it strong, right?"

"Thank you." He peeled the bags and dropped them into their cups. "Drink while it's hot. It will make you feel better."

"Yes." She leaned over the table toward him. "Will you help me?"

He reached for the sugar. "Your case is very difficult, Nadia Fedotova. You are a *defector*. That's very serious."

"I know. But please help me. *Please.*"

He stirred his tea thoughtfully, reflected light from its surface playing across his eyes. She waited, and after a long time he said, "Perhaps there is a way I can help you, yes. But you must do what I shall ask."

MEMO: FIRST DEPT, FIRST CHIEF DIRECTORATE
DATE: MAY 3
ATTEN: LT K. NIKOLEV
CASE: NADIA FEDOTOVA

THIS DEFECTOR HAS NOW BEEN ENTRAPPED
AND WILL BE DIRECTED TO EXPLOIT HER CLOSE
ASSOCIATION WITH AMERICAN NATIONAL
BRUCE CARLYLE PAGET, PRESIDENTIAL AIDE
AT WHITE HOUSE.

SOURCE: AGENT NVT, SOVEM, WASHINGTON.

CHAPTER FIFTEEN

At eight o'clock in the morning, Yefim Grishmanov approached the Council of Ministers Building inside the walls of the Kremlin and greeted the guard, who asked for his identity card and work permit.

Grishmanov had the identity card ready, and searched for his work permit while they were talking.

"Haven't you finished it yet?" the guard asked him teasingly.

"It's very sophisticated." Grishmanov was an electronics engineer, at present working on the alarm system in the filing office. He started going through his wallet again.

"I won't ever get you to do any work in my apartment," the guard told him. "I'd be dead of old age before you'd finished it!"

"If you had this kind of alarm system in your apartment, the *Komitet* would want to know what you were trying to hide. Then you'd be dead anyway. I can't find the thing," he added in annoyance.

"No work permit? No work, then."

"Son of a whore," Grishmanov said with feeling, and shuffled through his soiled batch of papers. "I've got to finish the job today, you know that."

"You know what they'd do to me if I let you through without a work permit, do you?"

"I don't care about that. I've got my job to lose too." He remembered having a drink at the bar around the corner from his apartment last night, and losing his wallet. Someone had found it before he'd left the place, and he'd got it back; the work permit must have dropped out then.

"I think I know where I lost it," he told the guard.

"Don't mean a thing to me." The guard caught movement in the distance beyond Grishmanov's shoulder; one of the Zils was coming up from Senate Tower Gate, and he noted the license plate. Comrade Chairman Rudenko was early again this morning; it had happened quite a lot, lately; you couldn't say he didn't know how to work for his living. "I can't have you hanging about here all day," he told the engineer, "you're cluttering up the place. It's a good thing I know you, but next time, mind, I want to see that permit, understand?" He beckoned the man inside.

"Fred?"

"What?"

"Urgent."

"Oh, Christ, I've got enough to do." He wiped printer's ink down his white linen coat and picked up his cigarette, taking another puff. "What is it this time?"

"How should I know?" Messengers weren't allowed to open envelopes; they'd have your nuts off for that. He dropped it onto the printer's bench and got a signature for it.

Fred took another draw on his cigarette and looked at the envelope. *XXX Priority* was stamped across the top, and he noted it with disgust. Forging was an art, and he hated rush jobs; it was a rush job that had landed him in the slammer that time: they'd seen the tail of the *y* was too long, on the signature and had held up the check. He hadn't liked his six months in the slammer at all, but it had given him time to do some thinking; maybe there was some kind of job going where they could use a forger, legitimatelike.

He opened the envelope and looked at the instructions, which were on Foreign Office paper. This had come through the diplomatic bag from Moscow. Then he looked at the dirty, dog-eared card they wanted him to copy. He couldn't read any Russian but they'd put the translation for him.

Working Permit No. 9146A, No. 1 Moscow District, Electronics Division, Main Labor Office. Operator Yefim Vasilievich Grishmanov, Identity No. 3A/1617/55/BDT/4.

There was a photograph on the card, and a photograph of a different man enclosed in the envelope. The instructions read: *Please change photographs and add franking. Change name to: Sergey Trifimovich Talyzin and remove signature. Remaining matter can stay. Utmost possible speed, please. MFJ.*

They were barmy, of course. Stark raving bonkers. This card was a good two years old and the signature was covered in stewed cabbage stains and the photo looked as if this geezer couldn't find any toilet paper—and those clots thought you could change the signature without finishing up with a card you could put in the pianola and play the Song of the Volga Bloody Boatman, stone the crows. He'd have to make a new card, and that'd take six or seven hours in the wear-and-tear machine, for a start. Utmost possible speed, please, my Aunt Fanny, they think I'm a bloody magician?

"Fred?"

"Bugger off, I'm busy!"

Yefim Grishmanov entered the Bluebird Bar and made his way between the rickety tables to the counter, his eyes already stinging comfortably to the smoke of black tobacco.

"What'll it be, Yefim?"

"I'll take a beer, Georgi."

"Coming up."

Yefim found a place for his elbows among the puddles of beer and squinted around him in the gloom, but couldn't see anyone he knew; he'd worked late tonight, and there were people here on different shifts.

The bartender brought his beer. "Got something for you, Yefim. We found that work permit of yours you was asking about last week." He dropped it onto the counter.

"Well if that don't beat everything!" Yefim picked it up and looked at it under the parchment-shaded lamp and put it into his wallet. "Where was it?"

"A customer found it on the floor."

"Well I'm damned! You know I waited three hours down at the Labor Office yesterday, trying to get a new one? Then they told me to go back there tomorrow! Who found it, Georgi?"

"He wasn't one of our usuals. Never set eyes on him before."

"If you see him again, give him a drink, on me."

"Will do."

Yefim Grishmanov sank his top lip into his beer, his heart full of gratitude for the benevolent stranger.

Three kilometers distant from the Bluebird Bar, Charles Clay got onto a bus along the Garden Ring Road and dropped twenty kopecks into the box and sat down, holding onto the seat in front of him as the wheels of the bus churned through the ruts of week-old snow at the curb. Twenty minutes later he got off near the Kremlin and walked along Kuznetsky Most Street, a narrow and ancient thoroughfare lined with bookshops and antique stores.

The man in the third bookshop from the intersection saw Clay come in and waited five minutes, taking down one or two leather-bound volumes and glancing through them with the doorway visible in his peripheral vision. Nobody had followed Clay in, so he went down the aisle between the shelves and the window and stood next to him for a moment.

"He's over there in the far corner, The one standing by himself, with the glasses. Okay?"

"Okay."

The man went out of the shop and Clay made his way between the shelves, taking a book here and there, putting it back, not hurrying. The woman in the heavy woolen shawl didn't look up from her book at the cash register; by the time Clay reached the man in the corner they were standing out of sight.

They spoke in Russian; in Moscow, foreign speech was still so rare that it caught immediate attention.

"They told you which house?" Clay asked softly.

"Chairman Rudenko's place."

"Right. How soon can you do it?"

"Tomorrow morning."

"Fair enough." A man passed the end of the aisle and Clay checked his face and the cut of his clothes and the age of his shoes and the way he was moving, and was satisfied. "Wait till Rudenko leaves. That's usually about 7:45. The TV set's on the ground floor, in the big room on the east side. Is the east side okay for you?"

"I can cover three sides, but not the north."

"That's the back of the building."

"Right." Talyzin paused as a woman went past the end of the aisle. "Where's the receiver going to be?"

"I've rented an unfurnished room for you, in a block due east of the Rudenko apartment. The distance for the radio beam is roughly seven hundred meters."

"You know what you're doing."

"That's right." Clay edged back from the aura of garlic.

Talyzin nodded. "Direct beam. Lovely. Did they send the work permit?"

Clay gave it to him and the Russian put it straight into his pocket. "I'll look at it under the light, soon as I can."

"It's perfect."

"That's good. My neck's on it." The bug was going to be easy enough—he'd done it a hundred times—the moment of truth was going to be when he presented that card. "I'll give you the word, soon as it's in."

"I'll be waiting."

Talyzin nodded. "Rudenko's place," he said softly. "This is something important."

"You wouldn't believe how important it is. You just wouldn't believe."

CHAPTER SIXTEEN

S ir James Braithwaite leaned forward slightly as the waiter
lit his cigar for him.

"Thank you, Cummings." As he sat back in the Queen
Anne wing chair he decided at last that something would have
to be done about Cummings, who was new to the club, who
saw fit to use a gas lighter for the lighting of cigars instead of
three Bryant & May matches—avoiding the stink of marsh gas
and at the same time precharring the leaf—and who was clearly
going to go on doing it until he was roundly taken to task. Yet
the fellow behaved like this out of kindness and an eagerness to
serve—rare qualities, these days, God only knew. So what could
you do?

He drew in sufficient smoke to ensure that the leaf was burning evenly and observed Lord Fresneigh across the room, doz-
ing over a glass of port. It had taken both Cummings and the
senior porter to get him into that chair, one on each side of him,
making the place look like an old people's home. The fellow
should be dead by now. Watching him from beneath his silvered
brows and noting Fresneigh's sagging posture, Braithwaite
thought that perhaps he was. And about time.

Steiger arrived punctually at nine, coming across the room
with an energetic step more suitable to a gymnasium, thought
Braithwaite nervously. The man walked with his head down and
his eyes up, as if aiming a gun—at this moment at the center of
Braithwaite's forehead, so that he almost ducked.

"Good evening, Steiger. Good of you to come. Let's sit over there, shall we? More secluded." Passing close to Lord Fresneigh, he gave him a searching glance. The fellow was still breathing. "I hope you'll join me in a brandy?" he asked the American.

"Thanks, sir, but I have to work out, later."

"Work out what?" Braithwaite inquired as they sat down.

"Uh—in the gym, you know?" He gave a keen grin, lifting imaginary weights. "Putting on flab, I guess."

"Ah." Sir James thought it best to order his brandy. In the company of this fit-looking keen-eyed young man he was beginning to feel his age. "So you're new to London. Like it?"

"It's great. And congratulations, sir."

"On what?"

"Your new lady mayoress."

Braithwaite looked pained. "M-mmm . . . breaks the tradition, of course, but there you are." He kept the small talk going until the tray and decanter were presented, with two glasses. "You're sure you won't change your—no, perhaps not. You look disturbingly healthy."

Another fresh grin. "Have to keep up, Sir James." He happened to know that the head of the British Secret Service, at sixty-four, could outrun most contenders on the polo field. "He plays dumb," Steiger's chief at Foggy Bottom had briefed him a week ago. "He's also very cunning at getting information he shouldn't have." As the new head of station at the US Embassy, Tim Steiger would be seeing a lot of the boys at D16, though not often the director-general himself. Tonight was pretty special—he'd received a personal invitation, and had signaled CIA HQ immediately. "He wants something," he was told, "or he's ready to give you something as a trade-off. If he's got something for us that's worthwhile, you can open up with him."

"How are you people getting on with Moscow?" Sir James asked him from the depths of his armchair. "Anything new?"

"I guess there's always something new, isn't there?" Tim Steiger pulled his own chair closer, which needed quite a bit of strength—it was more like a four-poster bed. He wasn't too happy about talking in public this way, even though the nearest person was asleep in the far corner of the room.

So the fellow was going to stonewall, thought Braithwaite. Well, he could easily change all that. "Pity about that man Terebilov," he said in a moment. "He was on our side, you know, really. He believed in getting on with the West without all this ridiculous saber-rattling." He swirled his brandy in its glass. "You people still have him on record, I suppose, as a drowning accident?"

Steiger's muscles drew taut. "As far as I know."

"Nobody knows much further than you, my dear Steiger, surely." He waited.

"We—uh—we still have him down that way, sir, sure."

"Then you'd better bring your records up to date. He was shot dead on the Turkish frontier, coming across from Bulgaria."

Steiger's head went down as he leveled his gaze at Braithwaite. "*Jesus . . . Christ,*" he said softly.

"Amen."

"When did you know?"

"Last March."

"Three months back?"

"Yes."

Steiger gave himself a moment to think. There was no point asking this guy why the Company hadn't been told; there was no agreement for the automatic sharing of intelligence between the CIA and D16. But when somebody as big as Arvid Terebilov got shot dead *crossing a frontier*, he'd have thought there was a case for passing it on. And why the hell wasn't this picked up anyway by the Company's own agents-in-place?

"Okay," he shrugged philosophically.

"You mustn't feel badly about it," Braithwaite said gently. "We really had a tremendous lot to do, covering it all up."

Steiger found his grin. "I'll bet." But just wait till he told his chief; an awful lot of people were going to get fired.

"It was easier for us," said Braithwaite, "in a certain sense, because—" he studied the ash on his cigar "—we were helping him across when it happened."

Steiger just went deadpan, on principle. He understood now: they hadn't wanted to admit to screwing it up.

"Rather embarrassing for us," nodded Braithwaite, picking up his thought. "But these things happen."

"Sure. He was defecting, sir?"

"Yes. He had something to tell us."

Steiger waited, feeling a sense of unreality. It was like saying that the secretary of defense, who'd apparently been drowned by accident on vacation in the Bahamas, had actually been trying to get across into Cuba. Unreal.

"But we didn't get it," his companion said. "Or not very much."

Steiger dumped his deadpan mask and tried to relax, like you had to do before a heavy game; there was an awful lot of hard playing to do tonight, he knew that now. "Jesus," he said as he loosened his necktie, "do they know over there that it wasn't an accidental drowning?"

"They privately believe it was suicide."

"They don't think it was the KGB? If he was trying to get across with some information—"

"Rusakov, head of the KGB, is not an opponent of Chairman Rudenko in terms of internecine rivalry for power within the Politburo. He would have been expected to inform Rudenko if it were a wet affair."

"Rudenko," nodded Steiger, and left a short silence; but the other man didn't speak, though he badly wanted to, now. Steiger knew what he was after. "Have you been watching him lately, sir?"

"Not closely. I thought you might have been."

"As a matter of fact . . ." he tugged his chair closer again, and lowered his voice.

It took only twenty minutes for them to understand that if they weren't ready to share what intelligence they had concerning Moscow, they'd be making a mistake. From Steiger's viewpoint, the British had been deliberately sitting on a piece of information that was going to send shockwaves right through the Company when they heard it, and this guy here was ready to show his deck—had in fact shown it, or what looked like most of it, Jesus, there couldn't be much else. From Sir James's viewpoint, since it was known that the CIA had recently started watching the Kremlin very closely indeed, even to the physical movements of the Soviet hierarchy around the city, it was probably a good idea to offer the Terebilov card in exchange for a showdown; the Americans must know a great deal more of what was going on in Moscow, because their network of electronic intelligence coverage was infinitely more efficient than the UK's.

And there was one other consideration that escaped neither of these men. Given the background, it could well be that if their two services didn't decide to cooperate at once, it might even lead to disaster.

"That's about what we have on Rudenko," Tim Steiger said as he took the first sip of his brandy. There wouldn't be any workout tonight. "And yes, to answer your question, we have talked about germ warfare."

"Because of the strange movements going on over there."

"Right. We believe they're looking for something to face us with, some kind of answer to the US space weapon." He spread his hands open. "After all, it's nothing new. The stuff was used in Afghanistan and plenty of other places. The US is working on quite a few exploratory projects itself, as I'm sure you know."

"We do. But we don't know to what extent."

"The Company doesn't know everything the Pentagon's up to, Sir James. I wish we did. Most of what we know is from statements by the Defense Department in response to needling by UPI and other news media. The Department naturally claims that research is directly applicable to the prevention of disease induced in military personnel and to a methodology that would ensure survival and continued effectiveness in a toxic environment. We can't argue with that, because it makes a lot of sense;

if an enemy in the field is going to spray our troops with botulism, malaria, anthrax hemorrhagic fever and stuff like that, we have to work out protective vaccines. We know they're trying to clone the squid gene for DFPase for organophosphorous detoxification. But there's—"

"Cloning," Braithwaite cut in, "is what we're really talking about. Isn't it? Forgive my interrupting, but this is what we believe might be going on over there, don't you agree? People as high in the Kremlin aren't visiting clinics and isolation hospitals simply to keep an eye on vaccine projects."

"Right. That's absolutely right. We're thinking on the same wavelength. From cloning the squid gene it mightn't be too far to cloning a known disease resistant to every known antidote or vaccine."

"Or worse."

Steiger leveled his gaze at Sir James again. "Or worse, right. That's absolutely right. In this kind of recombinant DNA work they could come up with something entirely new, entirely invulnerable. But it could only be used in limited warfare, tactical warfare."

"Of course. It would have to be containable."

"Right. They couldn't ever use it to knock out a whole island, or a whole continent. We don't have to lose any sleep over that."

Sergey Talyzin had a toothache.

There were something like a dozen cars in the parking lot behind the apartment building when he came bumping across the tarmac in his little Pobeda work van and halted it against the red brick wall. There was something ominous, he thought, about the wall. It wouldn't let him go any farther; it was as if he'd decided to cut himself off from escape. He could start the engine again, of course, and back up and turn around and leave the place; but then again, he couldn't. He'd told them he'd do this job, and he'd do it. And there was the money. Five hundred rubles wasn't monkeyshit; he'd be able to move out of that stinking little box in the workers' complex by the river and set himself up in the two-room apartment—*two rooms*—he'd been after for months now, where there wouldn't be so many screaming kids and he wouldn't have to listen to the Martynovs' radio through the plasterboard wall—all they wanted to listen to was bloody sopranos. Five hundred rubles could do a lot for you in this city.

He was sweating when he climbed out of the rickety van with its grimy corrugated aluminum sides and its rusted bumpers; it was a warm day, but that wasn't what the sweat was about; it was partly his toothache, because the very idea of going to a dentist gave him the running shits; and of course it was partly because of the risk he was going to be taking a few minutes from now. But then, he'd done this sort of thing fifty times, could do it in his sleep; the idea of going to the dentist was making him nervous, that was it, so he'd started exaggerating things to the point where he'd only managed to sleep for a couple of hours last night, sucking on a little cotton bag of cloves to help the pain while those bloody sopranos kept on caterwauling till past midnight.

Then again, this was Comrade Rudenko's apartment he was going to, chairman of the council of ministers, so there could be a few *Komitet* bastards around to keep an eye on things. And the Englishman had said this job was more important than he'd ever believe, so there was a lot of responsibility attached. It was a bad day for doing a job like this, you could say; he'd got no stomach for it. He'd only seen it happen once, but he'd never been able to forget it; he'd been working with one of his friends, Alek Shokin, on a perfectly legitimate job for the No. 3 Moscow Electronics Industry Work Center, when the KGB had come for him—for Alek. And this time it wasn't just a couple of shabby-looking gumshoes with a beat-up civilian car, it was half a dozen very efficient-looking bastards in a big gray-green van with bars at the windows, two of the men in uniform. They'd come across the sidewalk at a quick pace, almost in step, and Alek had tried to run, and of course that was fatal: they just grabbed him and spun him around and half-carried him to the gray-green van while he tried to shout something out, *what have*

I done, where are you taking me? and that sort of thing, but all there was left was the broken snow where their feet had been and the smell of the exhaust gas on the winter air. He'd never seen Alek again. He'd been running a little black-market deal in electric heaters, buying them for kopecks at the back door of the factory and selling them for half the price you'd pay in the stores. He'd be in a labor camp now, up north. For selling heaters.

What would they do to you if they caught you putting a bug in the apartment of the chairman of the council of ministers for a Western spy ring?

By the time he was standing in the lobby of the building the sweat had gone cold on him and the worst of the nerves were over; you could go only so far; you could let your imagination get right out of control till you didn't know who you were any more, till you found yourself praying to be a child again, with nothing on your mind; then you kind of recovered; and as the pale-faced snake-eyed security guard checked his papers, Sergey Talyzin felt drained, purged and in a sort of vacuum where nothing could happen to him, or if it did he wouldn't feel it or know anything about it. This was how a snowman must feel.

"Work permit?"

He held it out, keeping the tip of his tongue against his wisdom tooth. The guard held the work permit next to the identity card to compare the signatures, then he looked over the long green authorization sheet from the Ministry of the Electronics Industry, one of his bright black boots squeaking softly as he changed the weight on his feet, the stale smell of tobacco on his breath, his eyes staring at the worksheet like two glass lenses in a robot waxwork while Sergey Talyzin recalled how the snow had broken up to leave two narrow tracks where they'd dragged Alek's feet along, and how his shouting was sending an echo back from the metal shed on the worksite, things he'd never noticed before.

"Is there something wrong with the television set?"

"What?" The suddenness of the guard's question had sent a

flash along his nerves, just under the skin. "Not as far as we know. It's a directive from the factory in Tula—it says here, *Replacement of Part No. A/2738475/A1/37365-S.* That's the shunt switch to the—"

"I can read."

"Of course you can, I was just—"

"If you don't know whether there's anything wrong with the set, how do you know the part has to be replaced?"

"It's a mod. A modification. They've found out the switch overheats if the set's left on more than a few hours at a time. The way they think, if we replace—"

"Where is the new part?"

Talyzin got it out of his canvas workbag. "Here."

The guard took it and turned it over in his hand while Talyzin watched him, half expecting him to say it was the wrong switch, when in fact the bastard didn't know it from a bloody doorbell. It was funny, knowing he was just a pea-brained security man who couldn't tell a shunt switch from a doorbell but at the same time knowing that if he suspected anything wrong, even the slightest thing, he'd switch on his two-way radio and ask for assistance, and then they'd bring the gray-green van here and there'd be two dark streaks across the sidewalk where the black rubber of his shoes had been sliding when they'd dragged him away.

"What did you say it was?"

"A shunt switch. It's to take the load off the—"

"I know what a shunt switch does." He gave it back to Talyzin with a little tossing gesture, like throwing a bit of bread to a dog. "Open the bag."

The guard went through it thoroughly: screwdrivers, pliers, wire cutters, soldering kit, insulating tape, forked lugs, spade lugs, rolls of copper wire and half a dozen bits and pieces like relays, solid state blocks, alternator gear—*What's this?—And this?—And this?*—while Sergey Talyzin stood there with a snowball in his stomach, knowing he shouldn't have come here, knowing it was too late to do anything if this man, this other

human being, if you looked at it like that, if this *comrade* caught
the slightest whiff of anything wrong in his eyes or his voice or
his manner and slung his two-way radio around on its strap and
called for assistance and went on living his comfortable life
while Sergey Talyzin was shoved on a train with all the other
doomed souls who were going eventually to die of pneumonia
or rheumatic fever or dysentery up there in the icebound wastes
of the Gulag archipelago, with the bruises and the lash marks
still on their bodies and nothing but a hole hacked out of the
frozen clay to hold their bones.

"How long will it take you?"

"What?" For an instant he'd forgotten where he was, what he
was doing here. "I'd say . . . not long. Fifteen minutes." The
sweat crept down from his armpits, because the guard had noticed he'd been thinking about something else.

"You don't seem very sure."

"I can't say, exactly, see. But it shouldn't take longer than
that—it's simple enough."

"Then I'll expect you back here in fifteen minutes, is that
right?"

"That's right."

The guard stamped his temporary-pass book, tore off the leaf
and gave it to Talyzin. "Show it to the servant at the door."

By 9:27 on the morning of June 22 an American-made Scanar-
62 multiple-phase microphone/transmitter unit was installed inside the rear panel of the television set in the chairman of the
council of ministers's apartment, adjacent to the east wall of the
main salon.

Within the hour Sergey Talyzin entered the small unfurnished room on the seventh floor of the apartment block just
north of the Garden Ring Road, approximately seven hundred
meters due east of Chairman Rudenko's residence. Talyzin
locked the door after him and padded across to the cramped
bathroom, where he rapidly delivered himself of the physiological effects of this morning's acute tension; he then went to the

coffee-making machine that stood on the bare wood floor in a corner, and plugged it in. He was shivering now, partly with nerves and partly from the cooling effect of the sweat that had been creeping from his skin during the past ninety minutes, so he went to the makeshift bed on the floor and pulled the blanket around him, settling back with his shoulders against the wall and the Scanar-23 receiving set beside him.

> *EYES JB ONLY*
> *DATE: JUNE 22*
> *DESTRUCT REQUESTED.*
> *DECODE SERIES V.*
>
> *OPERATION BATMAN NOW RUNNING.*
> *AM STANDING BY FOR ANY MATERIAL.*
> *WILL SEND VIA EMBASSY CIPHER.*
> *CJC.*

"Steiger?"

"Yes."

"Braithwaite here."

"Hi, Sir James."

"Er—hi. That little matter I mentioned: all appears to be well. You may tell your people we shall be expecting some rather important results."

"That's terrific."

"Quite so. Good morning to you."

CHAPTER SEVENTEEN

On the evening of July 7, Chairman Mikhail Rudenko convened a meeting at his apartment between Sharaf Boytsov, Viktor Koslev, Ivan Rusakov—head of the KGB—and Tikhon Khitrov, the director of the Executive Action Department. Department V—the most sinister and therefore the most clandestine of the entire *Komitet*—was specifically responsible for *mokrie dela,* the "wet affairs" involving loss of life in foreign countries, including the sabotage of public utilities, transportation and communication systems with a view to endangering the populace at large and thus spreading confusion or inciting revolution.

Khitrov had started work in his youth as a railway lineman, graduating to engineer status and working on locomotives and rolling stock, which permitted him enough salary to afford a wife. There was no issue to the marriage, which embittered him to the point where he lost most of his friends after embroiling them in heated arguments and fist fights in the neighborhood bars, often because they hinted or even suggested that the barrenness of the marriage might be due to a physiological inadequacy on his part rather than his wife's. Her sudden death due to a train derailment in a blizzard near Tashkent at the age of only thirty-two increased his bitterness to a state of chronic depression, and for ten years he filled the post of itinerant inspector on the railways so as to divest himself of his few friends and to pass his life in the condition of monastic isolation that only a constant traveler can know.

He was by this time the kind of material for which the KGB was always on the lookout and to which recruitment was offered as a matter of course. At the age of forty-five, Tikhon Khitrov was taciturn, implacable and sternly self-disciplined; he also knew the topography of every region in the Union of Soviet Socialist Republics where the railway provided service. The work he was offered required a total lack of feeling for his fellow-men and an interest in causing them to suffer at the hands of the State—as he himself had been caused to suffer by his personal fortunes. He was to seek out those whose tendency to dissidence, malcontentedness or open defiance of authority invited retribution, be they at whatever distance from the capital of the far-flung railway system, spread like a web across the face of Russia.

Three years ago he was assigned to foreign operations, as a result of his zeal and dedication under training; he now spoke passable French, Italian and Spanish, and excellent English; he was also acquainted with the topography of cities as distant from Moscow as Sydney, San Francisco, Toronto and New York.

Two weeks ago he had been recognized by Rusakov, his chief director, as the perfect man for undertaking the primordial task in Project *Wasteland*, and recommended to Chairman Rudenko, who had subsequently invited him to the meeting that was this evening taking place in the apartment in Lenin Hills.

"It was suggested," Rudenko was telling his listeners, "that there might be a case for disseminating a limited amount of the L-9 material and knocking out one or two major cities in the United States of America as a demonstration of our power to subdue."

He means destroy, thought Boytsov. He'd noticed of late how Rudenko had started using euphemisms in their discussions of the fate that now irrevocably awaited the American people. A month ago Project *Wasteland* had been at a stage where major aspects could have been changed or aborted, where even the

entire enterprise could have been called off. By now it had
reached its point of no return; not only had the prodigious
amount of work by hundreds of specialists set the seal on the
future, but their indefatigable eradication of every obstruction
in the path to their goal had produced the confirmation that
Wasteland was not only feasible but assured of success. From
that time on, Boytsov had noticed, there'd come a change in
Rudenko's manner, even in his personality.

He'd begun speaking like a god. Where earlier he'd uttered
regret at the inevitable loss of human life entailed in his project,
he now spoke of the American people as creatures less than
human, to be "subdued," "sacrificed" and even "processed." It
had been this last choice of euphemism that had brought a chill
to the nerves of Sharaf Boytsov: it had called to mind the vision
of a meat-packing plant. And it had been from this time that his
doctors had warned him that unless he took a vacation and
turned his back on affairs of state for at least a month, his
stomach pains would one day incapacitate him, perhaps fatally.

He was now engaged in a gamble with time. No date had been
set for the launching of *Wasteland*, but from the tremendous
pace of the work in hand he knew it couldn't be long delayed.
Once it was done with, once he could take his place beside
Mikhail Rudenko as a leader of the new Soviet world, the acids
of guilt and self-revilement would cease pouring into his stomach; the Americans would have been sacrificed, yes, but in a
cause whose ultimate beneficence for humankind would be so
great, and—after the sacrificial act, so manifest—that his present misgivings could be forgotten.

Terebilov had felt these qualms, he realized, but had lacked
the courage to go on. Sharaf Boytsov, soon destined to assume
the heady status of a leader of the new Soviet World Presidium,
was damned if he were going to drown himself like a rat at this
stage of the game.

Reaching for a pocket, he quietly unwrapped and swallowed
another antacid pill as he listened to Chairman Rudenko.

"That might seem a humane proposal; but we are not to

achieve our high purposes if we are diverted by concessions to sentiment. To limit the dissemination of the L-9 material to any region less than the total area of the United States of America would immediately expose us to a nuclear strike, since the only reason for partial dissemination would be to announce to the Americans that we would subdue them totally unless they were ready to accept occupation." Pacing between the portraits of Lenin and Marx, his gold cuff links catching the light from the Florentine chandelier, his dark eyes shadowed by his jutting brows, his powerful shoulders hunched over the import of his argument, he swung a glance across the faces of his comrades at the long polished table. "We don't have to ask ourselves how long the Soviet Union would last, once the Americans were informed of our intended clemency. We are to create a Soviet world, not a silent planet with all life buried beneath a shroud of radioactive ash."

Still the orator, thought Viktor Koslev, and crossed his legs the other way. But there had emerged a strange kind of mathematical beauty to this man's unholy dreams. As soon as Koslev was out of the hospital and able once again to sleep the whole night through without having to get up and pee at intervals, he had launched himself into structuring the complex procedures that would begin with sending Colonel Khitrov into the United States to recruit and train the dissemination teams and end with the entry of the Red Army's salvage and rehabilitation forces into the wasteland. The problem of disposing of the dead had seemed insurmountable until Koslev's bank of computers and team of expert advisers had come up with not only a solution but a means of moving the major fishing grounds of the Atlantic and Pacific nearer the American seaboards; an earlier proposal to adopt the very efficient German methods of the 1940s to deal with cadavers en masse had evoked distaste. It would in any case be quicker to arrange transport to the extensive coastlines and provide a relatively decent burial at sea; moreover, the computers had revealed that after five months the fishing grounds would be found to extend in a seventeen-mile band close to each coastline from Canada to Mexico east and west, and along the southern seaboard from Baja California to Florida.

"You were asking me, Colonel Khitrov, about the efficacy of the L-9 bacillus compared with other contaminants such as anthrax, typhoid and other strains." Rudenko was now standing still for a moment, framed by the wide black marble fireplace as if posing—Koslev thought—for an official photograph. "The answer is simply that L-9 is not only resistant to any form of antibiotic or vaccine, but has a very short lifespan of only three weeks, on the average. The anthrax and other bacilli can remain lethally active for many years, making it impossible for our salvage and rehabilitation crews to enter the continent." He began pacing again. "I have also been asked by those concerned with humanitarian considerations—as indeed I am myself—whether death is preceded by distressing symptoms. I have been assured that this is not the case, pathologically." He moved to the table and looked down at his papers. "The onset of the disease is characterized by high fever, shock, mental confusion, swelling of the lymph nodes draining the site of entry of the L-9 bacillus, followed by prostration, delirium and coma."

"Pathologically," thought Boytsov. Trust Rudenko to insert a disclaimer. But what about psychologically? Shock, mental confusion and delirium—that was going to make an interesting scene, for instance, in the middle of New York City in the rush hour. *A nuclear bomb would be quicker.* The idea engrossed him for so long that when he surfaced from his fantasy, Rudenko was sitting at the head of the table and Koslev was on his feet, quoting from papers.

". . . And if we could encapsulate these prognoses into a bare scenario, it would appear as follows. The domestic airlines will already have been grounded as a result of the trigger conditions preceding the dissemination of L-9; similarly there will be no railway movement. But in the narrow time gap between the trigger epidemic and the dissemination of L-9 it will be beneficial to resume *domestic* air traffic and rail traffic immediately, so as to increase the spread of the dissemination." Koslev turned a paper. "You will realize that at this point the danger of global contamination is a significant factor. It is at this point when the Canadian and Mexican armed forces must be induced by world pressure to ensure that no living human crosses their frontiers. Under martial law, aircraft leaving the United States will be shot down; any vessel putting to sea will be attacked and sunk; any person crossing the border on land will be shot dead. It will be clear to the Canadian and Mexican governments that if these measures are not adopted, the lives of their citizens will be in jeopardy. It should be noted here that the L-9 disease is not zoonotic; it cannot be passed on to bird or animal life. Thus there is no risk of its being carried across borders by wild creatures."

Koslev paused to glance along the table, his thin, ascetic figure reminding Boytsov of a priest he'd once seen outside a cathedral in Smolensk, bareheaded under the winter snow as he gazed around him at the populace, his attitude expressing the zeal of the true fanatic as they hung on his words in silence, recognizing the saint in him. Koslev too had changed since they all realized that *Wasteland* was feasible. Earlier he'd been bothered, of course, by his prostate problem, but his whole approach to Rudenko's vision of world dominion had been to take it to bits on the computers and see how it worked. Today as he stood here with all those bits and pieces put together again in these papers on the table, he was describing for them the reality he'd constructed from Rudenko's visionary dream, and with the total absence of emotion that enabled him to look it in the face.

"Life in the major cities of the United States will cease after a period of five to six days, as the effects of the L-9 dissemination are intensified by panic, fire and the breakdown of communications and transport. The cessation of life in smaller towns and outlying districts will follow soon afterward, the pace of events being governed by the movement of citizens from region to region. We estimate that a minimum of fifty million persons will begin traveling soon after the initial outbreak of the epidemic, seeking to be with other members of their families."

Koslev spoke for a further twelve minutes, referring to notes as he completed his summary. "In normal times there would remain a number of citizens alive and untouched by the epidemic, self-isolated in the hills and deserts. In this case there will be a mass exodus from the cities as the inhabitants seek to escape the chaos and its attendant hazards. This exodus in turn will affect the contagion and subsequent demise of those in outlying areas. After the most rigorous and exhaustive computerized studies by the staff of my department and specialist advisers, we are able to estimate with reasonable accuracy that within a period of six weeks from the initial dissemination of L-9"—he closed the black folder—"all human life in the United States of America will have ceased."

"The final question," Chairman Rudenko was saying three hours and nineteen minutes later, "can now be given an answer." He was addressing Rusakov, Director General of the KGB. "Taking into consideration every conceivable possibility of delay, obstruction or change of plan that could be occasioned by unlikely circumstances, it seems probable that we shall be in a position to set this project running in four months from now, that is to say near the end of October."

So soon, thought Boytsov, and felt a pain in his stomach so piercing that his body jerked to the shock. No one noticed.

Rudenko turned to look at the head of the KGB's Department V. "Colonel Khitrov, you will shortly receive instructions to enter the United States clandestinely and organize the forces necessary to our project there."

Khitrov, thought Sharaf Boytsov, Khitrov the arch-terrorist, the chief of Department V, the *eminence noir* behind every Soviet-inspired assassination on foreign soil, behind every cut throat, bomb blast, and bullet wound in the dark back alleys and the embassy grounds and the underground parking garages of the capitals of the world. Khitrov the America-hater, soon to set his foot on the soil of that distant country, taking the first step toward turning it into a wasteland.

The first step, thought Boytsov, crouched over his stomach, *the first step. So it's come to that.*

Rudenko half threw her onto the great bed before she could even pull her clothes off, his hands tearing at her underwear in the gloom of the room while she lay with her strong pelvis arched toward him and worked at the buttons of his elegant pinstripe trousers to free this huge member of his that had plundered her body so many times here in the big chamber with the glow of firelight on the ceiling, here or somewhere else, in the kitchen late at night when the rest of the servants had retired, thrown down anywhere, her shoulder striking the big iron stove, taking her there on the floor among the pots and the pans and the cooking smells, there or somewhere else again, once in a Zil on the floor at the rear of the car while the chauffeur drove on through the night into the forests beyond the hills, her dark head against the carpeting with the strong thrumming of the wheels on the roadway below, her hair loosened by his restless hands until it lay across her face, across the floor, the tortoise-shell combs scattered in the corners, once in her bathroom upstairs when she'd been going to bed, the air heavy with the scent of attar that she used in the privacy of her own rooms, her shoulders bruised from the last time and the time before and the time before, but that was a part of it, part of the price for being chosen by the chairman of the council of ministers to fill his insatiable needs.

Was there love here? Sometimes she'd thought so, when it seemed he couldn't do without her. Did he feel some kind of love for her, or was it simply the convenience, the proximity? He took no other woman—she would know . . . ah, she would know! And if she didn't satisfy him he'd simply send her away and bring another woman here to work for him, to bring his food and wine and take his seed in the grunting, leaping shadows of the room. The whole building must shake at these times! The other servants knew what to do if they ever heard anything. Go to their rooms or be about their business. Once she'd been leaving his study and had seen a houseboy scuttling out of sight at the far end of the passage. She had caught him up and pinned him against the wall, her body still full of the fire under her disarranged clothes—*You work well here, boy, so for your own sake I'll tell you this: keep to your own quarters and don't listen at doors, because you'll get more than the sack if he finds out. You'll get sent to the camps and God help you.*

And did she love him, Mikhail Konstantinovich Rudenko, chairman of the council of ministers of the Supreme Soviet, when he was ringing the bell for her at a dinner party or walking past her on the staircase without a word or straddling her like this with his bull's strength driving her to orgasm after orgasm? She loved his power, yes, his raw and incontestable and unchallengeable power that held other men in its thrall—she'd seen it often enough when they came here on official business—and held her, too, in a state of willing enslavement since the first moment she had looked into those dark compelling eyes.

"Tatyana . . . Tatyana . . ."

It was always thus. Not a word to her before the tempest had abated, only the grunts and moans of animalistic rutting no different from what you heard in a farmyard, and then her name on his voice . . . *Tatyana . . . Tatyana . . .* as he woke to reality and reached for identity again, hers and his own.

Master . . . My master . . . with her voice as soft as his, just for a little time while they lay exhausted, and while she heard in his voice a tone that told her that yes, if he could love any woman it would be she.

Tonight she knew from the strength of his passion that the meeting had been decisive, perhaps historic. She'd known for months now that something unusual was occupying his mind; these meetings were unusual in themselves—before this year he'd seldom brought men of his own rank here to talk of the affairs of state; the chambers of the Kremlin were for that. Tonight he'd come to her with such a storm of tension in him that for the first time she'd been afraid for her own safety, and with good reason—it had almost amounted to rape.

"Tatyana . . ." he murmured now, "Tatyana . . ."

She murmured his own name back, and for another few moments he let himself linger in the aftermath of their frenzy, and then his thoughts swung away as they always did at these times, taking him through a phantasmagoria of scenes and memories, some of which never came to him at other times, others were seldom absent from his mind: the scenes where his life had been led—or occasionally wrenched or driven—into new directions, always to his greater advancement, the prize of his response to challenge.

In his early days, Mikhail Konstantinovich Rudenko had been in danger of his own rebellious nature, before he'd learned that ambition demands a token compliance with the status quo. One must climb on the backs of others without disturbing them, not snap at their ankles like a peevish dog, to be kicked away. He'd learned that lesson at the Soviet consulate in Florida, as a young man of twenty-three, a third vice-consul full of an overweening zeal to show these capitalists what it meant to be a brother in Communism, a comrade in ideological arms. He hadn't chosen a particularly impressive method of doing this, just three weeks into consular service. He'd turned up at a semiofficial party wearing a turtleneck sweater under his jacket instead of a shirt and tie. The glances of the smart young American contingent in their alpaca suits had pleased him enormously; they were taking note that a Communist can wear what he likes —it was his creed alone that mattered to him. After a while he'd found himself isolated, drinking alone at a corner table, and had felt for the first time the rather chilling effect of social disapproval—he'd been a little noisy as the evening wore on; it wasn't only his lack of a tie. Then his own consul had come over to him and ordered him to leave and come back "properly dressed," as he'd put it. Humiliated, he'd gone out to the car and found a policeman standing beside it; asked for his papers, he'd told the cop to look at the CD plate and leave him alone; asked again for his papers, he'd knocked the man down. Taken to police headquarters, he was again asked for his papers, which he then decided he ought to show: his consular chief was strict about protocol and could send him back to Moscow without thinking twice.

The American police made a report, told him roundly that although he was offered the hospitality of the United States of America as a diplomat he was nevertheless expected to behave like a half-decent human being while he was in a civilized country, and ordered him back into the street.

He had never forgotten that day. Despite the hardened carapace he had developed around his soul since then, the soft core of vulnerability was still there, and would always be there: the fear of humiliation. Since that day he had remembered that he must comply with the status quo in order, stealthily and from within, to undermine it. Since that day he had borne a hate for the Americans with their veneer of civilized behavior that covered their avarice and their inhumane materialism, their trappings of power as they stood dangling their martinis in their elegant suits, and who drove through the streets in their huge, powerful cars. Since that day he had gone to tailors and ordered suits like theirs, linen like theirs, adopting their trappings of power as in ancient myth a warrior would seize a helmet from an enemy to avail himself of that enemy's strength; and now he had power of his own, great power, soon to be omnipotence.

So one would wish, all these years, to destroy the citizenry of an entire nation because long ago they had ostracized him for his lack of taste? Hardly. But who knew what subtle and unsuspected processes were not set in motion deep within the psyche, spawned by some event of seeming insignificance, to work their way through the dark hinterland of the subconscious, feeding on their own obsession and gathering a monstrous force that would one day break into the light of consciousness and bring down mountains?

The woman stirred under him, and he looked down into her shadowed eyes. "Tatyana, our motherland is soon to be the genesis of great change in the world, great beyond any glory you could bring to mind. Go and fetch some cognac, and share it with me."

CHAPTER EIGHTEEN

The long black Lincoln sedan stood against the far wall of the A section of the underground parking garage, five blocks from the White House. Bruce had asked Nadia to sit low in her seat as he'd taken the ticket and passed the attendant's box. He hated having to treat her as someone he was ashamed of, but the pressure was coming on now from all directions.

"Your private life is your own, Bruce," President Hartridge had told him a week ago, "so long as you keep it that way. But you also owe a heavy responsibility to the public image of the White House, so I want you to bear that well in mind."

Bruce hadn't been surprised. Now that the chief had put it on the line, he realized he'd simply been kidding himself that his relationship with Nadia could go on forever without anything changing. The presidential aides had their picture in the media pretty often, and they were as recognizable in public as movie actors; moreover, their image was much more significant in the public mind: all you could connect with a movie actor was a camera, but an aide was connected with the White House.

It could have been that bitch in the *Washington After Hours* column who'd started the talk. *It's certainly fun to keep on bumping into the personable Bruce Paget these past few months in the discreetest of night spots, and with that nymphlike Nadia Fedotova on his arm. But I mustn't invite misunderstanding*

. . . we recall he was the gallant knight on hand at the White House when the talented ballerina defected, so what more natural that he should be keeping a protective eye on her? Let's call it unfinished official business . . .

Or it could have been Laura trying to bring him to heel. "I'm not reneging, Bruce. I know I said that most women would prefer it were 'someone else' keeping their husband late at the office, rather than the bloodless demands of the job. I'll still go with that, in spite of all those coy little toothmarks decorating our hero's manly body—I hope she's not just hungry for whatever she can find. But do you think you should be fucking a *Russian* girl while your boss the president is so busy telling the electorate what awful people they are?"

The thing that made him feel such an absolute shit was that Laura wasn't simply trying to pull him out of an affair—in this town a wife who did that would be thought of as eccentric. She was trying to pull him out of an affair that could wreck his career in government. His thanks for her loyalty was continued betrayal.

Two figures were coming into A section past the concrete pillars, silhouetted against the glow from the street outside; their footsteps brought echoes from the walls.

"Who are they?" asked Nadia, her dark head moving against his shoulder.

"Nobody we know." There were a few cars still down here, even at this late hour. He sank lower in his seat. The gossip columnists didn't have their spies out—they didn't need them; a lot of their muck was raked in from the ready soil of parking lots, hotel lobbies, elevators, cab stands—anyplace where the minions of the citadel worked, sometimes for less money than they received through the mail for their information.

Presidential aide seen snuggling with dancer in underground parking garage. Love will find a way.

The two men went across to the Buick that was standing against the opposite wall, and there was the jingle of keys. A squeal of tires, the taint of exhaust gas on the air, and they were gone. *This is sordid,* Bruce thought. He was earning seventy thousand dollars a year as a top official in the administration and he was sitting here in a stinking parking garage like a goddamned teenager who had to take his girl—his thoughts stopped sharply. Nadia *was* a teenager. What did she see in him, for Christ's sake, a guy of forty-seven who couldn't even make it everytime, who couldn't take her to a decent hotel anymore, who couldn't even *acknowledge* her? He was on the brink of a question that would need a whole lot of guts. *Nadia, what the hell are you doing here with me?*

It occurred to him for the first time that one day he was going to lose her. Maybe as soon as tomorrow.

She stirred against him, glad that the two men had gone away; strangers frightened her these days—any people who might come up to her and tell her something that would change her whole life in a moment, in a few words, sending her into a sickening vortex that would take her down and down into the final dark.

"Intelligence work has a bad name," Tarasov had said the last time they'd met, his faded blue eyes on her, his thinning gray hair catching the light over the café table, his short figure hunched in the shabby suit. "But you must remember that without spies there would be more wars. So long as each country knows what the others are doing, it can prepare to protect itself. The more knowledge, you see, the more hope of continuing peace. The cold war is a peaceful war, you must remember that." He'd ordered her another Danish, telling her she was losing weight, she must eat more.

She wasn't afraid of him anymore; he was kind to her, and respected her as a dancer, even though her performances were drawing cool notices, some even disdainful. But she was afraid of the huge machine behind him, the *Komitet,* whose power reached even this far from Moscow. The *Komitet* had the power to do harm or to do good, whichever was to its advantage.

I don't know what happened to my earlier letters, my love. You should have received them, but you say you didn't. There's so much to tell you, but first you must know that your sister and I are in good health again, and living in an apartment with four rooms (including the kitchen), and can hardly believe our good fortune. They tell us (there is a man who visits us occasionally) that they now realize that you wished to advance yourself in your art, and that your leaving your country was not an act of treachery, as it seemed at first. (We tried so hard to tell them that, earlier on! But they wouldn't listen.) Now they have changed their attitude to us completely, and we are left alone to go on with our lives.

That was two months ago, when Nadia had told Tarasov she would do what he asked; and the next time she had danced at the Met she'd received rave notices: her performance was "inspired," "spiritual," "on a new dimension." Then a week later she'd met secretly with Bruce again in a New York hotel, and had told him about the cousin she had in Moscow who was hoping to come to America, and was ready to bring with him whatever information he could.

"Tell Bruce your cousin is disillusioned," Tarasov had instructed her. "Say he is a stenographer in the Kremlin, with access to classified material."

From then on, as her meetings with Bruce had begun to fray her nerves, her performances had deteriorated and she'd begun losing weight, until now both Bruce and Nikolay Tarasov—unknown to each other, they knew her so well!—were telling her to eat more and look after herself better.

She didn't know how much longer she could go on like this. Her mother was the person closest to her heart in all the world, her sister was almost as close; and they were happy now, no longer harassed by the *Komitet*, no longer cold-shouldered by their friends, but enjoying their big new apartment. Bruce had been a stranger, such a little time ago; but he'd been there at the most traumatic moment of her whole life, when she had cut away her very roots and pleaded for the shelter and hospitality of these people, these Americans, whom she'd grown so quickly to love and to understand. Bruce had been her strength and her protector from the instant of her new beginning . . . *You don't need to worry about that; I'll fix it for you . . . No, you don't*

have to look for a place; we'll find you an apartment . . . No,
you won't ever have to go back if you don't want to; we'll see to
everything.

"Ask him," Nikolay had said softly over the café table, "if
there is any particular information he'd like your cousin to get
for him if he can. Ask him that."

Lying against the soft leather upholstery with her body
pressed into the curve of his own as they sat with his arm around
her and her knees drawn up, she began trembling uncontrollably, and felt his arm tighten at once.

"Are you cold?"

"No."

"What, then?"

"A raven perched on my tombstone."

"A raven . . . ? Oh. It'll fly away again."

"I don't know."

She wouldn't feel any peace until she made a decision, either
to stop betraying Bruce and bring misery to her family again, or
to protect them by exposing him more and more to the power
of the *Komitet.* It wouldn't help to go back to her own country;
once there, she'd be useless to them as a go-between, and no
longer privileged; her family would go back to a cramped apartment and she herself would be shut out from the Bolshoi and
the other great companies where she could develop her talents.

"Are you still bothered about leaving Russia?" Bruce asked
her.

"No. I love it here, Brutze. I love America."

"But it's bound to give you a few sleepless nights, even now. I
can understand that." He reached for her small, cold hand, with
its bones as fragile as a bird's. "You want out, Nadia?"

"Out?" Her head moved against him as she looked up.

"From me. From all this. From having to meet—"

"*From you?*" She held him tightly, burying her face against
him. "No, not ever. Why do you say this?"

"I guess I just needed to know."

"Then you know, now I tell you. I want to be with you forever. Even like this, with nowhere for us to be."

"What do you see in me, Nadia?"

"See?"

"Find in me. What am I to you?"

"You are all America to me, Brutze. Strong, and safe, and kind."

Okay, that worked; he was a father figure, and one that she didn't want to give up. It would have resolved this whole frustrating relationship if she'd told him that well, yes, she'd found her own feet now, and as a matter of fact there was a boy in her dance company who wanted to date her, and . . . That would make everything easy. Heartbreaking, sure, but easier to live with for everyone's sake, easier to go on living with until the day came when he could see her name on a ballet program and not want to die.

But right now he couldn't imagine life without Nadia, nor life with her, much longer. He supposed, sitting in the rear of the car with her now, her woman's body, child's body curled up across his own and unaccountably trembling, that if he'd known it was going to be this way when she had so desperately asked for his help that night in the White House, he would have just turned her over to the immigration people and told them to deal with it; another defecting artist didn't make much of a wave. It would have been so easy then. But in those first few moments the person she was had gotten through to him, her huge eyes pleading, her small body trembling against him, her defenselessness, her need of him—okay, of anyone who happened to be around, but it had happened to be he—and then later her wildness when they'd made love for the first time, and maybe most of all, her dancing, her lightness across the stage, her grace as she made her way through her life, the innocence in her that told her that to live was nothing more than to dance.

That was why he detested those bitches in the gossip columns, who made him sound like just another middle-aged Washington creep with a lech on for a teenager.

"I'll always take care of you," he said gently, "for as long as I can."

"For me there is no one else who can do this, Brutze."

"I know." He watched the figures on the digital clock flick to 3:00. "Have you heard from your mother lately?"

"Yes. Two days before. She is very happy now."

"And how's Boris getting along with his plans?"

She stirred against him, and in a moment said, "He is looking forward to come here."

Boris was her cousin, the stenographer who worked inside the Kremlin; the first time she'd told him this, he'd sat up straighter, but on reflection had done nothing about it. Stenographers inside the Kremlin were a dime a dozen, and what they called "access to classified information" usually meant very little; the CIA had people over there with a whole lot of coverage. But maybe he was missing something. Maybe it could even help him, if he could mention to the chief that Nadia was a useful intelligence source whom he could pass on to the Company as a Moscow connection.

"We'll be glad to help him," he said, "when he gets here."

She stirred again, as if her body were uncomfortable. "I will tell him. I hear from him a week before; he ask me again if you want to know anything he can find for you, you must tell me."

The figures on the clock flicked again. 3:01.

"Okay. Tell him we'd like to know anything he can tell us about Chairman Rudenko and his plans."

CHAPTER NINETEEN

Charles Clay stood in the signals room of the British embassy in Moscow reading the stuff coming through from agents-in-place and special-mission sources, looking for names that might trigger something in his thoughts. Batman was in operation and going smoothly, which left him nothing much to do except keep an occasional eye on Talyzin.

It was better to look at this stuff than do nothing, but most of it was a bore. After another ten minutes he turned around and looked at the cipher clerk.

"For God's sake, how much longer?"

"Any minute now." The clerk didn't get any tone of hurry into his voice; these bloody espions thought the whole of the signals room was here specially for them; they never considered there was a whole bloody embassy to run as well.

Clay went back to watching the report sheets as they came creeping off the machine, and saw a name that meant something at last. *Khitrov*.

"When you're ready," the clerk called to him. Clay went to the console.

"This is for JB via closed file. Signal is: *Meeting three nights ago, Rudenko's place, with Batman running. Tape retrieval soon.*" He looked up as a girl came in with a folder—blue eyes, fair hair, her nipples outlined under a thin cashmere sweater. Ashton, Clay thought at the edge of his consciousness, would

have gone for you, darling, all the way. "Change that," he told
the clerk. "Make it: *Tape retrieval seems imminent.*" Talyzin
had been showing his nerves.

"Okey-doke." The word-processor screen shifted the line and
made the change. "Is that the lot?"

"Yes." He turned away and noticed the girl again. "Are you
doing anything tonight?"

She seemed surprised, which surprised him. Didn't she know
what she looked like? Didn't she get asked the same question by
every man who came near her? It was a wonder she'd got to this
age without being raped or found on a wasteground with a
stocking around her neck, Ashton's type, my God yes, the spit-
ting image of that girl he'd seen—they'd all seen, those who
were watching from the dorm windows—walking with Ashton
into the staff building the time when he'd been up for the high
jump, found with a girl—a girl like *that*—in his rooms.

"Who are you?" she said—this one said—with a pert toss of
her head. Oh my God, you should never speak to them when
they were this blindingly attractive. There was so often nothing
behind the wave of fair hair and the slightly parted lips and the
erect nipples and the swinging hips, except a mind as banal as a
bus ticket. But you never learned.

"Mickey Mouse," Clay said and went out of the room, wanting very much to go and get roaringly smashed in some bor-
dello, *because if that tape picked up the Rudenko meeting
cleanly enough, London was going to know everything Terebilov
couldn't tell him when his blood was dripping onto the snow and
his clouding retinae were recording for him the last scenes of his
life on earth, the tops of some pine trees and an Englishman's
anxious face. It'd be a major intelligence breakthrough.*

He wandered into the room three doors along from signals,
and found his head of station in there, Blanes. "I was looking at
the stuff on the machine in signals," Clay told him. "What's
Khitrov doing in Poznan?"

Blanes scraped his pipe out and glanced at him sharply. "We
don't know. I was hoping you might tell us."

"Tomorrow," Clay said, thinking of little Talyzin sitting up there on his mattress with the door locked and a destruct unit ready to blow the tape into bits if it had to. "Maybe tomorrow."

By noon of the next day in London a routine Geninfo message came out of the scramblers and was taken immediately into Sir James Braithwaite's office by bearer, since a key name had been picked up by the computer.

Braithwaite read it and reached for the green phone. "Khitrov has gone from Poznan to Gdansk. Why?"

"We don't know, sir."

"Find out."

Shortly before 6:15 PM London time, Tim Steiger answered the phone in the cramped office they'd set up for him in the US embassy. The caller didn't give his name, but his accent was English.

"We've lost Khitrov, I'm afraid. Last observed in Gdansk."

"We lost him there, too."

"Oh?" There was a pause. "We're all being terribly chummy with each other all of a sudden, aren't we?"

Steiger gave a brief dutiful laugh. If this guy didn't know the Rudenko file had become a major team effort by the British Secret Service and the Central Intelligence Agency, he ought not to be on this phone.

"The only lead we got," the voice said, "is that he was seen boarding a Mexican freighter, the *Sánchez Roman*, bound for New York and Tampico. But we can't get any real confirmation."

"We heard it was a French tanker, the *Mistral*."

"Then he's obviously putting out a smoke screen."

"Let's keep in touch," Steiger said.

"Of course, old boy."

On July 16, nine days later, fire broke out on an empty coal barge on the Hudson River, New York City, a short distance from the Hoboken Terminal on the New Jersey side, almost opposite Pier 46 in Manhattan. A column of black smoke rolled heavily from the blaze, leaning southwest in the light river breeze and throwing its shadow across the moonlit water.

Within minutes the sound of sirens was making an eerie chorus from shore to shore, and three fire boats got under way, escorted by river police launches. The ship closest to the burning barge was across the Hudson at Pier 46, well out of range even if the fuel tanks went up. She was the *Santa Filomena*, registered in Brazil and flying a pennant indicating that she was in from Poland. The skeleton crew was lining the rails at the stern, their faces lit by the glow of the fire across the river.

It looked as if the fuel tanks had already gone up, because the blaze was out of control, a huge core of flame that sent its orange light pouring across the surface of the river while the water jets curved in frail archways across the night sky. Traffic was slowing along both shores of the Hudson as drivers caught sight of the blaze between the buildings; the crews and passengers on the ships from piers in the sixties to the far side of the Holland Tunnel were crowding on deck to watch; on the quayside the customs and immigration officers were staring across the river.

A small boat moved from the side of the *Santa Filomena*, in tonight from Gdansk, and drifted on the slow current for a time, the two men on board watching the blaze across the river, one of them standing up and shielding his eyes from the glare. After a while the boat was lost behind the pack of tugs going downstream, then later it turned toward Pier 32 on the other side of the tunnel, one man rowing steadily until the wash from the tugs nudged it against the timbers, and he reached for a rope, holding fast while the other man climbed out onto the deserted wharfside. Then they both set off among the litter of weeds and beer cans and paper wrappings, their heads down and their hands in their coat pockets, making for the dilapidated car that had pulled up on the West Side Highway, alongside the river.

As the two men got into the car the time on the dashboard clock was 11:32.

At 12:09 a signal was received by the CIA's European Liaison section to the effect that Colonel Tikhon Khitrov, chief of KGB's Department V, might shortly attempt an illegal entry into the United States. Docks, airports and the Coast Guard were immediately notified under the coding of a priority alert.

Soon after three in the morning a rowboat was taken in tow by the river police off South Brooklyn; it carried no identification of any kind, and was reported as abandoned.

CHAPTER TWENTY

The place stank like a bear cage.

Cans of sardines everywhere, coffee stains where the cup had left rings on the floorboards, empty packets of black bread, cigarette ends in the plastic box with the Scanar-23 serial numbers on it, what a mess!

Sergey Talyzin took a last look at it from the door. He'd never realized how untidy he was, but then, these last eighteen days had been unusual: he'd been trapped here on his own, with only a few phone calls from the Englishman keeping him in touch with the outside world. Sometimes his tooth had started up aching again so badly that he'd stood in the middle of the littered room shaking his fists at the ceiling—too much isolation and you'd go clean off your rocker, anyone would tell you that.

He tilted his head back and squeezed a drop of oil of cloves into his mouth, right onto the wisdom tooth, practice makes perfect. Tomorrow he'd go to a dentist, sit in the chair thinking how much he was going to ask that Englishman. They'd said five hundred rubles for this job, but they didn't know what was going to be on the tape when he'd finished. *How much would they pay to know that Comrade Chairman Rudenko was going to wipe out the whole of America?*

At the back of his mind as he went down the stone steps in the middle of the deserted building—stopping to listen at every tenth step, stopping to listen—he found himself picturing the cities over there with hundreds and thousands of people dying like flies in the streets, with airplanes falling out of the sky and ships running into the harbor walls and everything, it was terrifying, like the end of the world. But he couldn't do anything about it till he got the tape and gave it to the Englishman, *sold* it to the Englishman, and not for five hundred rubles, not for a thousand. He'd ask *ten* thousand—they'd pay anything for this!

It made him feel peculiar, though, as if he were somebody else. Here was this man going down the steps and into the Garden Ring Road on this fine summer's morning with the gold domes shining over the Kremlin down there through the trees, with the information in his head—inside this comparatively small round computer on top of his shoulders here—that was going to save the whole of the population of the United States of America. He was a *key figure*, you might say, *in world affairs*, the only one who knew what was going on, outside the ones who were actually planning it all. Supposing he got run down by a bus in a minute or two from now—the whole of the population of the United States of America would perish! What was the world coming to, when one man in Soviet Russia could press a red button and start a nuclear war that would finish everything off, or one man in America do the same thing, or one man could walk along the Garden Ring Road on this fine summer's morning and kill off everyone in the United States of America if he didn't watch out for the buses?

People went past him, a boy with his girl, a Red Army soldier, a knot of young men in black leather jackets and blue jeans, an old drunk with a stick, rattling it along the railings as if he were playing a harp. They didn't look at him. They didn't know how important he was. Sergey Talyzin, the savior of America!

He crossed the street—watching for buses, watching for buses—and approached the apartment block where Comrade Chairman Rudenko lived. And then another thought stopped him dead. How much would *Comrade Chairman Rudenko* give him for the tape, so the Americans wouldn't know what he was going to do to them?

He walked on again. Chairman Rudenko wouldn't give him anything for it. He'd have him thrown into Lubyanka and put against the wall in front of a firing squad.

The security guard was the same one who'd checked him the time before, which was good fortune. He didn't even keep him hanging around, this time, just to show his power over other people; he let him straight in, because Sergey had told him he'd have to be back "in a while" to check the shunt switch was working all right.

"Show this to them at the door." He gave Sergey the temporary pass.

"Fair enough." He lowered his voice. "You seen that housekeeper in there, have you? His housekeeper?" He made a gesture with his hands, encircling a luscious pair of tits.

"Be about your business," the guard said, and turned away.

It took five minutes to get the Scanar unit out of the TV set and stow it in the bottom of his toolkit; he left the tape in the recorder and shoved the mike into a spare connector box and told the woman he was leaving, the new part was working perfectly and he wouldn't have to trouble her again.

She showed him to the door without saying anything.

There was a gray van standing at the curb when he went down the steps, with two men waiting, and when the security guard behind him called out to them they moved forward at once with their hands coming out of their pockets ready to grab him. He thought immediately of Alek Shokin, and the time when the gray-green van had come for him and taken him away; he felt the breath blocking in his throat and his bowels letting go and then he was running with the toolbag clutched against his stomach, running very hard along the wall of the building as they shouted behind him, telling him to stop or they'd shoot, but he kept on running and saw another man, two men, three, coming for him the other way where there was another van standing by the curb, and then he stopped thinking about anything very clearly, just about their faces and the way the sun winked on their guns and poor Alek's boots dragging across the snow on the paving stones and leaving marks when they'd—*a gun went off*—when they'd taken him across the pavement like that—*another gun went off*—while he screamed at them something like he hadn't done anything—*another gun went off very close* and he felt the hot stinging in his chest and then his shoulders at the back and then something that came and burst inside his head and blew everything away.

Mikhail Rudenko was sitting at his desk when the KGB colonel was shown in, but gave no sign that he realized he was here. The colonel stood at ease in the middle of the room, his jackboots reflecting the colors of the Persian carpet beneath them. The security guard had gone out, closing the door quietly, and the silence here was intense. A fly buzzed in the vicinity of a window, and after a while the colonel moved his head slightly to see if he could see it; by the sound it was making, it was on a spider's web; as a boy the colonel had always enjoyed the spectacle of the kill, and had often caught a fly with his handkerchief, flicking at it so that it would only be injured, then dropping it onto a web and standing back to watch the drama. He couldn't, at the moment, see where the fly was.

"Colonel Brekhov."

He turned his head back smartly. "Comrade Chairman?"

"Were you aware that the man who placed the device in my apartment was to be taken alive?"

The voice was so soft, and so infinitely cold, that the colonel realized that the elegant dark-suited man at the desk in front of him was in a seething rage. Heads would fall.

"No, Comrade Chairman. I was not aware."

Rudenko gazed at him for a long time, his pale hands folded on the desk, his sable black eyes unblinking, his stillness reptilian. "Those were my orders, Colonel. That he should be taken alive." His voice was silky, a susurration that rustled on the silence with the effect of a fuse burning. Deep inside him, under the authoritative uniform with its insignia and braided shoulder straps, deep inside whatever was to be left of his rank after this, the colonel flinched.

"I will make the most rigorous inquiry, Comrade Chairman."

Half a minute passed, and he endured the gaze of the man in the chair by staring correctly a foot above his head, at the bottom edge of the gold-framed portrait of Lenin.

"Don't bother," Chairman Rudenko told him at last. "We're in little doubt as to who would attempt to secure information at the highest level. It would be the Central Intelligence Agency."

The colonel said nothing, since it wasn't a question. Katushev had been in charge of the Talyzin affair, Captain Katushev. According to the reports that the colonel had seen, one of the security guards at the apartment block had suspected something unusual about the man Talyzin: the report had said he was "nervous in his manner." The department had sent a television engineer to examine the set, and the bug had been found. The microphone had been deactivated and the whole unit left in place for Talyzin's return. The colonel hadn't seen the subsequent orders for his arrest; it was routine for a spy to be taken alive and grilled until he broke, and talked; someone must have blundered or, even with a dozen of them there, Talyzin must have run clean through them in his panic and looked like he was getting away.

Captain Katushev would be in for the chopper.

"I'm more interested, Colonel, in the report from Department V."

"Comrade Chairman." He unzipped his briefcase, took out the file and presented it smartly.

"Thank you." Rudenko ran his eye over the first few sheets, noting particularly the time and date of the signal received from the agent Tarasov in Washington. "Very well, Colonel. You may go."

"Comrade Chairman." He stepped back three paces and made his salute. He wasn't too surprised that he was here simply to act as a messenger boy; in the last few months it had happened frequently. Certain papers were in circulation among the heads of the Politburo that needed priority security by bearer of colonel's rank. Something big was in the wind, as everyone knew.

"What was the name," the chairman of the council of ministers asked him as he made for the big double doors, "of the officer in charge of this man Talyzin's arrest?"

"Captain Katushev, Comrade Chairman."

"I want him shot."

"Yes, Comrade Chairman."

When the colonel had gone, Rudenko studied the signals report in detail. According to the agent Tarasov, the exact words spoken by the presidential aide to Nadia Fedotova were: *Tell him we'd like to know anything he can tell us about Chairman Rudenko and his plans.*

Within the hour, Rudenko managed to pull Secretary of the Communist Party Boytsov out of a meeting with the minister of instrument making, automation equipment and control systems in the lower council chamber, and get him along to his office.

"You were quite right, Sharaf. The Western intelligence agencies will at some time begin to suspect unusual activity here. The matter of the device they found in my apartment is possibly unimportant, now that the danger is past; they weren't necessarily expecting to overhear meetings of the kind we recently convened. But the matter of this signal from the embassy in Washington is more significant. Their intelligence interest has reached presidential level." He waited for Boytsov to read the papers, pacing between the desk and the windows, pausing once to watch the death throes of a fly on a web in the corner of the window frame.

"This is too close," Boytsov said at last. "Too close for comfort."

"I agree. And I suggest two things. We should tell Department D of the KGB to feed a calculated disinformation report to the White House via the agent Tarasov and his contact Fedotova, and we should advance the launching of Project *Wasteland* to the earliest date possible."

"I was talking to Pugsley," said Braithwaite, "on the phone yesterday." He gave the menu to the waiter and looked at the minister again. "His opinion is that nuclear arms are simply an extension of conventional weaponry. If they *were* banned, we'd still be left with the eventual certainty of another world war in any case, with the usual millions of dead. What these protesters want to do is to demand that we find the *causes* of war, or there'll never be an end to it."

"No Chateau Duquesne left?" the minister asked the wine waiter.

"I'm sorry, sir. If we'd known you were coming . . ."

"Never mind. The Pouilly, then." He closed the wine list and said to Braithwaite, "That's a good point, of course, but since the very conception of a world war is an expression of insanity, how would we ever persuade the heads of government to put themselves under psychiatric care?"

Before Braithwaite could answer, he was called to the telephone. He crossed the room at a steady pace, resisting the urge to hurry. This was a call from his office, otherwise the manager would have fielded it for him, and the only matter important enough to warrant disturbing him during dinner was Batman. Clay must have signaled.

"Jim," asked the member for Kensington as he passed the corner table, "are you joining us for some snooker tonight?"

"Sorry. I've got to go to a ghastly party."

By the time he reached the telephone Sir James had reached the conclusion that Clay could only have succeeded, which meant that they'd know at last why Terebilov had tried to get across so desperately, and why Rudenko and his *troika* had been so suspiciously active these past few months. He was therefore uncertain as to how he was going to get through dinner with the minister and not tell him that he'd just pulled off what was probably the biggest intelligence coup of his entire career.

He picked up the telephone. "Braithwaite."

"I'm awfully sorry to disturb you, sir, but we've just received a signal from Moscow. I'm afraid Batman's been blown."

CHAPTER TWENTY-ONE

U ntil the Pleistocene period there were no horses in America. There was nowhere for the sturdy, short-legged strains of the species *Eohippus* to cross over from the immense landmass that is now Soviet Russia. Then, as the sixty-mile gap between Russia and Alaska froze over, the animals began crossing, their instinct giving them hope that if they wandered far enough they would come to a place where the grass was green.

Those in today's world of the horse who know of this prehistoric odyssey refer to the Bering Strait as the Ice Bridge of the North. Among the hardy fishermen along the easternmost tip of Russia on the Arctic Circle, the language still carries a remnant of this ancient history in the name they sometimes use for this narrow waterway, perhaps without understanding why. They call it simply, the bridge.

Fifteen hundred kilometers west of the bridge into Soviet Russia, beyond the Chukotski Peninsula and beyond the Anadyrskiy Range, the airstrip had been laid down during these summer months, in the center of a desolate area of tundra. In accordance with Chairman of the Party Control Committee Viktor Koslev's specifications, the airstrip and the camp that would service it were virtually self-supporting. The total complement of personnel numbered a mere thirty-two men, none below officer rank and most belonging to the air force.

Koslev and his banks of computers had reasoned that the launching of a project destined to remove Communism's arch-enemy from the face of the earth should be initiated under the most intense security blanket that could ever have been or-dered, even in war. It was also reasoned that a material capable of bringing all life to an end across the breadth of the United States of America should similarly be the subject of the most extreme isolation.

Within the overall Project *Wasteland*, the operation now es-tablished at the camp had the name *Springboard*. There was no name for the tiny huddle of army huts that now occupied less than a square kilometer in the thousands of square kilometers of this desolate tundra; it was simply called the Camp.

On this August day the noon temperature was a comfortable 39°; at night it would be considerably colder. The terrain here was so unbroken by anything higher than scrub that it resem-bled a gray-green ocean, and one could observe the curvature of the earth. There had been no jokes among the air force men since they had arrived here in military trucks from the railhead; no one had attempted to dub this desolate region the Elysian Fields or any similar name that would express what they thought of it. They knew, every one of them, that they had been hand-picked to serve an operation of such secrecy that they con-sidered themselves an elite force, however lost amid the vastness of this place. None of them would leave the Camp until the operation was completed: they had been warned of that. No others would arrive here until the bomber came to make its landing on the airstrip, though occasionally a high-ranking offi-cer or member of the government would be flying in.

Such was the case today, when Chairman Koslev arrived with a party of specialists to inspect the site and ask questions. They were greeted by Air Force General Ivan Pavlovich Goldin, who escorted them straight to the operations room, since they had last eaten only an hour ago on their long flight from Moscow. The ops room occupied the largest of the seven long huts, and its main feature was the horizontal relief map of the United

States of America laid out on a sand table in the middle of the room.

General Goldin picked up a telescopic aluminum pointer and indicated the Bering Strait. "This is our bridge. The bomber will fly at less than two-thousand-feet altitude to escape radar detection and land in this flat area here, between Umiat and the north Alaskan coast. Reports we've received from our agents there have satisfied me that we can put down the TU-28 on that terrain with no problem; she'll be taking off with less than half the normal complement of fuel to save weight, and that will be perfectly adequate to bring her back if the flight has to be aborted for any reason. If anyone has any questions, please interrupt as we proceed."

"It's that easy," a specialist in epidemiology asked him, "to escape their radar?"

"It's not *easy*," Goldin said with a confident smile, "but we know how. Their Semiautomatic Ground Environment network poses no problem: we need only to fly below ten thousand feet, and there are vector gaps in the seventy-five–station network if we have to change course. In Alaska itself, our destination, their thirteen-station network has a floor of three thousand feet. The thirty-one–station Distant Early Warning line reaches down to fifteen hundred feet, but that is not in our way. Drug smugglers," he said with another self-assured smile, "routinely penetrate the US radar defenses."

"What about their actual interceptor capacity, Comrade General?"

"It's none too impressive. We've known since 1964 that their mobile defenses were stripped down from fifteen hundred planes to some three hundred. In the meantime they've removed every battery of Hawk and Nike antiaircraft missiles and many of their ground radar posts. But we're—"

"Are they crazy?" someone asked.

General Goldin shrugged. "Since nuclear capability was developed on both sides, they've felt that there's no real risk of our sending bombers in, which is true; but if nuclear arms are banned by treaty, they'll certainly be crazy if they don't put back their original overlapping radar coverage just as soon as they can. But in any case, this doesn't concern us too much; for *Springboard* we're sending one aircraft across, and we see no problem."

Within two hours he and several specialists had outlined the main elements of *Wasteland*, referring most of the time to the huge relief map, where target cities were marked in red, with the initial access routes for the dissemination teams marked in the same color.

"We are concentrating mainly on the indoor sports stadiums," the chief of the epidemiological section told the other officials. "Ten grams of the L-9 material introduced into the air-conditioning systems during major-league games and similar crowd-capacity events will be capable of infecting sufficient numbers to incapacitate a city of one-half million people within our target time period." He led them over to the bank of computers along the end wall. "If you have any specific questions where accurate figures are needed, I suggest we put them straight into the computers for you, for almost instantaneous readout."

Before the visitors were escorted to the main canteen for refreshments, one of the psychologists specializing in crowd behavior put a final question to Koslev himself.

"As I understand it, Comrade Chairman, there will be no specific date for the launching of Project *Wasteland*. It will automatically follow the effects of what you call the 'trigger mechanism.' Do you feel it would be useful for me to know exactly what that mechanism is, so that I can have the overall picture? I don't like working in the dark."

Koslev considered this, his lean head angled. "A good point, Comrade General. Let me tell you, then, that before we can disseminate the L-9 material in the United States of America, we have to persuade that country to seal off its borders completely. Unless this is done, the L-9 contamination would spread throughout the world. So first we shall introduce an epidemic of Y. *pestis*—the plague. That is easily done." The light from the narrow windows flashed across his glasses as he turned to embrace the attention of the other visitors. "Y. *pestis* is readily put down by ordinary antibiotics, of course; we shall therefore need to arrange for the stocks of those antibiotics—streptomycin, chloramphenicol, tetracycline and others—to be tampered with on a mass scale, rendering them ineffective."

He looked back to General Goldin. "The contamination of the diluent for mixing with the antibiotics will be made with the agent *pseudomonas aeruginosa*. The batches will be switched at the source of supply: in the production plants of the pharmaceutical companies, during ostensible burglaries. Safes will be broken into, cash will be missing, and so on, to draw attention away. This will ensure a nationwide coverage for the contaminated supply. In addition, as the adulterated batches are discovered, *all* current stocks of antibiotics will be discarded—as happened over there with Tylenol—simply because the testing of every batch would take too much time and labor. This will produce an immediate and inevitable shortage of supply, while the plague epidemic runs out of control."

Goldin looked uneasy. "But surely they'll suspect us. As their potential enemy, we—"

"They'll suspect terrorists, yes, and they'll believe we are at the source of the operation. But what can they prove? And what time will they have, during a national crisis, to go into it? They'll already be coming under world pressure to seal off their borders. And they won't have any option, believe me. The moment they have isolated their country, you will dispatch your bomber, and within a matter of hours the dissemination of the L-9 material can begin—within the frontiers of a nation completely cut off from the rest of the world."

Koslev waited for another question, but he seemed to have impressed the general beyond further doubts. "I congratulate you, Comrade Chairman."

"Thank you. The plan is basically simple, and like most simple ideas it will work."

"So we can regard the plague epidemic, then, as a kind of—a

kind of fuse?" General Goldin had done his early soldiering in the bombardiers.

"If you like," Koslev nodded. "As a fuse, yes."

"And when will it be lit?"

Koslev glanced upward at the clock on the wall. "It's already burning."

CHAPTER TWENTY-TWO

W hat the hell for?" Clay asked with a tight mouth.
"I suppose he wants to know what happened."
"I'll tell you what happened—"
"Yes, old boy, but *he* wants to know, not me." Blanes watched him obliquely, feeling the rage coming off Charles Clay like heat off fire.

"Talyzin was blown because they suspected something," Clay told him, swinging away and swinging back, hands jammed into his pockets, his strangely blind-looking eyes not turned on the other man, his voice producing what sounded like a loud stage whisper as his nerves tightened his throat. "He wasn't blown because anyone blundered and he wasn't blown because they picked up his itinerary—he didn't *have* one, he was holed up at his base all the time—and he wasn't blown because someone put the finger on him."

Blanes assumed he was about to go on, but he didn't, so Blanes asked gently, "Then why was he blown, old boy?"

"What?" This time Clay's eyes were turned on him, and the other man felt a slight shiver. He never liked being too close to other people's emotions, especially rage, especially this man's. "He was blown," Clay said, "because he gave *himself* away. Somehow. I don't know how, but *somehow*. Maybe he let his nerves show or got his cover story wrong, how the hell do I know? *But that was the only way.*"

Blanes took a quiet turn of the small embassy room, waiting for more, not getting it. He said at last: "I'd get the next flight, old boy. Don't keep him waiting." The Chief hadn't sounded too cheerful, on the phone.

"What in Christ's name," Clay swung on him again, "is the point of my taking a fucking airplane all the way to London just to tell him I don't *know* what happened to Talyzin?" Blanes said nothing, so he added, more quietly, "How bad is it?"

"M-mm?" Blanes looked up, pretending he hadn't been expecting the question. "Well, you don't need me to tell you the score, do you? We were expecting some pretty big stuff from Terebilov, weren't we? He was a pretty big wheel. We didn't get it. Not your fault, of course. Then we were expecting some pretty big stuff out of the Rudenko bug, and we didn't get that either. And in the—"

"That wasn't my fault either."

Blanes let a moment pass, offering the unspoken suggestion that perhaps Clay was protesting just a shade too much. "Of course not, old boy. But in the meantime we all know that Rudenko is up to something that could be rather alarming, and we believe Terebilov was coming over to tell us what it was. And apart from routine electronic surveillance and a mass of useless-looking background info coming in from our agents over here, we remain completely in the dark. I don't wonder the Chief's a bit uncomfortable."

"So he wants my neck?"

"I really can't say." Blanes's tone was cool now; he was beginning to feel just a teeny bit fed up with this agent's particular brand of neurosis. Whether he messed things up on the Bulgarian frontier was not known, but he could easily have messed up the Talyzin thing, and was going through an orgy of self-blame. Blanes felt it would be much nicer if he stopped doing it here and went and did it all over Sir James Braithwaite instead. And the best of luck.

Clay went on standing at the window for a minute, a slight, straw-haired figure in the Moscow-made suit that had been going to pieces on him for years, his elbows worn out and the heels of his shoes worn down, poor little bastard, Blanes thought, he was a damned good agent, everyone knew that. Or at least, he had been.

"Do something for me." The voice came back off the window-pane, flat and toneless; the rage had died now.

"Anything I can, old boy."

Clay turned to face him, reluctantly. "If he wants to fire me, all right. But I don't have to go to London for him to do it. I'm going to stay here, whether he fires me or not, because here's where it all is, Blanes—Rudenko's here and his bloody *troika* and his diabolical plans, whatever they are—you know the Company thinks he's playing about with the idea of a chemical war? That's crazy, a chemical war's not containable, it must be something . . . I dunno, different, something . . . worse—any-way, this is where it is, whatever it is, and I'm going to stay here and find out." He paused and then said it again with a lot more force, "*I'm going to stay here and find out*, you understand that?"

"You don't have to . . ." Blanes looked for the right word " . . . redeem yourself, old boy."

Clay looked down. "That's my business."

"So what is it you want me to do?"

"What? I want you to get me off the hook, with the Chief. Tell him I want to stay in Moscow and break this thing open for him. Tell him it's going to waste time if I have to go to London and come all the way back again. *We may not have much time left*, Blanes, you know that?" He turned away a little, as if sud-denly needing privacy.

In a moment Blanes asked him, "What exactly do you intend to do, in Moscow?" He added quickly—"He'll need to know that."

Clay nodded. "I want to watch the stuff coming in—" he meant the all-sources background information that was coming in the whole time from agents-in-place and surveillance units "—and I want to analyze it and look for patterns in it. I want to talk to the a-i-p's myself, all of them, and get a picture in my mind of what they're doing, and try putting the picture together till it means something. Then I'll tell him what I've got, and what I want to do with it." A flash of the rage came back for a moment—"*Next time, Blanes, I'm going to bring it home, you understand?*"

Silence came back.

Blanes nodded. "Of course, old boy. Let me see what I can do for you." He stood looking at the wall for a minute or two after Clay had left, wondering if he should really try to get the Chief's permission for Clay to stay out here, or whether he should simply say, "If you want my opinion, sir, I think he's burned out by those two fiascos. I'm sending him home."

In his London office Sir James Braithwaite put down the telephone and sat for a moment wondering if he'd done the right thing.

He had very much wanted to get Clay here from Moscow and bite his head off, taking his time about it and making the man suffer. Clay might not have been responsible for the Terebilov debacle—in that kind of frontier incident there were always some bullets flying about, and from the reports that had come in, it looked like an unlucky shot; he also remembered that Clay had warned him about the moonlit conditions. But he was certainly responsible for Talyzin's being blown—and, mercifully, killed; Blanes had said a minute ago on the telephone that Talyzin had given himself away, according to Clay. That might have been so, but Clay should have foreseen the risk, and chosen a more reliable man for the job.

But the thing was, Braithwaite realized, that his own bitter disappointment in this second failure to find out what that bastard Rudenko was doing was the motive for his need to get Clay here and scalp him. That wasn't good. It could even prove fatal. There'd been a wildcat outfit in London known as the Clowns, with ultrasecret and wide-ranging powers at prime-minister level, and when it had been dismantled—for carrying out some of the most notorious "wet affairs" on the international espionage scene—there'd been a group of agents drifting around Whitehall without a job. Clay—whose code name had been dropped when he'd left the Clowns—had been one of these: clever, experienced, pampered by the privileged atmosphere of his previous work, and consequently arrogant and difficult to handle. The man's vanity was such that he was already going through his own kind of hell because of the Talyzin disaster, and Braithwaite had the feeling that if he had indeed got him here on the carpet and scalped him, Clay might well have gone off and driven his car into the Thames, or done something equally crass. Such an act had its precedents within the service.

So perhaps he'd done the right thing in telling Blanes to let the man remain in Moscow and see if he could redeem himself. And if he failed to do *that*, he'd probably drive his car into the Moscow River instead of the Thames, and that would be far less messy than if it happened here in London.

There was, finally, just a chance that Clay, driven by his own outraged pride, might get inside Rudenko's intelligence defenses and come out with some vital information; he would then, as far as Braithwaite was concerned, be eligible to receive the crown jewels, gift-wrapped.

He picked up the third telephone from the left.

"I'm leaving Clay in Moscow."

There was a pause while George Vickers considered this.

"Very good, sir, if you think it's wise."

"I don't, but there's no alternative."

Tikhon Khitrov, former railway lineman, childless husband and embittered lone wolf within the present hierarchy of the KGB, found himself on this humid August day in Washington, D.C., close to something he had never in his life experienced before. It was excitement. His work as a young man on the Soviet railways had been at best plodding, relieved only by his annual appearance in the May Day parade through Red Square as a heroic member of the Railway Workers' Brigade. Later, as a ranker in the KGB, he had discovered a certain satisfaction in his work as an arresting officer on mobile assignments throughout the city. There had been something rather pleasurable in observing the fear on the faces of the men he'd arrested—their wide eyes and their hanging mouths and their inability to walk properly on their way to the van, as if their muscles had lost their strength; their very helplessness had appealed to him surprisingly, and he could remember the several occasions when he'd noticed an incipient erection under his trousers as the doors of the van had been slammed on his victims. This had occurred much later, also, when as a full-fledged captain he had personally interrogated important dissidents, black-market operators and Jews in Lubyanka prison. Later still—as recently as last year—he had been present on the three occasions when an assassin's bullet had crashed into the skull of the selected victim (two presidents of small-time republics, and an African foreign minister) on his personal orders. He'd felt a strengthening throughout his body, as theirs had gone pitching down, as if in dying they had passed on their power to the architect of their death.

Today, as he stood in the ornate room of the Soviet embassy on Phelps Place, Washington, he had this same sensation of power within him, of great power, this time, and not only over another man, or even several men, but over *millions* of men and women and children, right across the breadth of this entire continent, the home of the most arrogant and the most corrupt pack of imperialistic materialists that Western society had ever spawned. He, Tikhon Trofimovich Khitrov, had been chosen by the chairman of the Presidium of the Supreme Soviet himself as the instrument that would shortly extinguish all life in this land where now flourished the most dangerous enemies of his own mother country. It was quite possible, he caught himself thinking, that he had not yet measured the degree of honor that had been bestowed on him, or the true significance of his status as the instrument in the hand of Rudenko, soon to be the savior of Russia and all mankind.

"What about our consulates?" the man in the chair asked him.

Khitrov emerged from his thoughts. "They'll receive the same medical attention, Comrade Ambassador. The entire staff of every Soviet mission throughout the United States will be given the appropriate inoculation against plague."

One of the nurses drew the hypodermic needle from the ambassador's bared forearm, pressed the cottonball against the skin for a moment and then covered the puncture with adhesive tape. "You can straighten your arm now, Comrade Ambassador."

"Thank you." He pulled down his shirt-sleeve and reached for his jacket.

Khitrov said nothing more until the medical team had left the room. "My instructions from Moscow are to keep you informed of our progress, Comrade Ambassador, without burdening you with information that has no particular bearing on what we are doing. Briefly, I have at this moment some one-and-a half-thousand subagents, most of them American Communists, working for me in the medical centers of fifteen major cities and townships. They have orders to ensure that they and all others loyal to our cause shall receive protection against the coming epidemic; they will also infiltrate medical centers, clinics, hospitals and production sources of plague inoculant, replacing certain batches with contaminated material."

Buttoning his dark jacket, Ambassador Viktor Sinitsyn listened without interrupting. He had decided to offer no comment on what Moscow was setting in motion; he knew only that an epidemic of the plague was to be spread throughout America, presumably as a prelude to some form of attack by conventional arms while the country was weakened and disoriented by the medical crisis. It could only mean, Ambassador Sinitsyn had assumed on hearing of this project, that President of the Presidium of the Supreme Soviet Vladychenko had gone mad, and that nobody in the Politburo or anywhere else could do anything about it. He would listen to this brute from Department

V, and would ask only those questions he'd be expected to ask. He would then, as soon as he could arrange it, take a plane with his wife and two children to Brazil, and remain there until this appalling madness had run itself out between the two superpowers.

He was an ambassador, a statesman; he was not a general of the army, a member of the Politburo or indeed any other kind of madman, and at this moment he wanted—as his good friends the Americans succinctly put it—out.

"The thirty-nine members of the cultural exchange group," Khitrov went on energetically, "arrived back in New York three days ago. It's likely that one or more will infect the other members of his or her family—the obsessive insistence on hygiene in this country leaves it wide open to attack by unfamiliar organisms—but whether any member of the group returning from Bombay infects his friends or relations over here or not is unimportant. My own medical infiltration teams are trained to contaminate food and water supplies with the plague bacillus; once it has taken hold, the health authorities will naturally suspect the cultural exchange group of being the carrier. My teams are to introduce the organism, of course, into the environment frequented by the members of that group, to establish the connection. One of them is close to the White House, and we shall ensure that no sources of the inoculant in that area are tampered with; we shall need President Hartridge and his advisers to remain in total power during the epidemic, since orders from the highest authority will need to be issued and obeyed. Do you have any questions, Comrade Ambassador?"

"Yes. I assume this epidemic is to weaken the social and military structure of the country prior to some form of conventional attack. Is that so?"

Khitrov's hands went behind his back. "We shall see."

The ambassador raised an eyebrow. "Very well. I have other questions, of course, but I shall refer them to Moscow, so as to relieve you of the responsibility of maintaining security." His tone was one of dismissal.

Khitrov hesitated. This puffed-up diplomat sounded unreliable, even untrustworthy; he was showing no signs of satisfaction at the idea of these whoresucking Americans going down like ninepins under the plague. Maybe a brief report to the *Komitet* was advisable.

"As you please, Comrade Ambassador." He turned for the baroque, gilded doors. "I should mention, with respect, that once a state of emergency has been declared in this country you'll receive instructions from your minister of foreign affairs that you will recognize me as a superior officer in the service of our nation. You'll be expected to obey my orders." A glitter came from the depths of his mud brown eyes. "I wouldn't wish you to be under any misapprehension, Comrade Ambassador, as to where you stand."

Three days later, on the evening of August 27, and five blocks across the park from the Soviet embassy on Phelps Place, Bruce Paget was sitting at the desk in his study when the telephone rang. Occupied with a memorandum the president had asked his opinion on by first thing in the morning, he waited until five rings had sounded: Laura was, as he knew, upstairs in her bathroom—where there was an extension to this line—and might just pick it up. But he also knew—by the terrible smell wafting through the master bedroom—that she was removing the hairs from her legs with a liquid depilatory and might not bother. At the sixth ring he picked up the phone.

"This is Bruce Paget." The number of this line was unpublished.

He knew, even before she spoke, that it was Nadia—she always gave a little light release of her breath when she heard his voice. Then she said very softly, "I know I shouldn't be calling you there, but I . . . it's been so long."

Instinctively he held the earpiece closer, though it made no difference. It was possible—*just* possible—that Laura, upstairs, had picked up her phone at the same time, and was now listening. That made no difference either, really; neither of them any longer pretended that he wasn't going through what Laura called a "torrid affair with that little Slav." But he still tried to respect the rules of Washington life; it would only be painful and embarrassing if any given wife picked up a phone—especially in her own bathroom—and heard the voice of any given other woman on the line. He'd therefore asked Nadia not to call unless it were something urgent.

"Are you okay?" he asked quietly.

"I think. But I miss you, Brutze."

"I miss you too." It had been almost two weeks since they'd spent their last night in a motel in New York, where Nadia had checked in and waited for him to find the room an hour later, avoiding the lobby. Underground parking garages and cheap motels, he thought bitterly: they were behaving like people out of a divorce detective's dog-eared file. Worse: he could no longer think of Nadia entirely as the dark-eyed nymph who had danced her way into his life from the distant snows; she was also his partner in a sordid intrigue. "Nadia," he said softly, "I have to go out this evening. If you're okay, let me call—"

"I am in Washington," she said.

His heart sank as he realized she'd been keeping it as a surprise.

"What are you doing here?" he asked her.

"All the company is here to see a lecture on Asian dance form. But I could meet you after, you see."

Bruce felt himself sag in the chair. The Chief had been keeping him and the other two personal aides on the run for the past three weeks, since the "accidental" sinking of the US Navy frigate in the Baltic Sea by a Soviet coast guard battery. Added to the pressure of work was Laura's insistence on as much social amusement as she could get him to share with her; she was patently trying to sap his energies in the hope of leaving him too jaded for assignations with "the little Slav," or to leave him so poor in his performance when they did meet that Nadia would look for someone younger. Even though it was perfectly obvious what she was doing, it was difficult to combat; it was a fact that tonight he'd no real appetite for lying to Laura for the hundredth time, facing her derision, and then stealing furtively away to some backstreet motel to try playing the ardent lover with a girl less than half his age.

For all that, he loved her. He loved her till it hurt.

"I don't think I can make it," he said, "not tonight. If you could have given me more warning, I could have—"

"Also I have news from my cousin," she said.

That too broke his heart. She shouldn't have to offer any persuasion. "Is it anything you can tell me over the phone?"

"No. I cannot speak of it here, where I am."

"I'll try to get into New York this weekend," he said on a note of hope. She might, in any case, have information from her cousin he could pass on to the Chief.

"You cannot meet me tonight, Brutze?" He'd never heard a voice so desolate.

"I have to go to the White House later," he said, and realized he was using the same excuse he'd used so often to Laura. "But tell me where you'll be, in case there's a chance of seeing you."

"We will be in the UNESCO Building, at eight o'clock."

"Which room?"

"I do not know. We will see the lecture on the Asian Dance Form."

Bruce made a note. "That's the title of the lecture?"

"Yes. It is by a culture exchange group, who have just come back from Bombay, in India."

CHAPTER TWENTY-THREE

Mikhail Rudenko stood alone in a room of the Council of Ministers Building within the Kremlin walls, his face lifted to the east window, through which he could see the clear blue sky above the Mausoleum in Red Square.

He had the look of a man watching a vision, his feet in their elegant polished shoes almost together, his broad-shoulderd body held perfectly still with his hands behind him and his head tilted upward a little, his eyes narrowed against the light of the morning and perhaps against the dazzling luminescence of the vision he watched.

He was aware of the history of this place where he stood. In this eighteenth-century building, Lenin had lived and worked, striving to set down the philosophies and the laws and the edicts and the social structure of the greatest edifice of government that had ever been known to mankind, where there was no king, no emperor, no potentate whose greed for power could be assuaged only by the exploitation of the people, by the draining of their resources and their very lifeblood in the cause of his own unbridled aggrandizement. Here, in this building where Mikhail Konstantinovich Rudenko stood today, Lenin had worked to bring about and make manifest the sovereign faith beside which all others paled: the true brotherhood of man.

On this summer morning Rudenko was more keenly aware of the history of this place, and of his own role in the unfolding history of mankind, because he had received a report that five cases of plague had been diagnosed in Washington, D.C.

So it had begun, and nothing could stop it. There had been a moment, when he'd seen the signal from Khitrov, of sudden doubt, even of horror at what he'd set in motion; but there had been many other moments during the past months when he had given pause in his mind during the inexorable onrush of preparation, and doubted himself, doubted his courage, his strength, even his sanity. Had he been somewhere else when he'd received the Khitrov signal he might have given way to panic, and arrested the progress of Project *Wasteland*, aborting it before the trigger epidemic could spread too far; but he had been here in this building, in this hallowed shrine to the man who had forged a new world for the peoples of Soviet Russia, Lenin, the man who this year had made his presence known to Rudenko from beyond the grave, and handed on to him the torch.

Nothing could now turn him aside from the masterwork that he himself had designed, in Lenin's name. Nothing.

Not even Klauson.

Rudenko had sent for him earlier this morning, and given him what amounted to an ultimatum. "I'm aware, Comrade Marshal, that you'd prefer to lead the Red Army into a more conventional war, to invade America by force of arms and take the enemy on his own ground. It would bring you much glory, I realize, if you could pull it off; but you can't, even during the crisis period of the coming epidemic; they'd know at once that we were responsible for the outbreak, and they wouldn't hesitate to respond with nuclear arms. That would be the end."

Klauson had strode up and down the carpet in his shining boots, listening attentively but playing the warlord in his decorated uniform and his tinted glasses (his "General MacArthur costume," as Boytsov called it) while Rudenko had told him categorically that if he were not prepared to undertake the salvage operation that would follow the extinction of the American nation he must say so now, and be replaced by someone with less taste for glory on the battlefield and more awareness of the greatness of the times, in which all must play their part.

"There are some among your advisers, Comrade Chairman, who are not my friends." Klauson had shrugged philosophically. "This kind of thing is unavoidable in the hierarchy of state administration. I'm not at all sure that you're right about our being unable to take that country by storm if we wanted to, during the epidemic; they know very well what would happen if they made a nuclear response: it would be the end of life on the planet." His boots had squeaked monotonously as he'd paraded up and down. "But it's not my place to argue the point, Comrade Chairman. The soldier is in the service of the state, which you represent." He'd come to an abrupt halt in front of Rudenko. "I only wish that Comrade President Vladychenko were informed of your plans. That, I admit, costs me a certain amount of sleep."

It wasn't the first time he'd said as much; he meant it as a threat, Rudenko knew, even as an instrument of blackmail. If the president of the Supreme Presidium got word of Project *Wasteland*, Rudenko would be slung into Lubyanka for treason and his grand design onto the rubbish heap. As it was, Vladychenko already suspected he was being fed disinformation by the close-knit *troika*. They'd let it be known they were exploring the possibility of invading South Africa and seizing the world's richest source of strategic metals. But the danger was past now. Last evening Vladychenko had phoned to say he'd be absent from the council chamber today: he was suffering from a mild attack of nervous debility, and Dr. Strautmanis had ordered a day's bed rest.

These attacks, as Rudenko happened to know, would recur with increasing frequency during the weeks ahead. The architect of an entire continent's imminent extinction would find little difficulty in procuring that for the one man who could ruin his enterprise.

"Comrade President Vladychenko was to be informed this morning," he had told Marshal Klauson. "You can hardly believe we could launch *Wasteland* without his knowledge and full approval. Unfortunately he's indisposed, but rest assured he'll be given our full confidence the moment he's himself again."

With patent insincerity the man had said, "It's not really my business, Comrade Chairman, as I've admitted. But—" with an expansive shrug of epaulettes "—as a serving soldier, my loyalties to—"

"You're perfectly right, of course. It isn't your business. But I've enough respect for you and your reputation to understand your feelings. As for your loyalties, Comrade Marshal, let me remind you that they should properly extend also to me, as chairman of the council of ministers, a custodian of the state. Those few who have failed to bear this in mind, Marshal Klauson, are no longer in office."

It had occurred to him, as he'd watched the bulky uniformed figure striding to the door, that he would probably be wise to have the supreme commander of the Red Army taken somewhere secluded and there shot. There was now too much at stake to allow any impediment from any quarter, particularly from the soldiery. Within a year from now, the Marshal Klausons of this world would be thrown onto the scrap heap together with their armies. The uncountable sums of money now vested in defense would be released, and rechanneled into programs for the final conquest of world hunger and for the exploration of space, where man would eventually spread his colonies. For so long it had been asked, how shall it profit the human species to leave this earth before war and sickness and hunger and fear have been eradicated? It was the question that John F. Kennedy had refused to hear, when he had launched his first astronauts into space; he had been taking the second step in the new and accelerating development of twentieth-century man, ignoring the first.

The first step was now being taken, and as Mikhail Rudenko stood at the window with his eyes lifted to the blue infinity of space, he felt within him a sense of cosmic order, the measured tread of a destiny that he alone had conjured from the turmoil and disarray that had for so long beset mankind.

When one of the telephones in the room began ringing, he didn't answer it; he didn't move. Perhaps, bespelled by the contemplation of matters so momentous, he failed even to hear it.

"He's not answering," one of Koslev's assistants told him.

"Never mind." Chairman of the Party Control Committee Viktor Viktorovich Koslev levered himself out of the chair behind his desk with the long-limbed articulation of a cricket, and crossed to look at the gunmetal blue computer in the middle of the main console. He knew the figures, but he punched in the coded data again to reassure himself. As a left-brained thinker he knew the value of confirmation. The first five cases of plague had been reported in Washington only two hours ago, and before he swung the project into its next phase he wanted to be sure of what he was doing.

It would have been good to have Rudenko's assurance as well, but Koslev had lately begun to think that the architect of *Wasteland* was withdrawing into a mood that sometimes seemed almost mystic. In terms of logic, this, Koslev thought, was understandable. There was an inevitably messianic quality to Rudenko's role of the savior of mankind, and you couldn't expect a messiah to behave like a bank clerk.

Had Koslev been left alone in his office to face the thought of what he was doing—of what all of them were doing—at this juncture in world history he would probably have put a gun in his mouth and pulled the trigger; and somewhere, deep in the flesh-and-blood computer banks within his domed and shining skull, he was aware of that. But he was not alone. Apart from his five highly intelligent assistants there was the same number of computers, a battery of technological expertise impressive enough to dismiss any reservations that might come to worry him. The data they were all feeding into the machines were true; the computed results were true. And in the presence of absolute truth, Viktor Viktorovich Koslev was able to live in peace.

From initial outbreak to nationwide contamination, the luminescent screen read out, *a time period of thirteen days*.

He punched in another question.

From nationwide contamination to proportions of epidemic appropriate to the declaration of a national emergency, twenty-seven days.

Koslev hit the keyboard again, his gray eyes calm behind their large-lensed glasses.

From the declaration of a national emergency to the decision to isolate the US from outside contact, given the established thought modes of President Hartridge, fifteen days plus or minus two.

The digital wall clock read September 4 in its date slot as Koslev glanced up at it. Then he shut down the computer and loped back to his desk, sitting for a moment picking at the quick of a nail before he selected the third telephone from the end of the desk and picked it up.

"Give me the Gestov-Klinik."

Vladimir Dobrynin, chief research supervisor at the Gestov-Klinik, was perched on a stool with his conscience as the fluorescent light tubes hummed above his head. A dark, squat man of no more than thirty-two, his brilliance as a biologist was well concealed under his football-playerlike appearance; there was an air about him of healthy aggression, of a bulldozing turn of mind in the face of opposition. Indeed, this would have been a fair estimation of his personality a few months ago, before the catastrophe. Since then—since, particularly, Aleksandr Lopatkin had vanished behind the doors of the Serbsky Institute of Forensic Psychiatry—there had appeared an extra element to his character, manifested in his behavior as a certain slowing down, a tendency to become lost occasionally in thoughts of which he never spoke.

The truth was simple enough. When the state had asked his good friend and fellow scientist Aleksandr Lopatkin if he would further his work on the DNA-recombinant organism now called L-9, he had said no, he would not. It was too dangerous, too "hideously and unthinkably dangerous"—as Lopatkin himself had put it in private to Dobrynin. And nothing had been heard of him since.

Nothing much was heard of Vladimir Dobrynin these days, either; but there was a difference. He was still here at the Klinik, promoted to chief research supervisor and granted privileges extending from a new four-room apartment in Lenin Hills to a *dacha* near the lakes; and though nothing much was heard of him in public academic circles, he was marked—according to Director Smirnov, his administrative boss—for "great honors." This could only mean a place in the Academy, as his good friend Lopatkin had had, before . . . before . . .

It was always here that Dobrynin faltered in his contemplation of his life today. At first, when the catastrophe had occurred, he'd thought of it as only that: a disaster, a crisis of potentially horrific proportions. Then Lopatkin had disappeared, and Director Smirnov had talked to Dobrynin and his colleagues, relaying information to them from state levels, assuring them that if they elected to continue work on the organism L-9 they would not only increase their prestige in the eyes of the state administrators but would also help their mother country in her unceasing struggle against the forces of political and ideological evil that threatened her from across her borders.

Today, as he perched on the high stool beside one of the assay benches with his face in his fists, Vladimir Dobrynin was prey to doubts that he had done right. Yet there was nothing he could do about it, except resign from the project and follow Aleksandr Lopatkin into the shadows of extinction. The only way he could control his mental equilibrium was to indulge sometimes in these bouts of soul-searching, between periods of unremitting and dedicated work, to which he could return, his conscience for a time assuaged.

Everyone had to have his *modus operandi*. This was his.

The only difficult times were when his conscience led him to visit Aleksandr's wife and daughter, Elena and Ludmila, in the single-room "apartment" in the workers' district east of the city. Elena was, of course, not strictly a wife any longer; everyone— herself included—now believed she was a widow, though she pretended to hope that Aleksandr was still alive in one of the forced labor camps in the northlands. Emaciated by grief, her beautiful eyes larger still in her wasted face, she never accused Dobrynin of doing work for the state that Aleksandr had refused as a matter of principle; it was as if she realized—as perhaps she did—that she made a mirror for his conscience.

Dobrynin didn't know what the state intended to do with the large batch of L-9 material it had ordered the Klinik to produce over the past two months. (The word "material" signified the actual organism contained in a survival medium of tissue culture.) There were rumors of the state's intention of ending the war in Afghanistan with a decisive *coup* of some kind; some people talked of the "inevitability" of Russia's invasion of South Africa for possession of its strategic metals and gold. Yet Dobrynin couldn't imagine that the L-9 material was to be used in either venture; he and his colleagues had warned the state repeatedly of the impossibility of containing the outbreak of an L-9 epidemic, once started.

Were they mad? Vladimir Dobrynin, sitting with his head in his fists, thought that perhaps they were. This was a mad world, and—

"We're to dispatch it."

He jerked around, one foot slipping on the rung of the stool and sending him off balance. He retrieved it. "What did you say?"

Smirnov, director of the Gestov-Klinik, was coming toward him between the assay benches, walking with his precise, measured stride that allowed him no deviation from whatever purposes he had in mind. "That man," Aleksandr Lopatkin had confided to Dobrynin once, "is liable to walk straight through a wall one day, if he doesn't remember to stop in time."

There was indeed an air of fatal irrevocability in the director's paced approach, or perhaps it was that his words had finally sunk into Dobrynin's consciousness, where it evoked instant alarm.

"We are to dispatch the consignment," Smirnov told him again. "I've received the orders direct from Comrade Chairman Koslev."

In a moment Dobrynin said quietly, "Very well."

"And you are to go with it."

"To go with it?"

"To ensure absolute safety." Smirnov took another step toward him, lowering his voice. "To guard it. If necessary with your life."

After another pause Dobrynin nodded slowly. "I see. Will I— will I have time to tell my wife? To explain—"

"Everything is arranged, Dobrynin. The consignment will leave here as soon as it can be loaded." He gave the chief of research an unfamiliar pat on the arm. "It's an honor for you, you know. This is an important assignment."

"Yes," Dobrynin said, "I know."

The convoy of three vehicles comprised a military armored car fore and aft, and a bullion transport van drawn from the gold-fields complex. Before midnight the ten squat cylinders had been taken from the laboratory on rubber-wheeled dollies and loaded into the van, where four officers of the Red Army had positioned themselves on folding seats. Vladimir Dobrynin joined them, not speaking, his head down as he tried to contain his terror. All the time the L-9 material had been under guard inside the Klinik he'd been able to sleep more or less easily, telling himself that it would surely never be used, that one day they'd receive orders to destroy it. But it had now emerged from its home and was abroad in the outside world—still encapsulated and still under guard, yes, but no longer safe in the Klinik where its appalling potentiality for evil had been understood by specialists.

Vladimir Dobrynin sat with his eyes closed and his head leaning back against the panel of the van, knowing in the most secret reaches of his soul that he had now become part of something so monstrous and so unthinkable, as the convoy rolled through midnight and the dark, that he was hard put not to give a cry of despair.

CHAPTER TWENTY-FOUR

G alanshin turned the nut another half circle and the spoke snapped with a loud musical note.

"Fuck," he said, but his expression didn't change.

Clay noticed that.

"Did you see Kazakov?" the Russian asked him.

"I've seen them all."

Galanshin scratched for another spoke in the box of junk and squinted at the thread and shoved it through the hole in the hub of the bicycle wheel and then through the hole in the rim. He was a short man with a bland face and a military haircut; he whistled silently between his teeth when he wasn't speaking. Clay had been passed on to him last night, when it was too late to talk to him—he worked as a clerk in the traffic office of the military airport seventeen miles from the city: *a real catch*, as Blanes had said, simply meaning that since he was inside the military he must have access to sensitive information. That was the trouble with Blanes—he'd never been on an active mission; his ass was stuck to a desk and a phone was stuck in his ear and he didn't even know that an agent-in-place could be right inside the military and still be a bloody amateur.

This man, though, didn't seem like that. Maybe Blanes was right, for once. *(Why do I hate that man's guts? Because he thinks I screwed everything up.)* He watched the little Russian as he got the nut straight on the thread and began turning it carefully. Footsteps sounded from the other side of the gapped, rotting fence, and Clay watched the man's eyes and saw they were listening, but that was all. He was beginning to feel more confident about Galanshin; he was slow-moving and deliberate, his hands steady; the only sign of nerves had been when he'd snapped the spoke, not concentrating.

The footsteps faded out. There were some kids playing not far away, and a woman was banging pans about inside the shabby little house; the actual yard was safe enough, not overlooked by windows because of the half-roof fixed to the wall—Galanshin would have put that there, and for that reason. Good.

Clay took another cigarette from the packet he'd put between them on the beer crate, and lit it, drawing in the smoke, feeling it in his lungs, greeting it. He'd started the habit a couple of years ago when he'd come in from his final mission and didn't have to keep his body tightened up to survival fitness anymore. Bad move.

"The flights are regular," Galanshin told him. "Once every ten days."

"Since when?"

"A month ago."

"Same plane?"

"Yes. They're all the same. Long-range bomber: the TU-28." He moved the spanner around gently, and the spoke sang as the torsion shifted.

"Who goes on board?" Clay asked him. Galanshin was one of those a-i-p's who never volunteered anything; you had to keep on asking specific questions. Of the seventeen agents Clay had seen in the past two weeks, a dozen of them had been like this; he respected the technique but it was wearing. It didn't matter now, though, because this looked like a potential breakthrough after two weeks of sitting at the raw-input telex and watching the stuff come in and sorting it out sheet by sheet through the coffee-swilling nights at the embassy and analyzing it and *analyzing* it and finding patterns and coincidences and sudden new directions that led nowhere, and then tramping all over the city and digging out the a-i-p's from their foxholes and persuading them to talk, to trust him, because they didn't like his faultless Muscovite accent: they thought he might be doubling for the KGB.

Then Brekhov and Lapin and George Fielding (God, his last mission had left him like a zombie!) and Sarkisyan and finally the busdriver, Kiselev, who'd said the man you want to see is Galanshin, whose brother runs the bicycle repair shop.

Next time, Blanes, I'm going to bring it home, you understand? But he hadn't hoped for a breakthrough as soon as this.

"Who goes on board?" he asked the man again.

"They vary. Some I don't know about, because it would mean asking questions. It's when I can get a look at the flight schedules that I can see who they are. They're mostly scientists. Three epidemiologists, two microbiologists, a doctor of pharmacology." He went on talking without requiring another question, because this one had a long answer. Clay squatted on his haunches beside the upturned bicycle, hunched over his cigarettes as he chain-lit them, dragging the smoke into his lungs and savoring it as he listened to Galanshin and then asked more questions and listened again until he started not to believe what he was being told.

"It sounds," he said, "like a whole shithouseful of stinking rotten disinformation, I suppose you know that."

Galanshin laughed softly, looking at Clay full in the eyes, which he hadn't done before. "You never know who you're talking to, do you?"

He went on whistling through his teeth again and Clay asked him: "Is it always the same KGB man on the flight?"

"So far."

"What's his name?"

"I don't know."

"Can you get it for me?"

"If he's on the next flight."

"When's that?"

"Tomorrow."

"If he's on the flight, get me his name. *Get me everything you can*, all right?"

"I'll try."

"Listen," Clay said, and waited till the man looked him in the eyes again. "For this stuff you're giving me, I can screw my bastards out of a really decent amount of loot."

Galanshin took another half turn on the last nut and dropped the spanner into the box. "That doesn't interest me so much. All I want is *my* bastards to get their balls burned. They've got my brother up there in the Gulag."

Two days later, on September 12, George Vickers walked through the rain to the Savage Club, having given up trying to get a cab in the evening rush hour. He arrived drenched, and shook his raincoat out in the hall, leaving it with the porter.

He found Braithwaite watching a news bulletin on television in the main smoking room: pictures of crowds gathering outside the emergency clinics that had been set up in Washington to ease the pressure on the hospitals.

"I don't understand why they can't seem to control it," Braithwaite said. "I thought we'd stamped it out in the West with antibiotics."

"The last I heard, sir, was that they've run short of serum."

"Run short? Dear God." He glanced up at Vickers, and saw the rainwater dropping from his soaked hair. "No cabs? What are you doing here anyway, George?"

There were a few other members watching the news, so Vickers asked his chief if he could talk to him somewhere more private. They went along to the dining room, which was almost empty, and chose a corner table.

"There's been a signal from Moscow," Vickers said. "Clay wants someone dispatched."

"He's out of his mind."

"That was my first thought, yes. But I've talked to Blanes since. He says Clay is on to something. And I suppose we've got to remember that he's had a lot of experience. He may have—"

he shrugged with his hands "—messed up the Talyzin thing, but he's still a professional. You sent him out there yourself, sir. And he's desperate to make up for what's happened so far, we know that."

Braithwaite watched the waiter who was serving the cheese-board to some people at the far end of the room, his back stooped, the First World War medals hanging from the front of his worn black jacket. Old Bradley, said to be past eighty now, an absolute institution here. Then the crouched figure changed and Braithwaite was looking at Charles Clay as his mind concentrated on what Vickers was saying. Clay, watching him back from the distance of Moscow, hands in the pockets of his mackintosh, a strand of hair blowing, his blind-looking gaze unblinking. Clay, wanting someone "dispatched," forgetting he wasn't still working for that wildcat outfit they'd called the Clowns, which had dispatched God knew how many people in the opposition. Clay, his body still—too still, considering he wanted a man killed—and his mind desperate for redemption, his vanity driving him on into danger, perhaps danger for them all.

"Whom does he want dispatched?" he asked Vickers.

"A KGB captain."

"Oh my God."

"He wants to take his place, sir."

Braithwaite jerked his eyes up to study Vickers. "Then he *is* out of his mind."

Quietly Vickers said, "I wouldn't say so."

"You've always had a soft spot for that fellow, haven't you?"

"I always have respect for those of our people who've done the kind of things he's done, sir. He's got an unbeatable record."

Braithwaite shifted in his chair, uncomfortable. He was never disturbed by the need for decision-making; he'd never balked at responsibility. But to give instructions, or in this case to give simply his permission, to dispatch a man, a stranger, someone he'd never know, was so cold-blooded. No rage, no desperation, just . . . *Very well, do it.*

"Do you *really* think, George, that Clay has *any* chance of finding out what Terebilov was trying to tell us when he came across? *Any* chance?"

Vickers didn't answer at once. If he were going to share the responsibility of a stranger's death—*a KGB captain's*—and the danger of appalling repercussions, he wanted a minute to think. Sir James waited, fiddling with the silver cruet on the table, knowing precisely the other man's need and giving him time.

At last Vickers said, raking his damp hair back with his fingers, "Yes, I'm pretty sure Clay has a chance, and even a good chance. He's well capable of going into a hazardous situation—in fact that's where he works best, as you know. He's well capable of passing as a Russian, even a KGB man—he's done it before. But what's even more important, sir, to my mind, is the *value* of his success, if he succeeds. And I think that far outweighs the risk."

"The Terebilov information?"

"Yes."

Braithwaite was quiet for some minutes while Vickers waited, his plump fingers moving restlessly on the linen tablecloth, finding a breadcrumb the waiter had missed, rolling it back and forth as he silently thanked God he didn't have his chief's awesome responsibility. (His wife had once asked Vickers in a moment of indiscretion, "George, darling, do you ever have to do really *nasty* things to people?" He hadn't answered.)

When his chief spoke again his voice was heavy. "Let Clay have what he wants."

Blanes leaned back against his desk, one hand in his pocket toying with his keys.

"We can't find anyone to do it," he said.

Clay turned his pale eyes on him. "Isn't Clark in Moscow?"

"Yes, but he's not willing."

In a moment Clay said thinly, "Time he went home."

Blanes said nothing.

"Henri?" Clay asked.

"He's going to get married. He doesn't want anymore—" Blanes shrugged "—operations on his conscience."

Clay said impatiently, "There's *no one?*"

"That's right. If you want it done, you'll have to do it yourself."

CHAPTER TWENTY-FIVE

Presidential aide Bruce Paget walked into the Oval Office and put the report onto Hartridge's desk.

"The Center for Disease Control in Atlanta recommends a declaration of national emergency, sir. They're waiting for your decision."

Hartridge picked up the report and checked the number of the last page. It was nineteen. "I'll read it now. Tell them that."

"You want me to stand by, sir?"

"Yes. God knows where this mess is going to wind up." He pulled a lower drawer of his desk halfway out and crossed his feet on it, starting to read.

Within twenty minutes he'd gotten a clear idea of the facts, though a few of the technicalities were out of his field. This thing had started out as primary bubonic plague in Bombay, India, on August 7. Three weeks later, a cultural exchange group from the US had returned from Bombay and attended a meeting at UNESCO, where they described their experiences of traditional Indian dance forms to some two hundred people. A man named Teschler, one of the group, had begun coughing uncontrollably, and had been escorted home at the end of the meeting; he was by that time running a temperature.

Within three days he was dead. In brief, the report stated that one reason for the rapid spread of the disease was that it was unfamiliar to medical staffs and health authorities; the incidence of pneumonic plague—which had developed from the primary bubonic form that had broken out in Bombay—in the USA was negligible, and earlier cases had been dealt with easily by antibiotics. *Until fifteen persons had died*, the report stated, *it was not recognized as pneumonic plague. Immediate action was then taken to isolate and appropriately treat new cases.*

On October 10 the epidemiologists flown in from Atlanta and Fort Collins strongly recommended shutting down enclosed sports stadiums, theaters, meeting halls and all places where crowds normally gathered. Of the approximate total of five thousand confirmed cases of *Yersinia pestis* in the pneumonic form, seven hundred victims had died. It was now believed that a resistant bacillus must be involved, since streptomycin, tetracycline, chloramphenicol and similar antibiotics would normally be expected to bring this specific disease under control within a matter of days, in conditions of strict isolation.

It was at this point in his reading that President Hartridge lowered the red file for a moment and looked across at Paget.

"Yes. We have to declare an emergency, and right now. What are the main recommendations?"

Bruce had been briefed in anticipation of this question. "Most sports centers and theaters have already been closed down, sir. We should follow this by radio and televised announcements to the public, urging them to stay in their homes as much as they can, avoid groups, meetings, social life, until the health authorities have gotten a grip on the problem. We should recommend skeleton staffs, and then only in essential industry and services; a sanction on all travel and population movement; and the encouragement of individual self-reliance in the home and street environment—mainly the stockpiling of food and essential supplies and the imposition of isolation as far as possible. We should also close schools and universities."

Hartridge put more questions for a further ten minutes, got three more of his aides into the room, called the Health Department and the Center for Disease Control in Atlanta, and told

Paget to get him air space on the three major television networks as soon as it could be done.

He went on the screens coast to coast at the prime time news hour at seven o'clock that night, giving a brief resumé of the situation and announcing a national emmergency.

"There's no way," Dr. Ron Voss told one of the interns at George Washington University Hospital on 23rd Street. "Either it's a resistant strain or it isn't. There's no way it can be resistant *sometimes*. Of the patients we've isolated since a week ago, around twenty-five percent have died while the rest have been completely responsive to therapy except for one or two cases of brief, self-limiting febrile episodes on the fifth or sixth day." He dug his hands into the pockets of his white lab coat, his voice slurred with fatigue. "They should *all* be alive, Bob, or they should *all* be dead."

There was silence for a moment in the long, brightly lit laboratory, except for the dripping of a faucet.

"You want to make tests, you mean?"

"That's exactly what I mean."

"Okay." The intern went over to the wall phone. "I'll set it up."

Ten minutes later they were watching the tiny disc of streptomycin under the microscope after streaking the plate with plague culture. The culture was unaffected: the bacillus remained alive, where there should have been an expanding zone of inhibition.

"It's resistant," the intern said.

Ron Voss pulled the slide out. "Okay. But resistant to what?"

They tested the chloramphenicol next. Then they tested the tetracycline. They tested six separate batches of each drug, making notes; and four hours later they called the hospital administrator, waking him from the first hour of sleep he'd managed to snatch for the past thirty-six.

"Two-thirds of the batches we tested," Voss told him, "are

okay. The rest are contaminated. We've been injecting a third
of our patients with adulterated antibiotics, and that's why they
died."

It took until midnight to alert every hospital, clinic and medical
center throughout the nation to this new and frightening danger; more people died before every batch of antibiotics on hand
had been tested prior to injection. Representatives of the manufacturers were flown in to Atlanta, Georgia, for urgent discussions with the top epidemiologists at the Center for Disease
Control, many of them in the track suits and sweaters and golf
jackets they'd hastily donned after being roused from their beds.
Teams of analytical biochemists from the Atlanta center and a
dozen subsidiary units were zeroing in on the pharmaceutical
laboratories where the faulty drug batches were manufactured.

"The figure I see," said a distraught PR man for J. K. Rand
Pharmaceuticals, "for awards of the court to the relatives of the
dead is around one billion dollars. So far."

"Who the hell cares, for Christ's sake? Our main concern is
to protect the living."

On the morning of the next day several facts had been established. No faulty batches of any drug had left the dispatch departments of the manufacturing pharmaceutical companies at
any time, since strict supervision was routinely maintained. No
faulty batches were discovered awaiting shipment, or in any of
the processing stages of manufacture.

Emerging patterns of nationwide delivery from the pharmaceutical manufacturers showed that despite the greatly varying
distances involved, as the airplanes and trucks supplied the hospitals and medical centers across thousands of miles, faulty
batches of drugs were discovered in almost equal quantities
from coast to coast and from the Canadian to the Mexican
borders. *The faulty batches had already been there in the dis-
pensing rooms at the time of the plague outbreak.*

At an emergency meeting of the FBI directors responsible for the inquiry into the drug crisis, Lou Fenner, overseeing the nationwide patterns of investigation, told the CDC:

"The faulty batches already were there for use in the hospitals at some time *before* the epidemic broke out. They were there, in my opinion, *in anticipation* of the outbreak. In upwards of fifty major hospitals from coast to coast, batches of genuine and effective antibiotics were switched around, and the batches of saline solution put in their place."

The word "sabotage" began going the rounds. Then the word "terrorists" superseded it. Then everyone in the health departments and the disease control centers and the FBI offices was making his own guess: it had to be the Iranians or the Cubans or the PLO or the Soviets. It had to be *someone*.

Two days later the shipments of antibiotics coming out of the manufacturing companies were escorted by teams from the National Guard, and at each reception center where the drugs were placed into storage there were armed security guards mounted in twenty-four-hour shifts.

The public was not told.

"It's bad enough," the press secretary at the White House told an aide, "with the population physically at risk and psychologically frightened about the plague itself. Tell them it's a case of terrorism on a mass scale and you'll see panic in the streets."

The little girl's eyes were wide with shock.

"*They killed Bonzo!*"

"It's okay, honey, it's okay, don't think about it." The child became engulfed by her mother's arms, a small bundle shaking with sobs.

"*But there was a man with a gun! He shot Bonzo! I saw him!*"

"It had to be done, sweetheart. Bonzo might have hurt somebody, see."

"*Bonzo wouldn't ever hurt anyone, ever! I saw the man—*"

"*Sshh*, honey, don't get yourself upset about it. It's happening everywhere, and it's really for our own good. The man didn't mean any harm. He was just—"

"He killed my Bonzo!" The small body shook with grief, with shock, with rage.

"Sshh . . . darling heart, *sshh* . . . It was just something that had to be, and one day you'll understand."

Nobody was making a count of how many dogs were being shot dead on sight in the streets of New York and Chicago and New Orleans and Los Angeles, in every city across the nation, as apartments and houses and mobile homes were left empty, their occupiers isolated and under therapy or already dead. The dogs had been left suddenly in most cases, with the abrupt onset of sickness, and were without food, pining for their owners and disoriented, forming packs in the streets and invading the grocery stores to seize what they could. There were increasing reports of children and elderly people being bitten, occasionally even savaged, and the emergency law—one of dozens now appearing on the notice boards of banks and post offices—was strict and explicit: any dog or cat seen unaccompanied in a public place was to be shot on sight. Both animals were exposed to flea infestation from rats, the primary carriers of plague. There was another danger: "On top of everything we've got," a weary health official told a reporter, "who needs rabies?"

By the fifth day of the declaration of a nationwide emergency—known succinctly among health and public services authorities as Plague + 5—the National Guard was supporting the police and county sheriffs to put down sporadic instances of civil disobedience, looting and the breaking of the curfew that had now been ordered nationwide. Fire services were under increasing pressure as people taken sick in their homes or removed by ambulance left electrical appliances switched on or a cigarette unextinguished.

The *New York Times* was the first newspaper to bring out editions of only four or six pages, most of which carried authoritative and factual reports of the crisis, plus an increasing number of federal and state government directives. Other newspapers followed suit, until many began closing down altogether, leaving it to the radio and television stations to inform the public more rapidly.

At the end of the fifth day the major Wall Street and Chicago stock and commodity exchanges gave notice that they would not reopen "until the general situation is under control." Trading had been falling off rapidly over the past three days, and finally the onset of panic had brought a stampede of short sellers desperately seeking to recoup their losses on the long side. A few fortunes were made, many were lost, and the man in the street with speculative investments was wiped out as the markets whipsawed. The price of gold in London had hit new highs and was still rising.

Confusion rife in the business world, was the headline for a TV news report. "What the hell are they talking about?" asked the editor of *Forbes Magazine*. "What business world? There isn't one left."

On Plague + 7 an emergency directive curtailed outgoing traffic from all airports and maritime docks. From the outbreak of the epidemic there had been an increasing rush by affluent and retired persons to leave the country before they could contract the disease. Following the emergency directive, only those with the most urgent business would be permitted to leave the United States, and then only if blood tests showed they were not already infected; they would also require the permission of the health and immigration authorities of the country of destination to land on their territory.

The emergency clinics set up at the major airports were inundated by requests for blood tests; the *No Vacancy* signs were lit up outside every hotel and motel in the area, and stayed that way. On Capitol Hill, congressmen were beseiged by callers protesting the emergency measures, and asked the telephone company for extra lines to be installed. They didn't get them: the telephone companies nationwide already were working against overload.

Incoming traffic to the United States had dwindled to ten percent of normal figures; foreign nationals were keeping away, except for those few who were prepared to put their business interests above the risk of perhaps fatal infection. The only American passengers on incoming flights and ships were those who in their turn were prepared to risk infection in order to rejoin their families and try to help them.

The whole situation was now changing with bewildering speed as reports of fatalities continued to hit the broadcast and televised news bulletins. On Plague + 9, the Canadian government took the historically unprecedented step of closing its frontiers to all traffic from the United States. Travelers seeking to land in Canada were required to prove that they had not been in the United States since one week prior to the outbreak of plague. Within twenty-four hours, Mexico also closed its borders, and the US armed patrols normally engaged in trying to keep Mexican nationals from entering America were now ordered to stop their own countrymen from crossing the border illicitly into Mexico.

Worldwide, urgent exhortations had been reaching the White House for the past four days, demanding that the United States close her frontiers entirely, on the tarmac of every airport and along the east and west coastlines. The World Health Organization was supporting this demand. President Hartridge was delaying his decision simply because the idea of sealing off the United States from the rest of the world seemed somehow ominous.

"If we close the gates," he told his aides, "will we ever be able to open them again? I have a feeling of—you know—*Götterdammerung*." His voice wasn't much above a whisper. For the past nine days he'd been speaking ceaselessly in the Oval Office and on the telephone as he had tried to keep pace with events and devise emergency directives aimed at containing the crisis as far as possible, and his doctors had warned him that his larynx was "like a forest fire" and that he must curtail his speaking to one hour per day. That was impossible. Hartridge's major concern was to pin down the source of the epidemic—not medically but politically. There was still no reliable evidence that the batches of antibiotics had been deliberately switched for batches of saline solution, but nobody doubted it now. No terrorist group had claimed the credit for the most severe crisis that had ever hit the United States except for war.

As long ago as Plague + 3—"The rate this thing's been going," a White House official was heard to say, "yesterday always seems like a week ago"—every unit of the armed forces had been confined to barracks and camp to keep down the risk of infection. Two days later the Pentagon, fearing that the rapidly weakening state of the country and the disruption of ordinary life might invite a nonnuclear invasion by inoculated troops, put the armed forces on alert status; all furlough was canceled, and on every base across the nation, practice drills were instituted for daily repetition.

Of the many strange aspects of the epidemic and its seemingly deliberate causation, two were vexing the special investigation teams of the FBI, whose reports were telephoned hourly to the chief executive. Across the vector maps on the walls of the Center for Disease Control, Atlanta, which showed the spread of the disease throughout the nation on a day-to-day basis, two clear areas were noted. *In the state of Alaska, only seventy confirmed cases of plague had occurred, and none of these had been fatal.* Epidemiologists were agreed that Alaska, separated from the continental United States by Canadian territory, had enjoyed a natural state of isolation; but traffic in and out of Alaska prior to the closing of the Canadian frontier had been routinely substantial.

The second area almost clear of the disease contained the White House and Capitol Hill. The fact that the White House and most government buildings had been isolated behind a *cordon sanitaire* since Plague + 5 hadn't precluded the risk of the disease spreading through the corridors of power. The single aspect linking both these clear areas was well established by the FBI. *In no hospital or medical center in either area had there*

been any tampering with the batches of stored antibiotics. Thus,
every case of plague had been swiftly dealt with, and the victim
restored to full health.

"It's kind of eerie," one of the FBI liaison agents in the White
House told Bruce Paget. "It's like the seat of government is
being deliberately left immune, so there's someone to go on
running the country. You know what I mean? And maybe even
more horrendous than that: so there's someone who can take
orders from the unknown enemy when our defenses are finally
down, and have those orders carried out."

Bruce only half heard him. The idea was too chilling, and his
mind was more preoccupied today than at any time before. He'd
taken a call from Nadia, and she'd been speaking from her bed
in Georgetown University Hospital.

"I am in isolation ward, Brutze."

"When did—?" He didn't know what to say, what the important questions were. Did it matter when? "What's the prognosis,
Nadia?"

"I do not know that word. I—"

"Okay. Get me your doctor on the line."

In an ordinary case it would have been out of the question—
every doctor in every hospital in the land was working under the
kind of pressure that was itself decimating their ranks—but this
was a call from the White House, and Dr. James Abram wasn't
to know it was unofficial.

"She's holding her own," he told Bruce over the telephone.
"It's all we can say."

"But now that you're able to use genuine drugs, it's only a
matter of time before she responds to them, right?"

"It could be only a matter of time," Abram told him wearily,
"before she and a whole lot of other patients find themselves
without adequate care, Mr. Paget. It's no longer just the plague
we're up against; this epidemic has weakened everyone's resistance all around, through the pressures of overwork, anxiety

and a debilitated immune system. All we can say is we're doing all we can."

In the background on the line, Bruce could hear a voice intoning: *Stat—paging Dr. Abram. Stat—paging Dr. Abram* . . .

"Can you tell me—" Bruce began.

"I have to go now. Sorry. I'll try and keep in touch."

When Nadia came on the line again, Bruce could only try to reassure her. "We're turning the tide, Nadia, right across the country. I get to see the figures, hourly. Since they found out about the spurious drug batches, all we've had to deal with is a bug that's easily killed by the real thing."

It was true that in several cities the mortality rate had peaked yesterday morning, and was in a slow decline, but the factors Dr. Abram had talked about were real.

"Brutze," her voice came huskily on the line, "I must tell you something. If—if I do not get better very much, and if I—perhaps can't see you again, there is something—" He listened to her voice breaking, and closed his eyes—"something you must know. It is a thing I could not help, because of my mother and my sister. But you must not believe my love for you was not real, because of this thing."

Sick and frightened, she lost her proficiency in English. "Nadia, I know it was—I know it *is* real. Don't worry about anything. Whatever it is, I understand." He wanted to go to her, but that was impossible; the private presidential staff was confined to the White House, and even if he could somehow reach the hospital he could never come back. The president was himself living and working in conditions of strict isolation.

"Brutze, I am afraid." Her voice was a whisper now.

"There's nothing—" he closed his eyes again, trying desperately to find something of true comfort to tell her instead of the stock blandishments. Of *course* there was something to be afraid of . . . she could be dying. "My darling, I want so much to come and see you, but I can't, for a little while. It's—"

"I know. You could give him infection, yes."

She meant Hartridge. "He's working—we're all working day and night to beat this thing, Nadia. That's why it won't be long before I can see you again." More blandishments . . . *Why was it that when you most wanted to give someone comfort, all you could think of was lies?*

The last time he'd seen her was only a couple of weeks ago, an entire world away in the distant past. He'd gone to New York for a meeting with the nomination committee, and spent the night with her in a motel, this time getting her to book the room while he went in through the door to the staircase, but thinking nothing anymore about the sordidness, the subterfuge: it was their life-style now. He'd taken a bag of cold chicken from a deli, and a bottle of Reisling; Nadia had seemed almost fey, troubled by something on her mind but determined not to let it spoil their evening: she had laughed too easily, and too often had fallen into silences, suddenly distant from him until she swung her dark hair and found him still with her, sliding her sinuous arms around him and clinging to him with more than passion, with a childlike need of his strength.

He had asked her once, was anything on her mind? All she had said was, "*Nothing can hurt us, Brutze. Nothing, ever.*"

It hadn't been true.

"Brutze," she was saying now, so softly that he cupped his hand over his right ear to shut out the background sound of the staff cafeteria. "I must tell you this thing, before it is late."

He waited, wondering if she wasn't going on because he must first say yes, he wanted to know. "You mentioned your mother," he said, "and your sister. Are they okay?"

Softly, so softly, "Yes. They are okay. And that is because of what I did for them, you see. I did not do it because my love for you was not real. I want you to—"

The line went dead.

"Nadia?"

He knew she hadn't hung up on him. It was happening all the time, when you were on the phone: the networks were overloaded and working short-staffed.

"Nadia?"

He hung up and called one of his secretaries in his office and told her where he was, and to try getting Georgetown University Hospital. Once she'd got the desk he'd take it from there.

Three times in the next hour he was put on the line to the hospital, but was told that Miss Fedotova was sleeping now and mustn't be disturbed.

It was midnight when he called the hospital again, and got the same answer. She was asleep.

"Is she making progress?"

"She's stable, sir. She seems to be holding her own right now."

He'd sent flowers, and a note; that was the most he was able to do—the *most*. There was nobody, no friend, no one on his staff he could send to visit her. She was in strict isolation. If she wouldn't speak to him on the phone, there was no way of persuading her.

Dog tired from overwork, he dropped onto the couch in his personal office on the second floor and tried to sleep. It didn't come easily; Nadia was clearer in his mind than she had ever been before: Nadia with her huge shimmering eyes, her quick smile, her smoky loins, her childlike excitements—*I did not know Christmas ever before, Brutze, it is the most wonderful thing!* Nadia the girl from the distant snows, her laughter as bright as her tears, her speech husky and filled with endearing mistakes that he thought sometimes she had no interest in correcting, because she knew he loved them.

Nadia the free spirit. *I love America because here I am free, Brutze . . . I can say the things I think, and nobody takes me into the prison for that . . . I dance, you see, and to dance is to be free, it is to fly, it is to live, and that is why I love your country, and why I love you.*

Nadia.

By morning, after only four hours' fitful sleep, he knew with daylight revelation that he'd been wrong last night when she'd suddenly stopped talking to him on the phone. She had, yes, hung up on him. To tell him what was wrong had been more than she could bear.

What had she been saying? That she didn't want him to think she hadn't really been in love—no, loved him—was that it, were those the actual words? *What had she actually said?* That her love for him was real, had been real. But the actual words?

Couldn't he even remember the last words she'd said to him, over a telephone?

He called the hospital again. They didn't have the time, or maybe the energy, to give him false comfort.

"She's losing ground."

Forty-five minutes later the president's four personal aides were standing in front of his desk in the Oval Office. Hartridge was pale and his eyes were restless, never fixing on anyone or anything, always looking somewhere else, somewhere new for solutions, even for the hope of solutions.

"We did the computerized study, sir." Edward Sneed kept the file under his arm; he wouldn't give it to the president unless he asked for it; the huge desk already was filled—you could say cluttered—with papers.

Hartridge let his red eyes rest for a moment on Sneed's, hoping for a solution there. "Tell me."

"We put everything in, Mr. President: the state of the nation's health, the state of the essential services—medical, police, fire fighting, water supply, energy supply, communications—and the increasing pressure from the World Health Organization and the health authorities of major countries. Also the effect of your decision on your rating in the primaries next—"

"For God's sake, forget the primaries. This whole thing's blown my chances to hell."

Sneed hesitated, then went on as though Hartridge hadn't spoken. Standing nearby, Bruce Paget thought the president was right. The time was over for false comfort, anywhere, for anyone.

"Sir, we put in just everything we could think of as being

directly relative—especially the political climate internationally vis à vis this crisis and the way you're handling it, the way we're seen by our allies. We—"

"The main thing," the man at the desk cut in wearily, "is to stop people dying."

"Yes, sir, we understand that. We gave the direct impact on health—" he gave a slight shrug "—survival, our maximum attention." He hesitated again, then said: "The computerized recommendation is very strongly in favor of closing the docks, shutting down all air traffic, and putting the United States under conditions of total isolation."

In the silence, Bruce Paget was aware of the sunlight that had come to lie across the floor from the tall windows; filtered by a high cloud-layer, it was so pale as to have an ashen quality, like moonlight, as if day and night had lost their orderly sequence, leaving them all in limbo.

"You mean," the president said heavily, wanting to get it right, "we should seal off the country from the rest of the world?"

"Yes, sir. Totally."

In a moment Hartridge said heavily, "Very well. I'll sign the necessary orders."

CHAPTER TWENTY-SIX

Toward midnight a wind rose from the north, and the headlight beams of the five military vehicles thrust their light through the blowing dust, so that it looked like a sandstorm. No one in this region saw it; here on the bleak tundra the nearest habitation was more than a hundred miles away in any direction. The convoy was as isolated as if it had been exploring an alien and lifeless planet.

Vladimir Dobrynin had come to terms with his fate. When they had reached Chelyabinsk, by road, and loaded the ten squat cylinders onto a wagon of the Trans-Siberian Railway train, eight days ago, he had been determined somehow to leave the convoy and make his way back to Moscow, pretending illness or a nervous breakdown, and regain his home without compromising the safety of his wife and children—as poor Lopatkin had done. But each time he'd brought himself to the point of putting his plan into action, his courage had failed him. If it hadn't been for his family, he would have simply left the four Red Army officers of the guard and disappeared into the night and into infinity, perhaps changing his identity and taking up a new life somewhere as a peasant. But he was a man of responsibility, and he couldn't bring himself to abandon those he loved.

From Chelyabinsk the great train had rolled eastward, and as he exercised himself by striding up and down the long freight wagon and jumping on the spot for precisely timed periods, he came to realize that his responsibilities were owed also to the state, which fed, clothed and protected his own and his family's welfare. If the state had decided that he should play his part in this secret and marathon journey across the breadth of Mother Russia, then he shouldn't question it. By the time the train had rumbled into the city of Omsk, he had managed to rid himself of the major part of his guilt. This was not to say that he was cheerful again, or confident in his knowledge that he was performing a patriotic act on behalf of all his countrymen; but he was now able to relax a little more, and see himself as a pawn in the service of the greatest chess masters in the world: the leaders of the Communist Party, an organization which surely held the future of the human species in its strong and steady hands.

Through Novosibirsk and through Krasnoyarsk the great train had rolled, its steel wheels alternately shining in the harsh glare of the sun and vanishing into the shadows of night. On the eastern side of Krasnoyarsk, north of the Sayan Mountains, the freight car containing the secret consignment had been switched onto a branch line and hooked up between two other wagons where more guards were taken on board. The cylinders of the L-9 material could not, as Dobrynin knew, be entrusted to an aircraft for this long, seven thousand kilometer journey toward the Pacific coast; an aircraft could crash, because of mechanical breakdown, human error or weather conditions, and whereas the loss of life in a jet airliner would be restricted to a hundred souls or so, the L-9 material, escaping from containers splitting under impact, could extinguish all human life on earth.

During the journey, Vladimir Dobrynin had eaten, slept, exercised, played chess with the army guards and read the newspapers they had taken on board at stations along the way. He had also found himself, despite these mundane activities, tending to lose his reason—in terms of linear left-brain functioning —as the hours and the days and the kilometers took him farther and farther away from his familiar world and into these desolate regions. Increasingly disoriented, he became subject to fantasies, finding symbolism in everyday events and in the long journey itself. He came to see the movement of the great train as the inexorable fate of humankind rolling through the light and shade of day and night toward its destiny, where all would at last be known, and too late.

At some of the railway stations the newspapers they picked up had carried news of an epidemic that had started in America, announced as pneumonic plague and later as pneumonic drug-resistant plague, as it took hold from city to city. As a biologist, and privy to the contents of the ten cylinders he was helping to guard, Dobrynin sensed a connection between the American epidemic and the journeying of the secret L-9 material from west to east across the face of Russia; for several nights he had lain sleepless, rocking to the motion of the wheels, striving to understand the implications, then finally giving it up. There were events afoot of which he could have no cognizance; events, he was now quite certain, whose significance would have sent him mad to contemplate.

In the early hours of the morning the railway journey ended in the small village of Novyy Onega, where the cylinders of L-9 material were transferred to a military armored car and escorted two hundred and five kilometers along the dirt road eastward, arriving just before dawn at the isolated huddle of buildings known as the Camp.

Dobrynin and the guard were greeted by General Ivan Goldin, in full uniform: the news of the arriving convoy had reached him by radio.

"Everything is in order?"

They stood in a weary group outside the operations room as the ten cylinders were unloaded from the armored car in the glare of floodlights.

"Everything," Dobrynin answered. "Everything is in order." He was aware of the airstrip that stretched in the moonlight across the tundra, with its pattern of lamps at this moment unlighted. He was aware that the consignment he had escorted over a distance of seven thousand kilometers was now less than fifteen hundred kilometers from the North American continent.

"Come along," General Goldin told him briskly. "I'll take you to your quarters. You must be hungry!"

Dobrynin followed him. "No," he said, though he'd not eaten for almost twelve hours, and felt that he would ever wish to eat again.

CHAPTER TWENTY-SEVEN

The cat moved again.

Clay noted it, that was all. The first time it had moved on the top of the wall he'd swung his body half-round to face it, thinking it was something dangerous. His nerves were not good tonight.

He had only done it twice before in his life, once in London on a freezing winter's day when the frost was thick on the roofs and the buses had stopped running because of ice on the streets; he could still hear the sharp explosion of glass below him, always below him, as the man had gone through the huge skylight over the ballroom of the hotel; he could still hear, sometimes, waking at night alone in a room, the man's breath catching when he'd realized what was going to happen to him. The second time was in Tunis five years ago, a desperate scuffle in the corner of the Casbah, the glimpse of a dark bared throat, the feel of rough rope and the jerk of the knot as the recorded voice of the muezzin came tinnily from the speakers on the mosque, calling the evening prayer.

Nothing very scientific in either case, but effective, that was the thing. But he always hated it. Hated them, hated himself, hated the bastards who made him do it.

Would Ashton Major have hated it?

Of course not, he'd have taken it in his stride.

The alley ran for some fifty meters, partly under trees. From where Clay stood to the far end there were seven trash cans, with rats moving among them; from here to the nearer end there were three. It was the rats that had caught the cat's interest, of course; it was watching them, sometimes producing that strange dry whickering sound in its throat; but it didn't seem to have the guts to come down off the wall and catch one; they were big bastards, their claws making a din as they ran up the sides of the bins and perched on the rim to get their balance, their long dark tails hanging.

There was moonlight tonight. Six months ago he'd told those idiots in London that the moonlight was going to be dangerous. Tonight he needed it.

Soon after nine o'clock the meeting in the timber-built hall began breaking up. He'd been briefed that it was some sort of KGB public whitewashing stunt, an attempt ordered by the more liberal Vladychenko to assure the good citizens that the *Komitet* really was their friendly big brother and would rock them to sleep at night providing they didn't actually try thinking for themselves. People began coming past him, a few yards away from where he stood in the deep shadow of the wall. KGB Captain Stukalin's small gray Moskovich was parked at the far end of the alley; Clay had been shown it by the agent an hour ago. Stukalin would pass the point where Clay was standing: the nearest alternate route back to the car was three times as long.

More people came past, most of them men, the harsh smell of their black tobacco hanging on the still night air. The agent had not come by. Clay would recognize him easily enough; he'd met him three times and there'd be no need for a sign.

Clay stood bathed in his own sweat and his mouth was like a husk. He felt the movement of the night air through his nostrils, the touch of the black motorcyclist's jacket on his skin, the beating of the pulse in his neck; it hadn't felt like this, before— there'd only been the guilt feelings afterward. This time he was questioning himself, questioning the need for the act, before it was done. A good sign, for humanitarian reasons. But this wasn't a night for humanitarians to be abroad; they'd be disappointed.

His nerves jerked as three more men came past the wall and he recognized the agent; he was walking alone, directly behind a thin, square-faced man in plain clothes with his hands swinging by his sides like hooks at the ends of his sleeves, not your typical KGB man with his starch-fed pallor and his heavy-footed walk; Stukalin looked more like an athlete, bouncing a little on his feet and making more headway than the others near him; the agent, wanting to keep up, was having to increase his pace by the time Clay moved from the shadow of the wall and followed.

So here we are then, we have the target in our sights and now it's a question of time. Everything has gone well: the encounter point was successfully worked out and we are met, my friend, by moonlight, and bent to our fell purposes. It is now up to me, to the rushing of this blood and the quickness of these hands and the effectiveness, the ultimate and lethal effectiveness, of the strike. What else is there to inform the moment? Conscience, perhaps. True, nobody as high as Terebilov would have been coming across the frontier without news of the most dire importance, news that would affect the world's millions who labor under the illusion of peace in our time and the brotherhood of man and similar bullshit. So this one minor cog in the machinery must rip out that other minor cog from the works— that one along there with the bouncing walk, Stukalin—in order to protect his fellow men from the machinations of the warlords. So, looking at it like that, my good friend, we are here tonight upon a mission of ultimate good, providing the means by which, perhaps, in some magical and mysterious way at superpower level, peace in our time might become a degree less illusory, and our children's children might stand a chance of dying in reasonable decency with their eyes unclouded by nuclear dust.

Three of the men turned right and took the road alongside the parking lot, leaving the agent moving between the lines of the cars and Stukalin behind him. A clear field now.

But the conscience of man, my friend, is easily comforted.

To kill without guilt he needs only the name of some god to brandish in the face of history: Buddha, Christ, Lenin, take your pick, it'll get you out of the trenches or into the missile post quick as a dose of salts and then bang-bang and you're dead and you can get away with it as easily as you did when you were a kid with a toy pistol. And when there are thousands doing it with you, how can you be wrong? That's the greatest god of them all. The crowd.

The agent was peeling off now, veering to the next aisle between the vehicles and jingling some keys. He knew Clay had noted the target; he knew Clay had earlier been shown the small gray Moskovich that was parked five from the end of this row here. Everything was going well.

When I left him, everything was going well.

But it's the personal confrontation, my friend, that finds the conscience naked. With no god to seek comfort in, with no crowd to carry you along, it's not so easy. Man on earth has never, you see, been able to order his life without gods and crowds; it would mean thinking for himself, and acting for himself, *and answering for himself* when the chips are down and the deed's done and they ask *who did this?* and being able to tell them, *I did, and if you don't like it you can fuck off.*

Not easy.

The thin man, Stukalin, was not getting his keys out. The small gray Moskovich had the license plate and insignia of an official KGB vehicle, and it wasn't necessary ever to lock it. He was pulling open the door as Clay went past and stopped, coming back a few steps.

"Stukalin?"

The man looked up. "Yes?"

"Fedorov. We were at the rifle school together. Are you going anywhere near the Novodevichy cemetery?"

"Close. Get in."

"You're doing well," Clay said as he dropped into the worn upholstery. "I have reports."

An effective officer, the briefing had said, *and ambitious. He*

*looks for special jobs, and likes praise. He respects rank, so throw
it. But watch his physique; he leads the gymnastic team at No.
5 Moscow Unit Barracks.*

Oil fumes blew from the bulkhead as the little engine raced.
Stukalin drove fast, advertising his expertise. "I agree," he said
above the noise of the car. "Our patrols would have an easier
time if the citizens trusted them more. Not that I'm in patrol
work, of course."

"I know. Officers of your caliber should never be in patrol
work; I'm always making recommendations."

"If you were at the rifle school with me, you've done pretty
well yourself."

"I'm like you—I work at it. Tread on a few necks!" He laughed
suddenly, and Stukalin made a point of joining in.

A mile from the cemetery he asked: "Where do you live? I'll
drop you there."

"Good of you. Two blocks down from here."

Passing the cemetery, Clay saw that the east gates were standing wide open; they would be closed, according to his briefing,
at ten o'clock, in forty-five minutes from now. He'd have to
hurry.

"There's a side street just here, Stukalin. You can drop me
halfway along, and I'll go across the yard."

"Right you are, comrade." It wasn't the usual term of address
in the contiguous ranks of the *Komitet,* and Clay caught the
shade of meaning. The man still couldn't place him, and wanted
to. Being ambitious, he also wanted to know if this Fedorov
could be useful to him later: which office did he work in? Was
he in administration?

The small car slowed.

"This will do fine," Clay told him.

"Fedorov," the KGB man said, "I remember the name, of
course, at the rifle school." He let the clutch out and pushed
the gear lever into neutral. "Would it now be *Captain* Fedorov,
or . . .?"

"That's right," Clay said and half turned in his seat and brought his right arm across in a ridge-hand strike to the man's throat with the force of all the fear in him that if he didn't get it right first time, this night would be lost and this death his; with the force of all the rage in him that to bring peace you still had to bring death because man was a mad monkey and would never learn better ways, with all the strength in him that had been building up in his muscles as the adrenalin had flooded into them during the short ride from the rendezvous.

He remembered, driving back and turning left and going through the tall iron gates of the Novodevichy cemetery, the way the man's hands had come off the steering wheel, the thin fingers opening instinctively to make a shield and then to make weapons as the signal had hit the motor nerves directly through the parasympathetic system, bypassing the cortex and shocking him into the defense mode in less than a second and much too late to do anything about a strike that was professional, powerful and accurate.

And Clay remembered the feel of the man's throat against his ridge-hand as the cartilage had been smashed inward and the force had driven its way through the fragile tissue of the thyroid area and sent blood flooding into the windpipe, blocking it.

He remembered these things because they would be a part of the guilt process during the coming days, the coming weeks and months; they would furnish his nightmares with the requisite phantasmagoria for the torment of his soul, until the day came, if ever it were to come, when he could look back and think, oh yes, that was the job I did in Moscow, in the name of peace on earth.

The cemetery was vast, and he drove the little gray Moskovich along the iron railings and the line of trees on the west side, passing the locked hut—*useless for cover*, the briefing had warned him—and the tall gravestones beyond. The open grave was near the center, with a pile of earth along each side and two spades leaning at one end.

Switching off the engine, he waited, moving his head to watch the environment, covering every degree and seeing no movement anywhere; traffic ran past the railings a long way off, some of it passing the entrance gates on the south side, some throwing light in the tunnel below the railway embankment; in the distance the lights of the Luzhnik Sport Palace were reflected in the river.

Stukalin was not heavy.

The grave, the briefing had said, *will have been deepened by two feet, to leave the normal room for the coffin. Remember to flatten the surface. The burial is for tomorrow morning, and someone will be there to see that all is well.*

Clay took the man's gun and his papers, dropping him in and using one of the spades, trying hard to recall the girl in the Roman nightclub he'd met last year, the most memorable girl he could think of, so that thoughts of her would keep away thoughts of this; he remembered her body, and the way it had moved, but her face had vanished, and all he could see was a skull.

Driving away through the little park and past the convent, he reached the gates and turned into the traffic stream with a strange and overwhelming sense of personal loss.

CHAPTER TWENTY-EIGHT

O n October 29—four days after the presidential order to seal off the United States from the rest of the world—a Japanese long-distance bomber approached the Californian coast at cruising speed and lowered toward Los Angeles. Just before noon it was given clearance by the US Air Force to overfly LAX at one thousand feet altitude.

Minutes later the first consignment of pure antibiotics from overseas was dragging from its parachute along Runway 5 under a fourteen mile per hour wind. The bomber signaled the tower and gained height, turning westward across the Pacific.

On the evening of the same day, at 6:05 New York time, the first consignment of drugs from Europe was parachuted onto the tarmac at Kennedy, under a light drizzle.

The following day, seventeen further consignments of streptomycin, tetracycline, chloramphenicol, and sulfadiazine, destined for abortive and prophylactic therapy in the critically depleted hospitals and emergency clinics across the country, arrived from Britain, France, Italy, Spain, the Netherlands and Soviet Russia, whose manufacturing plants had been working a twenty-four-hour schedule for the past three days to make up the loss as the medical centers ran short of the live-saving and life-protecting drugs that had so far kept the nationwide death rate down to one hundred fifty thousand.

Worldwide to date, one hundred and thirteen cases of pneumonic plague had been reported outside the United States. Most of these had been traced directly to travel movement from that country. All had been successfully treated with pure antibiotics, and no fatality had occurred.

Meantime the superfast military jets continued to approach the American continent from Europe and the Far East to drop their loads of freely donated yet priceless drugs and swing away again over the ocean.

Nationwide the figures of new cases were lowering into the hundreds day by day; fatalities were now declining as the new supplies of drugs reached the medical centers and the hypodermic needles.

"It's like hitting a burning house with fire hoses," Dr. Ron Voss said to a nurse at George Washington University Hospital. "Sooner or later it has to go out."

The nurse stood in the doorway, gowned, masked and wearing goggles against the risk of conjunctival contagion of Y. *pestis*. She raised a gloved thumb as a question.

In the bed below the narrow window, Nadia Fedotova gave a slow nod. The nurse went on her rounds.

"There's a stage," Dr. Voss had told the patient two days ago, "when the progress of the disease reaches a point where the antibiotics are going to have a real hard fight to combat its effects, and more importantly, where the patient's own body will have a real hard fight to repair the damage and restore order." Nadia had watched his pale, lined face, his eyes shrunken with the strain of long hours, long days, long weeks. But she watched mostly his dogged smile. "You've now reached that stage, little ballerina, so it's easier for you. All you have to do now is fight, and go on fighting, so that soon you can dance again, and go on dancing."

But she had decided not to do that. She had been lying here all this time trying to see a way out of the things that would happen if she went on living; and there was no way out. If she confessed to Bruce what she had been doing, and told Nikolay

Tarasov that she would help him no longer, Tarasov would report it to the *Komitet* in Moscow, and her mother and her sister would have to leave their new four-room apartment and be sent to a workers' district again and live as they had been made to live before, with their friends and their neighbors turning their faces away in the street and talking about them in whispers meant to be heard . . . *They are the mother and the sister of Fedotova, the notorious defector. It is said they goaded her into it. Don't speak to them.*

And if she agreed to go on helping Nikolay Tarasov, she would have to go on loving Bruce with a lie in her heart, betraying him, leading him closer and closer to the time when he would find out anyway, and be found out to have endangered his country. It would be very bad for him then.

The nurse came to the doorway again, saying through the gauze mask, "Feeling okay, honey?"

"Yes, thank you. I am feeling okay."

"You want anything, you just have to ping the bell."

"Yes."

The only way out she could see was if Nikolay Tarasov were to catch the disease and die of it, like so many people were doing. But she wished that for no one. Even to hope for it, as a way out for herself, might be in some way to bring it about. That would be a terrible thing. It would free her at last, and she could go on loving Bruce, and her mother and her sister could go on living in a nice place and with their friends around them. But it would still be a terrible thing, and she must not wish harm to Tarasov.

The next day was not good for Nadia. She knew, with the mystical ability of the body to know itself, that because she had refused to fight, and go on fighting, as the doctor had told her, she was now beyond the point of return to life. There was at first a fearfulness in this, and then, as the day drew out toward its end, a sense of peace, for this was the way out, and she had chosen it for herself. And she would die here in this country;

she would die free. Many people in America did not understand this, how important it was, because they did not question it. But she understood.

In the evening the nurse came, the one with the ginger hair who would stay most of the night.

"How're you doing, Nadia?"

"Very well, thank you."

The nurse checked the IV drip and took her temperature, then reached into a pocket and dropped an envelope onto the bed. "It was at the desk for you, honey."

"Thank you."

When the nurse went out of the room, Nadia opened the envelope and took out the single sheet of paper. The handwriting was very shaky, but it was in Russian, so she could make out more easily what it said.

Whatever else happened, I always admired you as a dancer, and always will. Your art, as an expression of life, is more important than life, do you not agree? Therein lies immortality. N.L.T.

When the nurse came in again, Nadia said: "The message was from a Mr. Tarasov. Did he leave it at the desk himself?"

"I'll go check when I can, honey, if it's important."

"Yes, it is important."

It was half an hour before the nurse could come back to her. "He didn't leave it himself, honey. It came through from Men's Isolation in B Wing."

Nadia moved her head on the pillow, to watch her. "He is in this hospital?"

"He—uh—well, yes. But he passed away just a little while back. Sorry about that. Was he a friend of yours?"

For the past two weeks the White House had been turned into what looked like a hostel for transients. President Hartridge's staff, from his personal aides down to his bodyguards, had been confined to the building and the grounds, and those in his immediate entourage had been permitted to bring their families into the White House as temporary guests. A schoolroom had been set up on the ground floor for the nineteen children involved; they were of course delighted, and busy preparing for their return to those lesser mortals who had once been their friends, with impressive stories of My Life at the White House.

Laura had been offered a small office near her husband's where she could sleep; the hours he was kept working made it impossible for them to share a bed—he would be constantly disturbing her, or vice versa. But they managed to keep up a semblance of normal married life, and felt closer to each other—until the phone call came from Georgetown University Hospital—in the midst of their common crisis, as most families did.

Laura was in the room when Bruce took the call, and knew immediately what had happened. They had both been expecting it, but hadn't talked about it; after twenty years together they caught vibrations easily enough.

But Laura felt that something should now be said. She couldn't leave him to deal with this thing in silence.

"I'm sorry," she said, and lit a cigarette.

He came away from the telephone. "Are you?"

"Of course." Their voices were very quiet. "I don't say things I don't really—"

"I know," he said quickly. "I just didn't expect you to feel sorry."

She shrugged. "For you. For her." She picked a shred of tobacco from her lip. "It's going on all the time, right? But I know that doesn't help." Watching the naked grief on his face she wanted to go to him and hold him as she once could have done; now she could only want to, but not do it. A man had to grow up some time, and one of the ways to do it was to let him handle, alone, the heartbreak of a broken toy.

"It's . . . good of you," Bruce said in a moment, "to take it this way."

"Probably." She went to the window and folded her arms,

looking across the expanse of the White House lawns. "Especially since I know perfectly well that you'd rather it had been me."

Her gaze was attracted to the flash of the late sunlight across the traffic on Pennsylvania Avenue, and her thoughts came back to this room only when she heard that behind her, Bruce was quietly crying.

She turned, impressed. So this had been a very expensive toy. Then as he spoke, she realized he was crying because of something entirely different.

"I'm going to spend the rest of my life," he said with his voice shaking, "trying to make you know that what you just said isn't true."

She watched him, interested.

"Okay," she said. "Good luck."

CHAPTER TWENTY-NINE

I don't think you can do it," Blanes said.

Clay didn't answer. Wouldn't answer.

"Have you talked to the chief?" Blanes asked him.

"No." It was no good talking to Braithwaite.

"Then I should do that."

"He'd try to put me off."

"Exactly."

"That's why I'm not going to talk to him."

Blanes picked up a paper clip and opened it out and spun it like a propeller. His eyes were moody. He'd been awake most of the night trying to judge where his responsibilities lay: to the chief, to this idiot here, to himself. He probably wouldn't get more than a bit of flak if Clay came unstuck; but it wouldn't be pleasant walking around the embassy with people knowing one of his agents had got himself killed—you were automatically to blame for bad briefing, bad organization, bad planning.

Braithwaite would know it wasn't his fault. Braithwaite knew what Clay was like. Impetuous, mission crazy, with no mercy on himself. Blanes looked up, straight at Clay, at Clay's hungry-looking, hollowed face (you could never look into his eyes—they were never there). What else did they know about Clay? What was there, inside that narrow, tilted skull, that they ought to know about before they told him yes, he could do what he wanted to do? What manner of rage, what vanity, what urgent need to push himself beyond the point where he could hope to survive was going on inside that damned skull of his, clamoring for gratification?

When Blanes had been told that Charles Clay was going to be attached to this station for mission availability, he'd said, "*Oh my God, what have I done to deserve this?*" The man was a bloody neurotic.

And brilliant. That was the problem.

"I think it's suicide," he told Clay.

"I know you do. It's just that you underestimate my capabilities." The narrow head swung toward Blanes and away again before Blanes could glimpse his eyes.

"Look, you screwed—" and Blanes stopped right there.

The head swung again. "What?"

Blanes didn't answer. Clay had screwed up the frontier thing and he'd screwed up the Talyzin thing and now he was going to screw this up. But it was no good telling him that. What Clay was after was redemption. To prove he could pull this thing off. To prove he wasn't finished.

"What were you going to say?" Clay asked him, moving a step toward him.

"You know what I was going to say."

Clay shrugged, looking down. "Yes. Well you're wrong."

Blanes thought for a minute and then went across to a cupboard on the wall and opened it and slid back a panel and turned a dial to the left and right a few times and opened the safe and took out a very small box with a number on it. He shut the safe and crossed to the desk and put the box onto it close to where Clay was standing. He never liked actually handing these things to people.

"Your instructions," he said, "are to use one of those if there's the slightest possibility of being caught. Are you willing to do that?"

Clay picked up the box and put it away. "There won't be any need."

"But are you willing to do it, if you're wrong?" Blanes sounded insistent.

"Of course I am."

"All right. You can sign the form as you go out. See Jenkins."

Clay started to say something, then stopped, and then just said, "Thank you," with a strange note of humility. Hearing it, Blanes felt himself as strangely moved. He was probably sending this stupid bastard to his death; he didn't want any thanks.

"There was another man like you," he told Clay reflectively, "about a couple of years ago, just after I'd taken charge of the station. He went off on some lunatic lark, too. He was found shot to bits in a sewer."

A stillness came into Clay, and when Blanes looked up at him he found himself staring right into those blind-looking eyes. "What was his name?" Clay asked him softly.

"I don't remember."

"Of course you remember."

"Have it your way." Clay knew perfectly well they didn't pass names around this place.

When Clay spoke again it was almost inaudible. "Was his name Ashton?"

"I tell you, I don't remember." He turned away. "Now go and sign that bloody form, and for Christ's sake try and look after yourself."

Chairman Mikhail Rudenko received Boytsov and Koslev in his office in the Council of Ministers Building inside the Kremlin walls, just before the hour of noon.

"Now we can proceed," he told them.

Viktor Koslev nodded. He'd been expecting this. The news had come half an hour earlier, that President Hartridge had decided to yield to world pressure and place the United States into immediate isolation.

Sharaf Boytsov said nothing. He was sitting in the black leather-upholstered chair with its back to the windows, his eyes in shadow. Unknown to his colleagues, a sensation was creeping into his body that he'd never known before. It was like the onset of paralysis; already he knew that he couldn't move his hands; soon his arms would be rigid, and his legs. The feeling wasn't moving, however, like a wave, from the hands to the arms to the shoulders; it was starting in the most sensitive areas: his heart was hammering inside his rib cage like a mad drummer; his tongue, he knew, would be useless if he tried to speak; his scrotum was shrinking, and so tightly that his testicles ached, constricted. This was nothing like the pain he normally felt, had normally been feeling for the past five months—the relentless cramping of his stomach as the acids seeped into it and burned there, despite everything Dr. Strautmanis could do. This was different. And it was frightening.

"I have given the necessary instructions," Rudenko told them. "As soon as it is announced officially that the United States is sealed off, I shall send the final order for those instructions to be carried out. That should be within the hour."

Viktor Koslev, sitting upright on the chair nearer Rudenko's huge redwood desk, nodded again. "Very well." He felt someone should say something. Yet he knew that in history's most momentous times, there was little, ever, to be said; words proved too fragile to carry the weight of great purposes. Here again, at this momentous time, there was nothing really to be said. The banks of computers had been spilling out the same answers for days now, no matter in which new form he had framed the questions. Operation *Springboard* was ready to go, and should achieve success.

The computers could not be wrong. Sometimes, when Viktor Koslev found himself assailed by doubts—not of fact or figures, but of the broader view in terms of the human heart—he had sought the clear and pristine reasoning of his machines, and was reassured.

"I invited you here this morning, my comrades," Rudenko told them heavily, "to inform you that I gave these final and irrevocable instructions without consulting you. I knew that you would concur, of course, and I wished to assume full responsibility for the consequences." He paced the parquet floor as he spoke to them, his dark, London-tailored suit immaculate, his gold cuff links glinting at his wrists, his polished shoes reflecting the light from the windows. He paced, thought Koslev, with the precision of a metronome; and Koslev was again reassured. Comrade Rudenko seemed fully capable of taking the responsibility of the megadeath he was to bring upon the world. It would have broken lesser men.

"It will remain for you," Rudenko continued, his tone sonorous in the high-ceilinged chamber, "in return for the prodigious labors you have undertaken for so many months, to share with me the ultimate . . . rewards." He had been on the point of saying "victory," but then it wouldn't really be that. There had been no battle, and no question of defeat. There had simply been the need for the courage to stand back, far back, and achieve the perspective of a visionary, to see man's place in the universe as a sacred estate, of which he had appointed himself custodian.

"Reward."

Rudenko and Koslev turned their heads to look at their comrade, Boytsov. It was he who had spoken, and in so strange a tone.

"Our reward, Sharaf, yes," Rudenko said. The man didn't look well. He was sitting as if clamped to his chair, his hands rigid along its arms.

Sharaf Boytsov stared up at the chairman of the council of ministers as if he'd never seen him before. Or more accurately, perhaps, as if he were seeing him for the first time—which, when you worked it out, wasn't quite the same thing. His good friend and comrade Mikhail Rudenko looked taller than usual, standing over the black leather chair, his thick shoulders hunched in their dark suit, like a perched vulture's, his sharp head tilted down to watch Boytsov with a gaze that would have sent a shiver through him if he'd not felt so paralyzed.

Two hundred million people.

Reward.

I have given these final and irrevocable instructions.

It wasn't only Boytsov's body that was suddenly under this gigantic pressure. His mind was struggling to put meaning to words he'd always thought familiar and comprehensible, and every time he managed to find the meaning again he found also that he couldn't put the words together, to make any sense.

I have given these final and irrevocable instructions, and our reward will be the death of two hundred million people.

But that couldn't be right. It couldn't mean that.

"Is it the stomach?"

More words, just as incomprehensible. Stomach? Food. Now what on earth did that mean?

Watching the huge man with the vulture's shape looming over him, Boytsov tried to shrink back into his chair, but nothing happened. His whole body was rigid now, and only his mind could move, as it spun and tilted and bumped against the inside of his rigid skull, terrified, desperate to escape. Because he knew what was happening now. They'd all gone mad, completely mad. They'd been planning this appalling act of mass murder for months now, without actually acknowledging the fact that they'd never really carry it out. It hadn't needed saying. They'd just been thinking what a splendid idea it would be to end once and for all this stupid and costly and never ending hostility between East and West, because nobody was sitting down at the table to talk anymore, and the arms race was spiraling upward into the very heights of insanity, and no one had a single clue as to what could be done about it. So it had seemed such a very good idea, because *any* idea that would get the world out of *that* kind of mess would seem quite splendid.

But we can't really do it.

He waited for someone to answer him, and when they didn't, he realized they probably hadn't heard. He'd said it only in his mind, because in his mind, as it raced and bumped around inside his petrified skull, was the perfectly clear understanding that if he told Rudenko they couldn't really do it, he'd get himself shot.

It had been going on for weeks now. He'd started keeping a count, then had given up, but it was fifteen or twenty, shot against the wall in Lubyanka, blindfolded and with the urine streaming down their trousers as the bullets had gone slamming into their ribs and tearing their hearts out, three of them full ministers, four of them chairmen of councils, unbelievable, and Vladychenko, Dmitri Vladychenko, president of the Presidium of the Supreme Soviet, now suffering such a degree of indisposition that he hadn't shown himself in public for the past ten days. Dr. Strautmanis said his spleen was infected, but that sounded too simple.

What was happening to everyone?

"No," Boytsov said aloud. "Yes." He'd got a grasp on what Mikhail had meant when he'd asked, "Is it the stomach?" And the answer of course was no, it wasn't the stomach this time, but on reflection, and taking into consideration the number of people getting shot every week for saying something wrong, the answer was indeed yes, it was the stomach, because Mikhail knew about the ulcer, and wouldn't want to shoot him for having it.

Koslev was exchanging glances with Rudenko. Boytsov didn't look at all well.

Boytsov knew what was going on. They were finding him rather peculiar this morning. He could feel it himself as the terror raced around in his head screaming to be let out. This sensation had come over him to a lesser degree before, but he'd been able to calm himself by calling Mikhail on the telephone and making some acceptable excuse and listening to that resonant, measured voice until he felt reassured. He had also gone to see Viktor Koslev at such times, like a sailor who, seeing from the rail that the ship was driving head on into raging seas, would go up to the bridge and be informed that all was well, they were still on course and had good steam up, not to worry.

This morning, reassurance was not within reach. Boytsov could not move, could barely speak. He may have heard of catalepsy, familiar to the rabbit in the headlights and to the apprentice steeplejack who for the first time looks down from a height, but it did not occur to him that this was his problem. He simply knew that everyone had gone mad, and that he must be very careful if he wanted to survive these calamitous times.

"My stomach," he said, stuttering over it but finally getting a fairly normal tone in his voice. "I'm afraid it's playing me up. I didn't mean to interrupt, Mikhail."

Half an hour later Chairman Rudenko was sitting behind the desk of President of the Presidium of the Supreme Soviet Vladychenko, on the lower floor of the Council of Ministers Building.

Vladychenko himself had suggested that until his condition improved, Rudenko should take over his office, subject of course to the support and advice of his other ministers. A secretary had been installed in Rudenko's own office to redirect essential calls. The telephone he was expecting to ring at any moment now was the red one at the end of the row of the eighteenth-century rosewood desk, known popularly the world over as the hotline. He had requested of President Hartridge through the Soviet ambassador in Washington that official word be passed over this specially protected line when the United States of America had completed its emergency plans to isolate the country by the suspension of all traffic. Rudenko had put it to his ambassador that he felt the president would consider this a reasonable and essential provision against confusion and misunderstanding at a time when world fears of conflict were unfortunately rife.

Rudenko was at this moment watching the big-screen television set at one end of the room. Everything seemed to be going according to plan.

Just ten minutes ago, the young woman announcer was say-

ing, *Kennedy International Airport in New York was shut down
to all except urgent or official traffic. Units of the National
Guard have taken up their positions there to ensure compliance
with these wide-sweeping orders stemming directly from the
White House.*

Standing beside Chairman Rudenko, an interpreter was giving him the translation as he watched the scenes at Kennedy
and, moments later, at Los Angeles, Washington and Chicago
as the young American woman read the electronically printed
bulletin above the cameras. *We have just received a news flash
that an airliner out of Rio de Janeiro, whose captain appeared
unacquainted with the orders in force, has just been diverted
from its approach path as it tried to land at Washington National Airport. The captain has been instructed to land at Nas-
sau, in the Bahamas. There have been many instances of this
kind of confusion during the past three hours, since the directive
from the president has taken the complex network of flight control stations across the country unawares.*

Everything was going according to plan. Here in Moscow,
Rudenko had been obliged to silence dissonant voices within
the Kremlin, but this had offered little difficulty. Marshal of the
Red Army Boris Ivanovich Klauson, that obstinate fool with his
medals and his General MacArthur sunglasses, had made a
token showing of insubordination an hour ago, complaining
that he and his beloved soldiers were being given the role of
garbage collectors across the American continent, once the second and final epidemic had run its course. But Rudenko had
not, this time, left his attitude unclear.

"You know the work that will have to be done over there,
Klauson. You know how to do it, how to amass your forces, to
detail their units, to pass your orders throughout the infrastruc-
ture of the army in the most effective way and with the most
dispatch—which, I need hardly tell you, is the essence of the
operation. If at this time, however, you feel that the task—that
any task—demanded of you by the motherland is in any sense

demeaning, you will please inform me now, before you leave this room, whether or not I can count on you in this critical hour."

"Comrade Chairman, you must please try to understand my—"

Rudenko had lifted his hand. "Let me remind you, finally, Comrade Marshal, that I have at my immediate disposal a corps of younger, stronger and infinitely more dedicated officers, should your answer prove unsatisfactory."

Of course the man hadn't a choice. He'd known that if he'd said no, he wouldn't have been dismissed from his post; he would have been shot.

Last evening a Japanese freighter, adrift in heavy seas off the Californian coast, was told that the Coast Guard would escort it into San Francisco if the captain wished to dock his vessel there, but that no one on board would be permitted to leave the United States until the period of isolation and eventual quarantine is over. Meanwhile, here is an update of those airports now closed to international traffic. Anchorage International . . . San Diego International . . . New Orleans International . . . Newark International . . .

Twenty minutes later, after Chairman Rudenko had dealt with five essential telephone calls from within the Kremlin and signed the third batch of special measures to be brought to him this morning, he interrupted his work to watch an attractive young black woman reading from the bulletin on the television screen, while the interpreter translated.

It's been announced that the White House is expected to declare the final sealing-off of the United States from the rest of the world in a few minutes from now. Please stand by.

Mikhail Konstantinovich Rudenko, chairman of the council of ministers, got to his feet and moved around the end of the massive rosewood desk, to stand watching the television screen, his feet together and his arms hanging by his sides, aware of a godlike potency within him as he awaited the news that the world was now delivered into his hands.

CHAPTER THIRTY

Earlier this morning, when Chairman Rudenko had still been asleep, a Tupolev TU-26 long-range medium bomber of the Red Air Force had lifted from the military base twenty kilometers from Moscow and turned eastward, climbing to twelve thousand meters and settling into its operational cruising speed of fifteen hundred kilometers per hour above the cloud layers of Siberia.

Captain Aleksandr Kokarev, a KGB officer on special assignment, had taken his seat at the rear of the compartment, which had been converted to passenger carrying more than a year ago to accommodate high officials on their discreet journeys across the face of Russia, offering them a transit speed of Mach 1.5 and a protective armament of remote controlled 23mm cannon and wing-mounted missiles.

No one had questioned the KGB officer's presence; he had of course shown his identity card to the captain of the aircraft before takeoff. He was replacing Captain Veniamin Stukalin on this flight and would assume normal duties. These included checking every other passenger for his credentials and letters of authority, watching over their behavior and reporting the slightest irregularity to his superiors in Moscow over the flight deck radio.

Charles Clay had done this once before, on his third mission in Soviet Russia, impersonating for a matter of twenty-four hours a KGB interpreter-agent during the visit to Moscow of former President Richard Nixon. He had learned one of the flaws inherent in a security system whose omnipotence was without question: even a KGB officer of street rank commanded respect and obedience that no one sought to challenge. The sole risk Clay had taken in boarding this aircraft had lain in the skill or otherwise of the printer in whose little back room within a mile of the British embassy the card taken from Captain Stukalin had been altered, with the photographs and signatures exchanged, prior to the artificial soiling and creasing process. One of the cyanide capsules had been loose in a side pocket of his civilian suit as Clay had entered the military base under escort; since last year, when an East German agent working for Bonn had infiltrated the Kremlin itself as an official interpreter and been discovered, instructions throughout KGB and military police branches provided for a personal search within minutes of arrest on suspicion: the East German had hit the floor of the Kremlin Palace of Congresses with his skin already turning blue before the officers of the guard could get him into a patrol van.

He'd been blown, as Clay knew at once when the story hit the UPI telex in London. You could leave things a bit longer if it were just a question of a suspect card or a routine check, depending on how many avenues of escape you'd got. But that man had seen it coming: they must have come at him in a group, cutting him off. The moment was always critical, because once they'd got to your capsule before you did, there was nothing on God's earth you could do to stop the ensuing interrogation, and the Soviets didn't have any form of interrogation that wouldn't drag the information out of you along with your guts.

The risk Clay was running now, as he sat in the rear seat on the starboard side of the TU-26, was critical only in the sense of timing. If nobody at the Novodevichy cemetery in Moscow noticed anything wrong with the earth in Stukalin's grave, he'd be safe for a while. (Stukalin's grave, and who else's? They'd put someone on top. Would they ever, in life, have been friends?

Lovers? *Requiescant in pace.*) But there'd be a time, in an hour from now, or a day, when someone at Stukalin's office noticed that he hadn't checked out officially for the flight, hadn't signed his clearance form or reported by telephone or locked his desk, any one of a dozen things; and they'd start asking questions. It would be like lighting a fuse, at that instant, and the explosion would happen here, or wherever Clay was. He had, in effect, a bomb strapped to his body.

Those had been Blanes's words, one of his usual melodramatic phrases. "I know," Clay had told him. Blanes had been trying to frighten him off the mission, that was all. The thing was, it had been a rush job. If Clay were right, and there was something out there in eastern Siberia for him to do, then someone would have to go there, and fast. Nobody else would take it on; nobody else would even dispense with Stukalin. You couldn't expect any kind of perfection in a rushed job, which that bastard Blanes couldn't see.

It didn't matter now. Clay was here, with the foam seat cushion expanding under him slightly as the aircraft shut the power down and began its long approach path from cruising altitude with the sun southeast-by-south through the small square window. They'd been flying four hours, which at cruising speed would bring them somewhere over the Chersky mountain range, north of the Sea of Okhotsk. *What the hell were they doing out here?* There was *nothing* out here, except mountains and the bloody tundra.

Clay felt the flexing of the seat under him, and heard the faint ticking of plastic as the interior panels vibrated; when the door to the flight deck slid open behind him he tensed, and his right hand dropped to his pocket. He'd gone over it in his mind so many times on the flight out: *Captain Kokarev, we've just had a radio message I don't quite understand. Your office reports that Captain Stukalin should be escorting this flight.*

It hadn't happened yet, but it could happen at any time. The thing was to know what to do when it came.

"We're now making our approach," the captain was calling

out as he came past Clay's seat. "I want you to fasten your seat belts. We'll be going down through cloud and moderate rain. There'll be air pockets."

Clay got the ends of his belt together and clipped the buckle. Through the small window the sky was almost black at this altitude, with so little atmosphere to refract in the sunlight; but below them was a white haze rising as the aircraft lowered.

Twenty minutes later the windows became streaked with rain, and a ridge of mountains showed to the south; later still there was the glint of wet rock out there, and the rush of scattered scrub, then the aircraft shuddered as the flaps went down and the fuselage tilted nose-up a few degrees before the landing wheels hit the runway and bounced and hit again and rolled, with the jets' thrust reversing and sending out a wave of thunder as the brakes dragged and everything shook until the power was shut down again and Clay sat watching the runway lights slowing past them, and a human figure standing there in the rain, waving.

One thousand five hundred kilometers east of the camp in Siberia, a dark blue Dodge pickup with twin rear wheels was turning off the highway in central Alaska and bumping over a hard-top minor road through the mountains. In an hour it met a dirt road that ran straight to the north through low bush and desert.

The driver was Tikhon Khitrov. Earlier today he had flown from Washington, D.C. to Anchorage, and there rented the pickup, loading it with fishing tackle, maps, two sporting rifles, a pair of field glasses and provisions for a week's sojourn in the desolate land that now lay ahead of him.

He was not afraid of isolation. During his years as a railroad inspector across Soviet Russia he had learned to live on his own, in between his meetings with railroad engineers. Later, in the capacity of a KGB officer on special assignments, he had isolated himself even further, spiritually as well as physically, as his work set him apart from his fellow men, demanding a cloak of secrecy.

He would not, in any case, remain alone for long, as the blue pickup moved northward through the scrubby desert of Alaska. Nor would he lose his way: he had been here before, ten days ago, to verify that the landing place chosen by the Soviet Air Force surveyors was suitable for the speed, weight and surface requirements of the TU-28 medium-range bomber that was scheduled to arrive here at midnight, in seven hours' time from now.

By eight o'clock in the evening, Khitrov had surveyed the terrain and was sitting on the roof of the pickup's cab with the field glasses raised toward the south. He was gratified to note that the field team of ten Chevrolet vans would reach here precisely on time: he could already see their headlights.

They reached the landing area within ten minutes and moved immediately into the tapered linear pattern on both sides of the flat, scrubless landing site, dousing their headlights. At midnight, now in three hours and forty-six minutes, they would provide illuminated runway marking.

From his pickup truck, Khitrov informed his agents in Anchorage by cellular telephone that everything was in good order for the reception of the Soviet bomber. If any state ranger or private hunter chanced to move into this area, he would first note the insignia of the National Aeronautics and Space Administration on the sides of the vans, and the words *Field Survey Unit*. He would then be requested by those members of the team wearing the uniform of the National Guard to leave the area. If for any reason he objected or appeared suspicious, he would be shot.

The anemometer mounted on the roof of the foremost van on the south side of the landing site was spinning slowly, registering a seven mile per hour wind from the north, moving inland across the sea. Khitrov conveyed this information in his signal to Anchorage. He then used his telephone to call Moscow direct, with the information that the conditions at the landing site were satisfactory and that a state of complete readiness existed.

At this time, signals in code via satellite were reaching Moscow from the Soviet embassy and consulates throughout the United States, similarly reporting their readiness to receive the Chevrolet vans as each arrived separately in one of the ten major cities designated to it, for the immediate unloading and dissemination of the L-9 material.

At fourteen minutes past eight o'clock, Khitron cradled the telephone in the cab of his pickup truck, having made his final call direct to Moscow, and direct—as he knew—to Chairman of the Council of Ministers Rudenko.

Mikhail Rudenko was alone in his office in the Council of Ministers Building. The time registered by the blue onyx clock on his desk was fourteen minutes past eight in the morning. After putting down the overseas-line telephone, he moved with precise steps into the middle of the eighteenth-century chamber and lifted his head to the window, as he had done more than once before. He felt drawn to the sky, to the oblong of blue space beyond the casement, to the visible universe in whose awesome vastness he was soon, in a matter of hours now, to bring a significant change.

Perhaps there were civilizations out there already. If there were, he was this day to initiate the long journey that man must undertake in order to reach them, and greet them as a brother. If in that vastness he now watched from the surface of the planet Earth there was no one, no creature, no intellect of any kind, then he would this day create the beginnings of man's dream to venture abroad from his miniscule home in the firmament, and plant his seed wherever it would flourish. And if it were that mankind, at this moment in time, found itself alone in that vast cosmos, he would, over the eons, lead to its gradual population, bringing the creature *Homo sapiens* to his many-splendored domicile among the stars.

And the memory that would endure throughout those eons, as man made his way through the cosmos and carried with him the tidings of earlier times, would be the memory of this one man, of this one name. Of this man. Rudenko.

Rudenko, the creator of cosmic life.

Such was the effect of this thought in his mind that suddenly he saw himself floating there in the oblong of blue sky, a human figure, insubstantial yet unmistakably bearing his own face that gazed back at him, aglow in an aura of celestial light. Stilled, bespelled, he stood in thrall, his mouth coming open and his hands going out to the vision beyond the window; and when a telephone began ringing on his desk it was a long time before he went to answer it, staggering like a man drunk.

CHAPTER THIRTY-ONE

GROUND ZERO

At 6:45 Eastern Siberian time, the dolly containing the ten sealed cylinders of L-9 material was wheeled from the hut adjoining the operations room at the Camp toward the big delta-wing TU-28 medium-range bomber. The evening was cool, and a light wind was blowing across the tundra; a three-quarter moon hanging low in the eastern sky cast an ashen glow along the roofs of the huts.

Five men worked steadily at the dolly, keeping it straight on the dried-mud terrain; others watched, among them General Goldin, the biochemist Dobrynin and the KGB captain who had reached here four hours ago on the last flight from Moscow.

Charles Clay was standing at the edge of the group. Earlier he had gone into the operations room with the rest of the visiting party, where Goldin had briefly announced that Operation *Springboard* was going according to plan; he had shown them the relief map that had taken up most of the planning table.

Clay had also talked to some of the aircrew, and had listened to other people talking among themselves, one of whom was a high official on the Moscow flight, addressed as Comrade Chairman Koslev. Clay's first thoughts were of sabotage, but he was already beginning to understand the odds against it. The alternative was to try sending a last-ditch signal to the embassy in Moscow, but that too would be close to impossible.

He walked slowly across to the bomber, whose matte black paint work had the sheen of sharkskin under the moon. Each cylinder was being manhandled from the dolly onto the loading ramp with great care, three of the air force officers using ropes slung from the sides of the ramp to keep the cylinder upright. General Goldin had also moved from the operations room to watch the loading procedure. It was with this lavish care, Clay thought, that Big Boy must have been loaded into the bomb bay before takeoff for Hiroshima.

As a KGB officer responsible for civilian security here at the Camp, Clay had moved unmolested through the working quarters and around the huts, but he had no excuse for going into the Tupolev-28, which was strictly air force territory with its own security guards. He was armed with only a single revolver, the Soviet Mikoya version of the Colt Python .357 Magnum, holstered under his jacket. The full air force complement here comprised thirty-two men, all of officer rank and carrying side arms.

The only conceivable way of stopping the takeoff of the TU-28 with a single revolver would be by taking General Goldin hostage with the gun at his back and demanding the bomber be disabled. But even if that could be done, it would only postpone the flight. A single man against thirty-two trained military officers under the command of a full general wouldn't have a chance of holding out.

Clay turned away from the aircraft and was in the operations room when General Goldin called the final briefing. He addressed mainly the crew of the TU-28.

"Every report from Moscow and from Alaska is satisfactory. After takeoff you will of course receive continuous information from our weather station in Anadyr, in addition to reports from our agents in Anchorage. I shall be in touch with you personally from this base and will make whatever decisions necessary in the event of problems."

Clay noticed that the general's face was bright with sweat under the long tubular lamps; he wasn't a young man; he was long used to command, but perhaps not used to leading a proj-

ect of this magnitude into its final phase. He knew what the
outcome would be, if successful; they all knew, these people
here. There was an atmosphere of solemnity in the camp; voices
were quiet, and it was difficult to get anyone to meet your eyes
when you spoke to them; people moved with the unhurried yet
measured pace of a sacrificial ritual.

"If you have for any reason to abort your flight in the sea,"
Goldin told the captain of the aircraft, "do not use flares. Do
not send any signal, not even *Mayday*. Your predicament will
be known to me, and I will initiate all possible procedures for
your rescue."

He spoke for fifteen minutes, taking the aircrew over the landing and return-flight procedures and using his pointer on the
large-scale map. Finally he looked at his watch.

"You will be taking-off in three hours from now, at 2145 local
time. Until then, you will remain here in the operations room,
and I shall be here with you to answer any questions or reiterate
any instructions." He wiped his face with a blue-gray handkerchief. "There will be refreshments," he said with an attempt at
cheerfulness. "Let us not be too gloomy, comrades."

At 6:40 PM, Charles Clay went outside and walked fifty yards
or so to the signals hut and showed his card to the radio officer
and requested communication with Moscow.

"I cannot permit that."

The young air force signaler was sitting half around in his
chair, watching Clay.

"My orders, " Clay told him, "are to confirm to KGB Headquarters that *Springboard* is going according to plan." He
dropped his identity card onto the radio table.

There was no chance, no chance at all, of getting inside that
bomber out there; it was under military guard. And there was
no chance, not a chance in hell, of trying something exotic like
taking General Goldin hostage and braving it out. *No chance*.

So the best, the *most* he could do was get a signal through and let Blanes take it from there. And even that looked so risky, and so fragile: one slender thread spinning out from here to Moscow, from Moscow to London, from London . . . . But it was all he could do, alone here in an armed camp with one gun and five bullets in it.

Blanes, you bastard, this is all you're going to get, so for Christ's sake make the most of it.

The young radio operator picked up the KGB card, looked at it politely, and handed it back. "I'm sorry, captain. You'll understand that this signals post is under the highest possible conditions of security." His cool, clear eyes rested on Clay's. The matter was over with.

How old was this young and dutiful Soviet soldier, with his certainty in the military protocol, in the sacred inviolability of his rank, his uniform, his authority? Twenty-five, twenty-eight, thirty? Did it matter? Was there a wife somewhere, minding the children at home? A sweetheart, looking at his photograph somewhere, waiting for him to come back to her? Did it matter?

It wouldn't have to. One had reasons of one's own.

"I want you to call up Moscow," he told the young man, and the young man stared into the muzzle of the gun.

Clay knew how to do it, but he wanted the young man to do it for him. If that first understanding could be reached, it could save a life later.

The Soviet got slowly to his feet, still staring into the gun. Clay let him get up; it was a concession to manners.

"I refuse."

Manners were going to be important. One had to save something from the wreckage.

"I will count five," Clay said, and lifted the gun a degree to shift the aim to the point between the young man's eyes. From outside the hut he could hear the dolly being wheeled back to its storage. "You have five seconds," he told the radio operator. "Then if you won't obey me I shall shoot you dead."

The man's face was growing pale, and his eyes were changing.

He was beginning to know that he was no longer looking into a gun, but into the face of death. At his age, it would be difficult to recognize, with so much life to spare.

"One."

There was a stillness in the little room, a silence deeper than silence, almost a communication.

"Two. Three. Four."

Clay felt sickened now. This was going to be Stukalin, all over again. He always hated it.

"*I refuse.*"

Duty. Obedience. Loyalty. One couldn't ask more from this soldier. He would be called a Hero of the Revolution.

"Five."

"*I refuse.*"

"You're a good man," Clay said. "I salute you." The young Soviet had started coming for him when Clay shot him between the eyes and caught him as he went down, easing his body to the floor and then hitting the console and raising the embassy, hearing the response and turning the volume up.

"*This is Clay, Siberia. Get Blanes there. Get Blanes.*"

The stink of cordite filling the hut.

"Will do," the voice said. It didn't sound real.

Five seconds, ten, fifteen on the dial of the console clock, the thin black hand sweeping around. Twenty.

"*For Christ's sake, get Blanes.*"

Blood seeping across the wooden floor. A good young man. A hostage for two hundred million.

Thirty seconds. That shot would have been heard. There'd been nothing he could do about it. The risk was calculated, the only chance left.

"*Get Blanes there—*" and he choked it off. Panic didn't have a place in this. Panic could kill.

"Blanes at the console. Hear you, Clay."

"I might be cut off. Put this on tape. A consignment of a lethal bacillus is to be flown into Alaska in three hours from now, for dissemination across America. There is *no* antidote to the bacillus and there's *no* protection against it, anywhere. *It's a DNA-recombinant gene, you understand that?*"

In a moment, "Yes." Blane's voice hardly recognizable.

"The bomber is to land in Alaska, coordinate sixty-nine degrees north by one hundred fifty-three degrees west—six . . . nine . . . north by one . . . five . . . three . . . west—and the ten canisters of bacillus will be put on board vans marked with the NASA emblem, for transport and release in ten major cities —*is that tape running, Blanes? Is that*—"

"Yes. Tape running." His voice sounded very quiet. That was Blanes, you could say this for him, he never panicked.

Someone was shouting, outside the hut. That had been expected.

"*Listen, I haven't got long now.* The aircraft you have to watch for is a TU-28 medium-range night-bomber. It'll be going in below radar range across the coast, and will—" but the door of the hut was swinging open with a bang and a Soviet stopped short on the threshold as he saw the radio operator on the floor with blood coming away from him. "*Blanes, you've got to understand what's happening*—" he swung his gun into the aim and fired at the man in the doorway as the man saw him and drew his own gun from its holster, blood springing from his throat as Clay's bullet went in—"*Blanes, they're trying to wipe out America*—" as the shot came and hurled him back from the console with the shock spreading through him and the darkness coming, the darkness coming down and somewhere in it a voice crying, fainter and fainter . . . *Ashton* . . . fainter and fainter . . . *Ashton* . . .

At 6:50 AM in London, Sir James Braithwaite was jogging past the Round Pond in Hyde Park. He usually avoided Rotten Row because at this hour there were always a few riders out, and among them Brigadier Styles, who had sometimes tried to stop and talk. Effective aerobic exercise wasn't achieved by halting halfway through the session and disturbing the breathing rhythm by talking, especially to that old fool.

Braithwaite wasn't entirely unaware that despite his age, the lean body in its royal blue striped track suit presented somewhat of a dashing spectacle, and he occasionally veered off course to pass close to one of the nursemaids who began parading their perambulators at about this hour; he would then call a hail good morning to them, and to hell with the breathing rhythm.

His Nike running shoes, with their smart Olympic insignia, kicked up the autumn leaves as he turned and jogged parallel with Kensington High Street. It was then that the beeper clipped to his track suit began sounding.

He didn't alter course, but kept straight on to Princes Gate and turned along the pavement, jogging steadily until he reached the first policeman he could see, almost halfway to the Hyde Park Hotel.

" 'Morning, officer!" He showed his card. "I need to use your telephone down there at the gate. Come on."

The policeman tried a fast walk as Sir James set off, but couldn't keep up.

"Come on, man! Can't you run?"

"It's against regulations, sir."

"Good God! give me the key, then!"

Braithwaite set off again and opened the police phone box, identifying himself and asking the station switchboard to give him a public line. Within ten seconds he was talking to his signals room.

"Braithwaite."

"Yes, sir. We've just got something in from Moscow. I'll run the tape."

As the head of the Secret Service listened to the translation, a nursemaid went past the telephone box, wheeling her pram into the park; he didn't notice her. His breathing had slowed since he'd stopped jogging, now it quickened again as he stared into the distance at the Albert Memorial. The young policeman came up at a steady walk and began asking something; Braithwaite silenced him with a look. When the recording was finished, he asked:

"What's the source of that signal?" He noticed his voice was shaking.

"Blanes says it was Charles Clay, sir."

"Is he *certain* it was Clay?" This was vital.

"Blanes made a point of saying so. He's quite certain."

"Very well. What was that sound of shooting on the tape?"

"Blanes thinks Clay could be dead, sir. It sounds as if he'd broken into their signals room."

In a moment Braithwaite said, "Dead. Yes, I see. All right, I want you to run that tape over the special line to the CIA—*to Steiger personally*. Tell him I'll expect to see him at my office if he'd like to talk to me. Then give it direct to their headquarters on line 5, as soon as you've rung Steiger." Line 5 went straight and exclusively to Foggy Bottom in Virginia. "I shall be along very shortly." He hung up and told the policeman: "Use your radio. I want a patrol car to pick me up here right away. Tell them it's life-or-death."

As the man switched his radio to transmit, Braithwaite turned away from him, the full significance of this thing half stunning him. Life or death, yes . . . *but how many lives . . . and how many deaths . . .*

At six minutes past midnight in Washington, D.C., the telephone on the small, special-situations communications panel beside President Hartridge's bed woke him with its low, fluting note. The room was cold, which was the way he liked to sleep, with two of the windows open and a double blanket on the bed. The sound of late traffic reached him from Pennsylvania Avenue, then it was muted out as he listened to the voice on the phone. The call was from Gordon Walsh, director of the CIA.

"I'm real sorry to wake you, Mr. President, but I think you should hear this tape. It's a signal we got in from London a couple of minutes ago."

"Play it," Hartridge said, and reached for the glass of Perrier water on the side table, lifting off the plastic cover. When the tape was finished he asked Walsh in a strained tone: "How much credence do you put on this signal?"

"It has Braithwaite's name on it, sir. He's the head of their—"

"I know. And *he* says it's genuine?"

"The source is an agent he sent out to Moscow personally. The way I see it, Mr. President, this looks like a logical answer to all those questions we've been asking about the Rudenko *troika*, the Terebilov defection, the camp they've been setting up in Siberia, and the epidemic of plague right here. We've—"

"*The what?*" Walsh said it again, and Hartridge remembered the words on the tape: *There is no antidote to the bacillus and there's no protection against it, anywhere. It's a DNA-recombinant gene, you understand that?* "You think this is why they got us to seal off the United States?"

"It figures, Mr. President."

"Jesus *Christ* . . ." Hartridge stared into the glass of water as the enormity of the situation hit him. "Look, Walsh, I want you over here just as soon as you can make it. I'll clear the landing pad for you right now."

"Yes, sir."

Hartridge hung up and spoke to the switchboard. "I want these people in my office right away. Mr. Sneed, Mr. Paget, Mr. Napier, General Cummings, the chief of staff, the deputy chief, the secretary of defense and the secretary of state. Have you got that?"

"Just a minute, sir." The operator read the names back. "Is that correct?"

"Yes. And tell them to come as they are: this is a national emergency. Tell them that."

He hung up and threw the bedclothes off.

Alexander Dynan, secretary of state, had gotten into the map room with the help of a security guard and brought along a large-scale relief map of Alaska. It was lying across the president's desk.

Hartridge was in a red jumpsuit and slippers; Robert Perrins,

Defense, had buttoned a fleece-lined jacket over his pajamas and found a pair of sneakers; Michael Simpson, chief of staff, was in a bathrobe.

"We have approximately two hours," the chief executive said. He looked for the biochemist among the crowd of twenty or so people standing around his desk. "Dr. Levy, could you tell us the risks?"

"Yes, Mr. President. They're very real." He came closer to the desk, a short man with a black beard and a birthmark the size of a dime on his temple. "If it's a new organism created in a laboratory, there's nothing we can do about it, absolutely nothing. If—"

"Can't we simply shoot down the plane?" Perrins, Defense.

Hartridge lifted a hand, not looking away from Dr. Levy. "If what?"

"If enough of that stuff were disseminated, then yes, it could wipe out life on a massive scale. Possibly all life on earth."

Hartridge took a slow breath. "Okay. If we shot that plane down, what might happen?"

"If the containers are massive, which they should be, they could simply be cracked open by a direct hit from a missile, and the bacillus would be released into the atmosphere and carried on the wind. That would be catastrophic."

Hartridge glanced at Robert Perrins: his question had been answered.

"If we blew the plane up as it landed?" the chief of staff asked Levy.

"Even a low ground wind would spread that stuff around."

"But if there were a big enough explosion, wouldn't the actual heat destroy it?"

"Oh, yes. It's an organism we can't destroy medically or chemically, but it's still a living organism, destructible by fire. But we don't know the strength of those containers. It's—" he shrugged "—a crap shoot."

The president looked at Perrins, defense chief. "Bob?"

"Could we force the plane down in the sea?"

"Without blowing it up?"

"Yes, sir."

Hartridge looked at General Cookridge, commanding the US Air Force.

"No," Cookridge said. "No way. Unless of course the pilot agreed to ditch it, under threat of destruction. But he'd have weapons of his own he could call on: we might not be able to offer him a credible threat."

"Could we just hit the crew," Perrins asked him a little desperately, "with cannon fire, and bring the plane down without blowing up the containers?"

"That would entail a minor air battle," the gray-haired veteran of World War II told him. "The containers would almost certainly get hit, without necessarily getting destroyed along with their contents."

In the lengthening silence, President Hartridge said wearily, "If anyone wants to smoke, do that." Time was running out, and nerves were fragile.

"Suppose we let them land the plane," Perrins said, reaching for his cigarettes, "is there any way we could force the crew to —you know—come out with their hands up?"

"If I were running that operation," the CIA chief told him, "I'd give them orders to release that stuff out of the containers at the slightest sign of opposition, once they were on American soil. We have to regard this as a kamikaze-type operation: those guys don't necessarily expect to live."

After another silence someone said angrily, "I wouldn't have thought it'd be so goddamned difficult for us to shoot down one goddamned plane in our own airspace."

General Cookridge glanced at him. "It's like trying to disarm a bomb, son. If we shake it, it could go off."

From outside the building there came the sound of another helicopter arriving.

One of the military advisers lit up and blew out a plume of smoke. "Kill that plane on the ground."

"In Russia?"

"In Russia."

"We know where the airstrip is," the president nodded, and looked around for comment.

"With a missile?" Perrins asked.

"Sure. It's within easy range, for a Big Mac." The military adviser, General J. G. Hoeffner, had their attention now.

"Jesus," the chief of staff said slowly, "that'd be taking quite a risk."

"Of a showdown?"

"Absolutely. They could—"

Hartridge cut in, "But we still have the problem of releasing that goddamned stuff from the containers, even with a direct hit, don't we?"

"Not with a nuke," said General Hoeffner.

Hartridge stared at him. "With a *nuclear* warhead?"

"Is there any other kind, on a Big Mac?"

Everyone was suddenly looking at the biochemist, Dr. Levy.

"Would that do it?" the president asked him.

"With a direct hit, sir, yes. We'd have sufficient heat."

"And the absolute certainty," Perrins nodded, "of getting it inside the containers."

The silence drew out.

"Jesus," said the chief of staff under his breath. "That won't have happened since . . ."

"Nagasaki."

"Right. We—"

"Suppose that signal we got from the British agent was just wrong information," nodded Dynan, state, "or—" he shrugged "—I don't know, maybe false in some way, maybe *dis*information, but just suppose. We'd be sending a nuclear missile onto Soviet soil, and I can't imagine doing anything more precipitous. It'd look like a first strike!"

"But for Christ's sake, Alex," Perrins told him angrily, "those bastards are aiming to wipe out the whole of the United States! Don't you think *that's* a little bit precipitous?"

"But I said *if* that signal wasn't genuine."

President Hartridge kept his tone steady, as an example to the others. "We're assuming it's genuine. We're assuming it's reliable. We can't afford to do otherwise."

Paget, one of his aides, lit a cigarette from the butt of the last. "It could be a device, sir, by the Soviets, to make us attack."

"And give them the excuse to try an overkill?"

"Yes."

In a moment Hartridge said briefly, "Our relationship with them right now precludes that. They're not in any position to counterstrike without calling me first on the hotline to find out if our shot was just an error."

The first man to speak again was Paget. "Then why don't you—" he stopped as the president stared up at him with a jerk of his head.

"Exactly," Hartridge said. Their eyes remained locked as the same thought went on circling between them. "Exactly." In a moment he stood up and moved around a little, his hands jammed into the pockets of his jumpsuit and his massive head lowered in thought. Nobody interrupted. When he'd got it right he sat down again and looked at the telephones. He wasn't going to put this out for comment. They'd thought of everything else and they weren't getting anywhere, and the time on the desk clock was now 1:09 AM. "What I'm going to do, gentlemen, is order a nuclear missile shoot, to hit that plane on the ground in Siberia. At the same time, I'm going to call on the hotline and explain why I'm doing that." He could feel the blood leaving his face, but he kept his voice perfectly under control. "Let us pray he's intelligent enough to see it doesn't offer him grounds for a counterstrike."

He picked up the telephone nearest him.

At 2140 hours, Eastern Siberian time, the crew of the TU-28 bomber climbed on board through the hatch and took up their stations in the cabin. One minute later the twin reheat turbojets began whining, the low wind carrying the sound away from the huts.

In the signals room, General Goldin was speaking at the console.

"I cannot explain it, Comrade Chairman. They were all trusted men, security-screened."

Goldin shifted his position on the chair, his boot grated across the loose dirt that had been thrown onto the pool of blood. The body of the radio operator was still on the floor, face staring upward; the body of the KGB officer leaned against the wall, as if the shots had flung it there. The body of the air force lieutenant was face down across the threshold. The hut stank of cordite and death. Outside the door a group of men stood awaiting orders, murmuring among themselves.

"You cannot explain it?" The voice of Chairman of the Council of Ministers Rudenko sounded strangely remote, though the radio reception was loud and clear.

"There's been no time yet, Comrade Chairman, to investigate. I reported to you personally the moment this—this incident occurred. I trust I did correctly."

In a moment Rudenko said, "Yes. Yes. There was some kind of dissension between these men, you believe?"

"That's a possible explanation, Comrade Chairman."

The general was treading with extreme care. If he added that some kind of breach of security was also possible, the chairman might order the operation delayed—a far-reaching decision, considering what was at stake—and if later there were no such breach of security established, Goldin's head would be on the block. In the past month, rumor had it that Rudenko would have you shot as soon as look at you. And yet, if the operation failed, and it was later found that a breach of security had in fact occurred, to account for that failure . . . He drew a deep breath. "I shall investigate at once, Comrade Chairman."

There was another pause. "Yes. But everything else is ready, General? The aircraft is ready to take off?"

"Yes, Comrade Chairman. Everything is perfectly on schedule."

"Then nothing must delay us now. Do you understand?"

"My orders are to proceed, Comrade Chairman?" He waited, watching the blanched face of the young radio operator as it stared at the ceiling—his own face, if he made a mistake at this most critical of all times. *Suppose some kind of signal had been sent?* To whom? Saying what? These men weren't civilians, hooligans, traitors; they were officers of the air force, of the KGB. Suppose—but his orders were to proceed, and they had come from the all-highest. Nothing must delay them now, the chairman of the council of ministers had said, and in precisely those words.

"Yes," the voice came, remote and distrait, as if something else were on the chairman's mind, some vast concern than a puzzling skirmish between three lowly mortals. "Yes, General, your orders are to proceed."

General Goldin listened to the low whine of the turbos outside the hut. In less than ninety minutes, *Springboard* would have been completed. To question those orders at the last minute would be madness.

"Very good, Comrade Chairman."

Chairman Rudenko, sitting behind the desk of the president of the Presidium of the Supreme Soviet in the Council of Ministers Building, lowered the telephone.

He stared at the red plastic phone which connected him directly to a similar telephone in the Oval Office of the White House and the president of the United States of America. But he had nothing to say to the president of the United States of America, nothing at all. Following the dissemination of the L-9 material throughout that country, there would never be any need of what was popularly known throughout the world as the hotline. Such a device was already obsolete, an archaic relic of a world where two great warring factions had held the future of man's life on earth in a balance so precarious that the teeming millions of men, women and children had been unable to go to their beds at night with any certainty of life the next morning.

That was an unthinkable condition for a creature as intelligent as man to suffer, year after year, decade after decade. He would change it, soon now. He would remove fear from the world, and restore dignity to the preeminent species of all life on earth, of which he would become the leader, the savior. He, Rudenko.

His reflections were interrupted as a knock came at the door and it opened without his invitation. Sharaf Boytsov came in, crouching a little over his stomach, as he'd been doing habitually of late, because of his ulcer. Rudenko watched him as he approached.

"It will soon be over, my good Sharaf," Rudenko told him. "The creation of Soviet America will begin in a few moments now. The aircraft is due to take off." His black eyes glittered, reflecting the four great ceiling lamps, but his voice was gentle. "When all is done, you'll feel better again, and you can take a vacation—perhaps in Florida, or California. Anywhere you choose, my friend, anywhere in the world. *In our world.*"

"Yes," Boytsov said, "that would be nice." He stood not far from the desk, his arms folded across his stomach to ease the pain. He knew he would never be without it now, whatever happened; it had grown into him like a malevolent root, never to be torn out again. "So the aircraft hasn't yet taken off?"

"I've given the order. It's a matter of minutes now." Rudenko spread a gracious hand. "Sit down, Sharaf. We'll enjoy the occasion together. General Goldin is to report to me as soon as takeoff has been made. We shall—"

"There's time to cancel it, then." Boytsov's face was clearing, and there was a strange note in his voice; he reminded Rudenko of the men he'd seen in an asylum for the insane, when he'd paid an official visit years ago; the happiness on their faces had been bland, and mindless, the light of reason shining on beyond reason's dying. Sharaf had been under a great strain, of course. So had they all. "I want you to cancel it, Mikhail," Sharaf told him. "Cancel the flight."

"Sit down, Sharaf." His tone was no longer gentle. "You don't know what you're saying."

"I came to tell you we must—" But one of the telephones began ringing. A light had started flashing, on the one at the end of the row, the red one.

Rudenko stared at it for a moment, then picked it up.

"This is the chairman of the council of ministers, Rudenko."

Sharaf Boytsov watched him, his arms folded across his stomach, his body twisted slightly into the position where the pain always seemed eased a little. He saw the pallor creeping into Rudenko's face as he listened with the red telephone held to his ear. It wasn't from fear, as Boytsov knew; Mikhail Rudenko had never been afraid of anything in his life. It looked more like rage.

"But you cannot do that," he told the man at the other end of the line.

Boytsov could hear nothing of what the caller was saying, but he knew it could only be the president of the United States, speaking through his interpreter.

"You cannot do that," Rudenko was saying again, his voice hollow with rage. "I shall regard it as a deliberate act of war." He listened with the telephone pressed so hard against his ear that the knuckles of his hand were blenched. "I shall order an immediate response by nuclear force, do you understand me, Mr. President?"

Something was going wrong, Boytsov thought. Something was going badly wrong with Rudenko's new Soviet World. He was slamming the red telephone back onto its cradle and snatching up another one, the one nearest it. His face was wax white, and there was a light in his eyes that reminded Boytsov of the eyes of a wolf he had once seen in winter, backed into the corner of a wall by a hunter, the light of deathly defiance.

"Get me General Kirilenko."

Boytsov was frightened now. Kirilenko was the chief of the Counterstrike Center, Missile Command. There wasn't much time left.

Boytsov unfolded his arms and aimed the gun and fired, and watched the dark hole appear at the side of Rudenko's head, and then the redness gushing out. He fired again and again until there was a dull clicking noise, then sank wearily into the chair that Rudenko had offered him, letting the gun fall to the floor.

This was a start, then, but there was going to be so much else to do. Koslev and the others, all the other madmen would have to go too; then he would talk to the Americans, go and see them and try to explain, to make them understand that this must be the last time that misunderstandings between the two superpowers could lead to the brink of megadeath before the rest of the world could do anything about it. The last time, in the name of life on earth.

The Big Mac homed in to the target zone, impacting on the surface of the earth at a point 68° North by 177° West, its eruptive force reaching, in the next millisecond, the black bomber as it became airborne, flipping it over before the fireball burst and its million degrees of heat consumed it, together with the containers that comprised its cargo, reducing to atomic debris the thin spiral organisms that in their swarms were to have made their deadly trespass into the bloodstream of the peoples who lived beyond the Bridge of the North.

The column of dark smoke rose until it stood a thousand feet above the tundra, marking the grave of a madman's dream.